The Book of Lost Fathers

\\\

Johns Hopkins: Poetry and Fiction
John T. Irwin, General Editor

ALSO BY ROBLEY WILSON:

Novel
The Victim's Daughter

Short fiction
The Pleasures of Manhood
Living Alone
Dancing for Men
Terrible Kisses

Poetry
Kingdoms of the Ordinary
A Pleasure Tree
Everything Paid For

The Book
of Lost
Fathers

\\\

Stories
by Robley
Wilson

The Johns Hopkins University Press

Baltimore and London

This book has been brought to publication with the generous assistance of the G. Harry Pouder Fund.

Printed in the United States of America on acid-free paper
9 8 7 6 5 4 3 2 1

The Johns Hopkins University Press
2715 North Charles Street
Baltimore, Maryland 21218-4363
www.press.jhu.edu

"California" was first published in the *Iowa Review*, "Hard Times" in *Epoch*, "A Simple Elegy" in *Poet & Critic*, "Remembered Names" in the *Gettysburg Review*, "A Day of Splendid Omens" in *TriQuarterly*, "Dorothy and Her Friends" and "Parts Runner" in the *Santa Monica Review*. "Barber" was published in various newspapers under terms of the PEN Syndicated Fiction Program.

Library of Congress Cataloging-in-Publication Data

Wilson, Robley.
The book of lost fathers : stories / by Robley Wilson.
    p.   cm. — (Johns Hopkins, poetry and fiction)
    ISBN 0-8018-6717-7 (acid-free paper)
    1. Psychological fiction, American.   2. Paternal deprivation—Fiction.   3. Fatherless families—Fiction.
4. Fathers—Death—Fiction. I. Title. II. Series.
    PS3573.I4665 B66 2001
    813'.54—dc21   00-012113

A catalog record for this book is available from the British Library.

Remembering my own father (1898–1989)
and my mother (1902–1971)

Contents

The Book of Lost Fathers

\\\

Trespass

The driveway that leads to the house where his ex-wife lives is designed as a slalom, which is to say that as Jarvis Kimball enters it a screen of tall cedars blocks his view to the top of the hill. It isn't until he is halfway up the drive, has veered left and right and then left again, that the house reappears with its long, low roofline, its light-blanked bay window that opens out of the country kitchen, and its three-car garage that reaches away from the main building at an angle, like a protective arm. Jarvis remembers designing the house himself, sitting long afternoons in the dim study of the place they rented in town, while Eileen perched on the chair arm, looking over his shoulder, brushing the forelock of hair back from his brow in a gesture both distracted and affectionate.

He is here this morning because she has called him—the phone on the nightstand rousing him before six, the cat jumping down from the bed in alarm.

"We have to talk," she said. No explanation. "It's important, or I wouldn't have called at this hour."

"What's the matter?" he said, but she'd already hung up.

So Jarvis has driven out here in a kind of dread, drawing up worst-case scenarios, his stomach churning the way it used to in the last married days, when the anxiety attacks were debilitating and as regular as waking. Off and on over the past year Eileen has threatened to take him back into court, on the grounds that he is holding back on his alimony payments; he is supposed to pay her a percentage of his income, and she believes—or says she believes—that he is cheating her. Sometimes Jarvis thinks she only makes threats as a way of keeping him in her life, a displacement her therapist probably approves of.

He can no longer remember the particular contributions Eileen made to the plan of this house, except that he recalls her saying, "Those doors—you see where the door from the garage, and the one down to the basement, and the one from the half-bath all come together in this little narrow hall—are going to be a real problem." And of course they always were a problem. He had to give her that. In the end the only thing they could do was put thick rubber caps over all the knobs to protect doors and walls that got in each other's way.

Today, he thinks, the house looks terrific. The new siding, put on the summer before the divorce, has weathered nicely—an even, silvery patina that would have mottled if he hadn't had the decency to pay for the application of sealer, long after the formal settlement was agreed to. Five years ago, that was. Now, still scarcely eight o'clock in the morning of a day in early October, everything about the house spells out nostalgia; it fairly bathes the place. Everything is proper and at its best: the time of day, the season, the golden weather only beginning to seem autumnal.

As he reaches the end of the driveway, a half-dozen pheasants—female, all of them—flutter up from the undergrowth east of the lane; he smiles to hear their insulted squawking. This is harvest time; Fred Bartlett, who owns 240 acres across the way, has already cut his corn, and the pheasant flocks have escaped to the shelter of this side of the road. When the snow comes in another few weeks, Eileen will buy cracked corn at the Farm Fleet to feed them through the winter.

He parks the car in the graveled space in front of the garage, gets out, stands for a moment or two stretching his back and looking south across the five acres that used to be his. They are still half his;

if Eileen ever decides to move, half the equity will come to him—
but it will be only money.

He walks across the drive to the front door, passing under the
bay window. From this different angle the light changes and the
glass is no longer opaque. Out of the corner of his eye he can see
Eileen, seated at the kitchen table, looking out the window, smoking a cigarette. Perfect. It is the one consistent image he has carried with him since he moved out: Eileen, smoking one cigarette
after another, her gaze set upon the world beyond the window, her
mind God knows where. The image is unsettling and comforting at
the same time: it reminds him that no matter what happens in the
rest of their lives, he will always in some perverse fashion be connected to this woman.

||| As he passes the bay window, Eileen stands. He gives her a nod,
a small wave. She looks at him, but doesn't return the greeting. She
is already on her way to the door. Standing in the entry where brass
carriage lamps decorate each side of the front door, he fumbles au-
tomatically for his key, but almost in the same instant he remembers
the lock has long since been changed. The change was a symbolic
act, part of Eileen's insistence on a complete separation of their
lives—though Jarvis was never a threat to her, would never have entered the house without her consent. "I am not that sort of man,"
he once said to her. "If I'd known what sort you were," she responded, "I'd never have married you."

But she did, he thinks. Twenty-five years of marriage to his sort.

The door opens inward. Eileen steps back from it to let him
enter.

"You were quick," she says.

"It sounded urgent." He goes into the kitchen, looks around.
Eileen closes the front door and follows him. The kitchen is spacious, cathedral-ceilinged, divided into an eating area and a cooking
area, with a counter between. The built-in electric stovetop on the
counter is one of Eileen's ideas. It has four ceramic surface units and

a grill; the fan draws cooking vapors downward and expels them through a vent under the kitchen window. This morning a Chemex coffee flask, half empty, is sitting on a trivet over a front burner.

"May I have a cup of coffee?" he says.

"Help yourself."

He finds a cup and fills it. "I forget where you keep the sugar."

"I don't use it," she says. "Under the counter, left of the sink."

He opens the door and finds himself looking at Eileen's liquor supply—tall green and white and brown bottles half-full or quarter-full: Dewar's, Bushmill's, Beefeater—the porcelain sugar bowl squat on a narrow shelf above them. He takes out the sugar, finds a spoon in the silverware drawer, stirs in the half-teaspoon of sweet he needs to take the hard edge off Eileen's morning coffee.

"I don't suppose you've thought anymore about a key," he says.

"What key?"

"To the house. This place is half mine. It only makes sense that I should have a key to it, in case something goes wrong while you're away. I wouldn't abuse the favor."

"No," she says, "you wouldn't, because I'm not giving you a key. The place is half yours if and when we sell it. Not before."

"Suit yourself."

He puts the spoon in the sink alongside an empty ice cube tray and carries the coffee to the kitchen table. He sits with his back to the bulletin board—another of Eileen's ideas, originally a place to display their son's grade-school artwork. At one corner of the refrigerator door the low morning sun lays an uneven gold rectangle that spills over onto the wall beside the entrance to the half-bath and laundry. Jarvis thinks mornings are best in this room: it is the only time the light is strong enough, ample enough to fill this area made spacious by its absence of doors, its high ceiling, its massive Chicago-brick fireplace intended to serve both kitchen and living room—except it has never drawn properly, the fireplace the one structural thing he didn't design.

Eileen sits to his right with a fresh cup of her own. She looks tired, nervous, her eyes avoiding his. "How are things at the firm?" she says, and lights a filtered Chesterfield.

"So-so," Jarvis says. "You know the economy."

"Doris Boyer says you guys have done wonders with that building of yours. She says she wouldn't mind living in a place like that."

"It turned out nicely," he says. "But it's still a place of business."

"Doris says everything is top-dollar: oak woodwork, a crystal and brass chandelier, Colonial decor, real parqueted floors—"

"Jesus, El, you can't expect architects to work out of a tarpaper shack." This is one of the moments when Jarvis wishes he still smoked. It would please him to make an abrupt gesture, light a cigarette, exhale an angry cloud of smoke. It happens that he is proud, probably excessively so, of the building he and Harold Boyer bought at just about the time the divorce became final. It was originally a railroad depot and sits beside the long-abandoned roadbed in the west end of the city, an angular red-brick building of two and a half storeys with a wonderful, quirky interior space whose remodeling he used as a way to keep his mind off Eileen and her bastard lawyer.

"You and Harold must be doing very well," Eileen says. Smoke slides from her nostrils; she flicks ashes with the tip of her forefinger.

"You would know," Jarvis says. "You cash the alimony checks."

She gives him a cool, opaque stare. "You bet I do," she says.

A frigid silence lies between them like etched glass. Eileen compresses her lips into a line that shows barely any color and squashes the cigarette into the pale blue ashtray that was one of his long-ago gifts to her, an anniversary present, but he cannot recollect which one. He cradles the coffee cup in his palms, for warmth, for self-control.

"Maybe you ought to tell me why you called," he says.

|||| His ex-wife lights a fresh Chesterfield, shakes out the paper match with a brusque motion of her wrist, takes a sip of her coffee and exhales a stream of yellow-gray smoke toward the bay window. Waiting, impatient, he hates her.

"This isn't easy," she says. "Your father died this morning."

The words are shocking; for a moment he imagines them to be a lie, which in a moment will be unsaid. He wonders at his ex-wife's motive. Then the brass ship's clock in the living room strikes once. Time recommences; Eileen does not take anything back.

"How do you know?" His reaction—the pitch and roll of emotion Jarvis can feel in his stomach, under his heart—surprises him. When was the last time the two men talked? He tries to think how old his father was.

"The nursing home called here."

"Why here?" he says. "Why would they call you and not me?"

"Apparently you didn't give them a new phone number after you moved out. This is the number they had."

"Damn it," Jarvis says. His father was eighty-seven, almost eighty-eight.

"They said it was heart failure," Eileen says. "They called twice, actually. The first time was around eleven last night. The nurse said he was sinking, said they weren't sure he would last the night."

"Why didn't you call me then?"

"I did. I got your machine." She smokes, sips coffee. "I don't talk to machines."

His mind is racing. The nursing home is in Maine, in the town where he grew up. He will have to book a flight to Boston, arrange for a rental car, find the phone number of his father's attorney. He wonders, should he ask Eileen if she will let him phone from here?

"The second time was just after five o'clock this morning. They said he died in his sleep. I called you as soon as I'd made the first pot of coffee—as soon as I was really awake."

"I've got to get a flight," Jarvis says. "Someone has to take care of the funeral arrangements and stuff."

"I've already made a reservation," Eileen says.

Surprise. "That was thoughtful," he says.

"I made it for me, not you. I talked with Aunt Edith in Portland. She's meeting me."

"Oh?" he says. Edith is his mother's baby sister—he thinks she must be in her late seventies by now.

"Edith says your father pre-planned his funeral, so there's not that much to do. She and I can take care of any odds and ends, talk to the lawyer, find out about insurance, the will, things like that."

"And what am I supposed to do?"

She lays the cigarette across the ashtray and makes her lips familiarly narrow—an expression that calls to mind the distance, the demeanor of disapproval she increasingly put on during their later years together.

"You never paid that much attention to him," she says. "And need I remind you that he never forgave you for dumping me."

"*Dumping* is not the word I would use to describe what happened between us," Jarvis says.

She sighs, puts out the smouldering cigarette. "Anyway," she says, "I've delivered my sad message. Now I have to get packed. My plane leaves at noon."

"You're really going without me?"

"Really," she says. "If you want to make your own plan, go ahead, but does it make sense for both of us to spend all that money on airfare?"

"He was *my* father," Jarvis says.

Eileen stands, preparing to show him out of the house he has no key to.

"No one can take that away from you," she says.

\\\\ It is not yet nine o'clock, far too early to go into the office on a day when nothing there is pressing. He has a client errand this afternoon, a meeting downtown this evening, then a late dinner date with a woman he met last week at a charity book sale. Diana Watts, the secretary he and Harold share, doesn't come in until ten.

He stops at the Citgo station on University Avenue to buy gas, putting the nozzle on automatic, watching the digits run up. When he was in high school he used to put gas in the tank of his father's

green Buick—fifty cents or a dollar at a time—and mornings after
he'd driven the car he was obliged to listen to the old man complain
that the gas gauge always showed empty. "Fifty miles on the odome-
ter," his father would say. "Where the deuce do you kids drive to?"
Nowhere. Truly nowhere: up and down the main drag, looking for
anybody else who had no destination. Gas was cheap then; you really could go fifty miles on a dollar's worth. That was what he and
his father talked about: the car, whether he should smoke cigarettes
in the house, what was wrong with the Red Sox. "They can't stand
prosperity," his father would say when the Sox frittered away a lead,
when they left the bases loaded, when they brought in the wrong relief pitcher. Nothing of substance in the father-son discussions,
nothing you could pretend was worthwhile or important. And his
mother: a background figure only, a pale sweet face among darker
faces. "Ask your father," Jarvis remembered. A refrain. A verbal
shrug. She died twenty years ago; breast cancer. That was a funeral
Eileen had declined to attend.

|||| He drives home from the gas station, showers and shaves, puts
down fresh water for the cat. The last time he was in Maine, he visited his father in the nursing home, a place smelling of disinfectant
and talcum and the terrible staleness of age. Father ensconced at one
end of a plastic-cushioned sofa, facing an oversized television set;
the room linoleum-floored, with a south window that let in too
much garish daylight; other residents ranged about the room in
wheelchairs. It was late summer, years ago; baseball danced on the
big screen. The sound had been oppressive. Jarvis wondered at the
reason for the volume, then remembered that it was compensatory:
his father had long since been declared legally blind, could see
movement, shadows, changes of light—no more than that.

Later, sitting opposite him in the tiny room with the two
straight-backed chairs and the metal hospital bed, Jarvis attempted
to talk about the game—the Sox had lost it in the ninth to a pinch-
hit home run—then gave it up. His father hadn't been paying at-

tention despite the volume of the play-by-play. Even now the old man's eyes were vague. Not blank, just not zeroing in on anything.

When Jarvis was a child—before television, before almost everything technological—you never "saw" the Red Sox games unless they were at home. When the team was on the road, there were telegraphic re-creations. The announcer in a studio in Boston read a tape spooling from a machine and pretended the action of the game while the printer tapped away in the background. A good announcer had to be an actor, had to read ahead, building suspense before the home run or the double play he already knew was coming. You didn't need eyes. His father sat in the leather-upholstered rocker beside the radio and read the Portland papers, *Life* magazine, the *Saturday Evening Post*, while the game clucked along out of the speaker static.

"Do you remember taking me to see the Braves play the Dodgers, when Jackie Robinson was with the Dodgers?" Jarvis thought it might work; he had gotten reactions in the past. "I must have been ten or eleven."

"I don't know," his father said. The voice was thin, phlegmy. "I recall the old Boston Bees."

"That was before my time," Jarvis said.

"Baseball isn't the same," his father said. "Not the same at all. Though I don't see so well now. I admit that."

"Sure you do," Jarvis said. Three words whose ambiguity echoed in his head until he made his excuses and left the old man sitting alone in the white room.

"The players have no loyalty," his father said after him.

That was the last time he saw his father. It pleases him to have located the occasion, disappoints him to realize how trivial it was.

\\\\\ "It's a strange feeling." Jarvis is telling Howard about the events of the morning. "It's as if she's kidnapped my old man—just up and stolen him from me."

"You could have flown out yourself," Howard says. "You still can, if you want to. There's not that much going on around here."

"I could," Jarvis says, "but what's the point?"

"I can't say I'm surprised by all this," Howard says. "Doris sees Eileen quite often, and I get to hear about her comings and goings—and what she thinks of you, old friend."

"Oh?" says Jarvis. It is Howard's position that Jarvis doesn't deserve the unkindnesses Eileen visits upon him; his impulse is always toward sympathy. The sympathy is consistent with the man's physical appearance—soft, slightly overweight, what used to be called "portly"—and it is what makes him so good with clients: he wants what they want. It is as if Howard taps into their emotions and sees the world they aspire to, while Jarvis concerns himself with the practical—what they need, what it will cost. Eileen once described the partners as "an architectural Laurel and Hardy." That was when she still loved Jarvis.

"The latest is that she's selling off as many traces of you as she can," Howard says. "Books, tape cassettes, anything you left behind when you moved to your own place."

"How did that come up?"

"Eileen and Doris were in that second-hand bookstore on Maple. Eileen asked the owner to drive out and give her an estimate."

Jarvis shrugs. "That won't make her rich," he says. When he gave up on the marriage, when he knew he could not revive in himself the love he had once felt for his wife, he used to sit in his study late at night and make lists of property. Things he could give up, things he could not. He was amazed to discover how much he was willing to leave behind in exchange for what he thought of as rescue.

"Or make her happy," Howard says. "What she doesn't sell, she's throwing away. Old photographs. Ticket stubs. Crushed flowers. Doris says she mixes them both a drink and weeps over everything that reminds her of better times between you two."

"I'm sorry for that," Jarvis says.

Ever since the divorce, Howard's wife has become a curious link between his present and his past by remaining friendly with his ex-wife. She is a messenger service of sorts, reporting from the enemy camp. He cannot understand her motives, if she has any—her insistence on telling Howard everything she knows about Eileen's comings and goings, knowing Howard will pass the information on. He cannot tell if Doris thinks she is keeping the lines open for a possible reconciliation between the Kimballs or if she is simply a gossip, compulsive about broadcasting other people's lives.

Now he sits in his office, in the corner of the old depot that used to be the baggage room. The windows are Tudor, the upper panes forming a flattened half-circle, the lower panes small and almost square. The room has oak wainscoting, and above the panels the walls are painted a flat white; posters bought from the Boston Museum catalog are hung there in Doris's tasteful and uncrowded arrangement. A ceiling fan turns slowly overhead, silent, stirring the afternoon light. If he looks out his open door that same light glistens like water across the parquet of the lobby and reflects off the oak front of Diana Watts's reception desk.

There isn't much on Jarvis's docket—a word his father used. "What's on the docket for today?" his father would say, the two of them sitting at the breakfast table. He was a high school student, his father an accountant; the word *docket* had come from his father's father, who'd actually been a lawyer and a judge. Jarvis's meeting has been canceled, so that on his docket is only the client errand: a brass lock set sits in its box on his desk, waiting to be delivered to the Sheridans, whose country house—west of town, not more than two miles from Eileen's—is almost ready to be moved into. After the errand he is free until seven, when he has the dinner date he already regrets having made. The woman he left Eileen for is long since gone; why on earth should he risk complicating his life all over again?

Shortly before five Howard appears in the doorway, a look of concern on his round face as if he is worried about Jarvis.

"What do you say we shut up shop and go over to the Alibi for a drink?" Howard says. "You oughtn't to be sitting here brooding about your dad."

Jarvis shakes his head. "Give me a raincheck," he says. "I have to take the proper front-door lock out to the Sheridan place. Then I've got this dinner date." He wonders why he hasn't in fact been *brooding* about his father's death. Shouldn't he at the least be grieving?

Howard has raised an eyebrow. "Dinner date, eh?"

"Nothing serious." But Howard will tell Doris, Doris will tell Eileen—when Eileen is home from the East, the funeral. *Jarvis has a new girlfriend.* But it isn't true. "I'm thinking I might beg off," Jarvis says.

"Well," says Howard, "if you feel like a nightcap, just give us five minutes' notice."

"Maybe I will," Jarvis says, though he knows it is the last thing on earth he is likely to do.

\\\\ It is still early when Jarvis gets home from his dinner with the woman he met at the book sale. Her name is Marta, she sells insurance, and at thirty-one she is approximately half his age. It has not been a successful evening, as even Howard would concede if he had witnessed it. Jarvis talked endlessly, uncontrollably, about his father and about his ex-wife's betrayal—how she stole the old man from him—while the young woman listened and sipped white wine. He knows he won't date Marta again; any future sale of second-hand books would be spoiled by the possibility of picking up—and of course buying—books that had once belonged to him. What aggravates him now is that as he talked he began to realize that the "betrayal" was his father's in the first place. He remembered, in this restaurant, across from this child, exactly when and where he had been *dumped*—Eileen's word, only this time properly applied—by his father.

It was Easter, seven years ago: a restaurant between York and Kittery, a white frame place where they didn't accept credit cards and where the waitresses were older—motherly gray-haired women with opaque stockings and discreet hair nets. *How long since he'd seen hair nets?* It was a place his father had picked.

"This is a nice restaurant," his father had said. "They serve the best chowder. Fish. Clam. Lobster stew."

The old man had eaten slowly, deliberately, filling the spoon too full and letting milk dribble over his chin and onto his shirt front. The white shirt was yellow with age and stained by the fallout of other meals.

"Maybe I shouldn't mention this," his father said, "but it looks like you're not wearing your wedding ring."

Jarvis remembered making his left hand into a loose fist and looking at it as if he were noticing for the first time that the ring was missing.

"I've gained a little weight," he said. That had been true. "It needs to be re-sized."

His father was nodding, a gesture that said *Yes, yes, go on*, not *Yes, yes, I see.* He wondered at the time how well his father could see him, how well he could read the expression on his son's face.

"And anyway, Eileen and I have been separated for a while. We're getting divorced."

"I wondered," his father said. "I thought it might be something like that."

His disapproval was plain, and it endured for the rest of his life. He liked Eileen, called her *daughter*, after the divorce bought her a cruise in the Caribbean. Jarvis tried to joke about it with Howard: *Eileen got the alimony, half the house, and my father.*

He stands in the narrow kitchen of the townhouse he has rented since the divorce and pours himself a modest Scotch with a splash of water. *Damn it, Howard*, he would say, *why do we never perceive the real design of our lives?* Though the insight would be wasted on Howard.

To compound the failures of his day, Jarvis hasn't delivered the Sheridans' front-door lock after all; it's still sitting in its box on the

backseat of his car. He will have to put it on the docket for tomorrow. He is about to write himself a reminder note when the phone
rings. It is his ex-wife, calling from Maine.

"I don't have to do this," Eileen says, "but I thought you'd be interested to know that everything's taken care of. He'd even picked
out his casket."

"That's just like him," Jarvis says. He imagines his father and his
father's lawyer choosing the box at Hurd's funeral parlor, down in
the basement room where so long ago he stood with the old man
to select a coffin for his mother. Polished wood, white satin, half-
lids open like laid-down Dutch doors. His father took forever, de-
ciding. *What the hell do the dead care?* It was something Jarvis wanted
to say, but didn't.

"The service is day after tomorrow," Eileen goes on. "It's a Masonic funeral; it's what he wanted."

"Of course."

"Aunt Edith is in fine fettle. We drove down to Vallé's for lobster."

"I envy you." He finds a notepad and writes: *lock*.

"Did you decide about the funeral?" Eileen says. "Are you flying
out?"

"No," he says. "You're right. It's extravagant, and there's no
need."

"I think you're being sensible," she says. "You two weren't close,
this last few years."

"No. We weren't close."

"Well, that's all I called for. If there are any details I can't handle, the lawyer will get in touch with you. I gave him your actual
number."

"That's good," Jarvis says.

"You're not in your father's will," Eileen says. "I can already tell
you that much."

⦀ At ten he watches the local news, and at ten-thirty he gets into
his car and for the second time that day drives out to the house he

built with—and *for*—Eileen. There is a full moon; everything—the cedars, the siding of the house, the trees and shrubs around the yard—is touched with silver. He tries to remember if this is the harvest moon or the hunter's moon or what. Whatever it is—isn't there a wolf moon?—its light glistens like metal.

For five minutes, ten minutes, he sits in the car in front of the garage, the headlights out, the engine off. The thin steel of the hood ticks and tocks as it cools—irregular, random, like time disjointed. He imagines the impending funeral service for his father: the Masons dolled up in their embroidered aprons, medals on wide ribbons around their necks, self-conscious in front of the casket and stumbling over words they haven't troubled to memorize. He imagines the mourners: two or three feeble old men who have outlived his father, a few younger men and women he did taxes for before he retired. He even imagines his father: the thin auburn hair that never grayed, the paleness of the brow made more stark by the embalmer's blush on his cheeks, the square-and-compass Masonic ring too bulky for his finger, the 32nd-degree-everything Lodge decorations showy on his chest. Perhaps the old man will be buried in his tux. He always looked distinguished in a tuxedo; it was appropriate to him, Jarvis thinks—his aloofness, his lack of easy social graces.

Sitting in his ex-wife's driveway, not quite knowing why he is here, he wonders if he has been seen by the Bartletts, across the way. They wouldn't recognize the car, which is new since his divorce; might they call the sheriff? No, he thinks not. The Bartletts are an older couple, and old people retire early, get up early; it is long past the Bartletts' bedtime. Besides, all cars look alike nowadays, all designed in wind tunnels, not one with a trace of individuality. You could talk with an architect and get a house tailor-made, a home uniquely your own, but try that at an automobile dealership. This house he built for Eileen—no mistaking it for any other, was there? The wainscoting in the hallways, the built-in bookshelves, the efficient layout of workrooms, the generosity of the leisure rooms. Perhaps one day he would build it again, selfish, just for himself.

Jarvis gets out to walk around the house. The moon casts his shadow on the colorless gravel of the driveway and silvers the cloud of his breath in the crisp air. As he walks across the front yard he can see through the bay window that Eileen has left a light on in the kitchen; a small rim of fluorescence glows from the top of the cupboards. The other windows at the front of the house—the study, the master bedroom—are dark, giving back the pewter sky and a few faint starpoints. He visualizes the arrangement of the rooms and wonders if there is any way in, if Eileen has perhaps left something unlatched. He tries one of the study windows, his hands like claws at the edge of the frame, but it is a silly exercise. All the windows are casements; even if they were unlocked, how does he think he could open them? Then he thinks of the garage door. It is automatic, as is the one where he now lives; it requires a remote control device, one of which is clipped to the driver's-side sun visor of his car. He knows the transmitting frequency of the remote can be changed, and he knows—though he has never done it—it is a matter of manipulating the tiny dip switches inside the plastic case. How many frequencies can the remote be capable of? Surely the number is limited; he remembers how his son as a teenager used to drive through unfamiliar neighborhoods, targeting garage doors as he went. A surprising number of the doors opened.

Jarvis completes his circle of the house and goes to sit in his car, the door opener dismantled on the seat beside him. He adjusts a switch, aims, and nothing happens. He repeats the operation three or four times—different switches, different combinations. It occurs to him that he ought to have made note of the original switch positions—how will he get into his own garage?—as finally he cracks the code and the door rolls open to him.

The garage is extraordinarily empty, a space wide and deep where he had imagined he would someday maintain one or two classic cars. He remembers his grandfather's automobiles from their photographs—an old Studebaker "Dictator," a black LaSalle sedan,

a Packard touring car—no mistaking them for anything but themselves. Even his father's Buicks from the late fifties—maybe they
were ugly, but still they were themselves, unique. The garage even
has a grease pit, though he never actually used it. Now, with Eileen's
car at the airport, the space is empty except for a dozen or so cardboard cartons stacked against a far wall.

He gets out of his car, goes inside, uses the button beside the entrance to the kitchen to reclose the door. Now he is inside his ex-
wife's house; now he is trespassing.

|||| As he comes into the kitchen he is struck by the silence. Empty,
the room amplifies his own breathing, the rub of his clothes—sleeve
against sport jacket, one trouser leg against the other—the scuff of
his shoes across the coarseness of the kitchen carpet. The air in the
house is close and smells powerfully of cigarettes; Jarvis remembers
what it was like to wipe off the screen of the television set, collecting the yellow-brown residue on the white dustcloth. His ex-wife's
smoking is a presence, pervasive and eternal, in the permeable fact
of the building he designed.

This is the first time he has been free to walk through the house
since the divorce, and everywhere he looks he is struck by how dated
are his old choices. That electric stove—today he would put in a gas
range, a convection oven. Now he would never tolerate the wall-to-
wall carpeting—a breeding ground of allergy and filth—but opts for
wood floors or tile. He avoids composites for countertops, in favor
of stone or butcher block. If he could redo this house, he would replace the living room's false ceiling beams with real, and anyway it
has been years since he liked cathedral ceilings. In short, the house
has become a paradigm for the marriage he left: a relationship of du-
bious choices and changing styles, a tired environment.

In the front hallway, just outside the door into the master bedroom, a floorboard creaks under his weight; Jarvis remembers how,
after the house was completed, he stood in the basement and looked

up to find random slips of paper forced between joists and floor-boards—the contractor's quick fix for careless workmanship. *I was young*, Jarvis reminds himself; *I didn't know how to judge the men I hired.* But though he learned quickly, his first house is forever flawed.

Doris has told the truth: Eileen is getting rid of his books, his old phonograph records and tapes. Perhaps that accounts for the cartons in the garage. The bookshelves are half empty, small groupings of hardcovers surrounded by bric-a-brac: decorative ashtrays, bud vases, a pair of jolly Hummel figurines, the brass clock in its ma-hogany cradle. The shelves are built around an alcove for the spinet. He plinks a couple of keys with a forefinger; the piano wants tuning. At eye level is the set of Christopher Alexander's books on environmental structure—at least she hasn't sold *them*, and he thinks perhaps he will take them, steal them, when he leaves.

He strolls down the hallway and enters his ex-wife's bedroom, flicks on the overhead light, sits on the bed with its heavy patchwork comforter. It has been ten years since this bed was his, ten years since he moved across the hall into the guest room—a symbolic act, but a genuine uncoupling. Only once afterward had he shared the bed with Eileen: the last time his father visited and occupied the guest room, when it would have been awkward to explain Jarvis's sleeping on the sofa. Awkward, he remembers, to lie awake beside a woman he no longer loved. Within a year, he moved out.

Now his father has moved out—out of the nursing home, out of the world, out of life—and Eileen is visiting him, to see him settled, standing graveside. Not to weep, surely, but doing a solemn duty she believes her ex-husband cannot be trusted to carry out. She and Aunt Edith will stay until the end of the ceremony, hug each other, lay a single last flower at the grave. Then the two women will drive to the ocean, find a nice restaurant; Aunt Edith will order a manhattan and her cheeks and forehead will flush, just as Jarvis's mother's used to. It will be like a celebration: the disowning of Jarvis. Tomorrow the lawyer shares his father's will, Jarvis not mentioned. He thinks he might get the proceeds of his father's life insurance policy—twenty-five hundred dollars, ordered from an 800 number flashed on television. Eileen will have three-quarters of whatever estate there is; Aunt Edith will have the small remainder.

He sighs, slaps his knees, stands up. His old study is adjacent to the bedroom and amazingly unaltered. Here are the drafting table, the wide-drawered cabinets, the cranelike lamps, the fake-German beer mug loaded with pencils and penholders. The walls are oak-paneled, excessively dark after sunset; the room was always like a cell, a comfortable womb whose pulse was an all-night music show throbbing from the transistor radio on the windowsill. He drags his fingers across the table and feels the dust. Eileen ought to sell this house, move into something smaller; maybe that's why she is selling the books, the music, the reminders of his living in a house to which he no longer has a key.

Now he remembers the lock set he was supposed to deliver to the Sheridan building site, and without giving much thought to his reasons he opens the front door and walks out to the car. He takes the lock assembly off the backseat and brings it into the house. He sets it on the kitchen counter and pulls open the narrow drawer beside the sink. The tools are still there, just as they have always been: a small hammer, two or three screwdrivers, a pair of pliers. At the back of the drawer are odds and ends of nails and screws, all of them loose and rolling noisily as he slides the drawer out. A yellow flashlight is pushed toward the deep end.

⑂ It takes Jarvis a good twenty minutes to dismantle the lock in the front door, and another fifteen to unwrap the new lock set and slide its pieces into place. He uses the old outside handle—a perfect fit into the new mechanism, its brass still unmarred, perfectly usable—and doesn't replace the original striker plate. By the light of the flashlight propped in a corner inside the front hall, he tightens the new screws, and latches and locks the door. Finished, Jarvis returns the flashlight and tools to their drawer.

He takes down a tumbler from the kitchen cupboard, fills it with ice cubes from the freezer compartment and pours himself whiskey from the Bushmill's bottle under the counter. Tomorrow, Eileen and Aunt Edith will drive to Kittery for shopping. The next day they will watch while his father's casket is lowered into the cold Maine earth, and Jarvis will be sitting at this kitchen table, absent and orphaned.

California

\\\

Early one Sunday morning when Elaine Prentiss was twelve years old, a UFO touched down in the field behind the local high school. It was an event that perplexed the town—Ransom, Iowa, population 1,377—and Elaine went with her father that same afternoon to see where the landing had taken place.

"I don't believe any of that stuff," her best friend, Beatrice Adams, said to her the next day. "You have to be crazy to think something like that could happen."

Elaine didn't know how to respond. The field was a forty-acre tract of land that the school board owned and leased to Harvey Andersen so he could grow timothy and brome for his horses, and it was almost ready for the second cutting. The exact place where the spacecraft landed was an uneven black ring, fifty feet across, in the precise center of the field, where the ship's engines had burned their alien signature into the green of the ripe hay.

And what was to be made of that? She had already seen, in the Des Moines *Register*, aerial photographs of a tornado's path— an unruly spiral carved by 300-mile-an-hour winds across the furrows of a freshly-plowed field—and been impressed by the evidence of powers beyond human control.

Eleven years after, coming home to Iowa too late to say goodbye to her dying father, she drove to the school to see if any record of the space visit had outlasted time. She was distressed to find that the school was gone, "consolidated" with two other rural schools in the county, and that a dozen or so shake-shingled ranch houses occupied much of Andersen's field. But she was gratified to discover across two of the few vacant lots of the housing development a perfect half-circle of goldenrod that glowed like flame out of the summer-high prairie grasses.

ꟽ She had moved to southern California in late January, six weeks after her graduation from the university at Ames, and rented a one-bedroom apartment in Upland, in the San Gabriel foothills. She found a job with the state Board of Equalization in Ontario. She bought a Hyundai, red with white vinyl upholstery. And she wrote her parents, telling them how happy she was to be free at last of Iowa winters.

Yet for a long time she wished she hadn't left the Midwest. She thought at first she would never get used to this odd desert country. The days were unexpectedly warm, the nights unjustly cold. Sometimes she would wake in the middle of the night to strange noises on the roof—a loud thumping and scratching, as of animals fighting—and was told by her new friends at work that it was probably a possum she heard. They also told her they were afraid to let their cats out after dark, for fear coyotes down from the mountains would kill them.

Then, in mid-February, she felt her first earthquake; she was in the bathroom, just stepping out of the shower, when the floor began to tremble under her and she heard a low growl, like the sound of a distant train or a jet plane taking off from the airport nearby. By her own actual count—she could not think what else to do, standing on the mat with the towel held to her mouth and her free hand clinging to the towel bar beside the tub—the quake went on for nearly ten seconds and then subsided into stillness. The radio was on in her bedroom. While she was dressing, a jocular announcer came on to say, "Well, I suppose you folks felt what we felt just a few minutes ago," as if the event were only one more of the shared pleasures of being Californian. Two weeks later, Elaine started bolt upright at three in the morning, roused by the sound of a high wind in the pines and live oaks that surrounded her. It was a Santa Ana; she had never heard such energy in a wind. Next day, trees were fallen in the neighborhood; the streets were a litter of branches and cones and torn shingles.

Her apartment was called "the annex," and it stood behind a large stucco house owned by a woman from India, Amita. Amita was an immediate aggravation to her: a restless, haunted creature perhaps in her late fifties, up every morning at daybreak to water the lawn of her back yard, moving the hoses every half-hour to a new sector of thirsty grass, prowling the gardens to pluck dead blossoms and fuss at unruly leaves. Day after day, Elaine woke to the rumble of water from Amita's hose splashing against the walls and windows of the annex, and each time for the first few minutes of her waking she could not imagine where she was, what was happening. Privacy, she would think; privacy. There were no curtains at the windows of her workroom. A shadow would cross her vision; she would look up from reading a book to see Amita in front of the picture window, deep in consultation with the Hispanic gardeners who came every Wednesday to mow and clip and to tend the exotic flowers—camellia and gardenia, bougainvillea and bird-of-paradise were the only ones Elaine had learned to recognize—and she would draw the collar of her bathrobe up to her throat in a reflex against being so vulnerable.

Worst of all, she had to share the telephone. In the beginning, when she knew no one, the nuisance was minor, but as time passed and she had new acquaintances, the inconvenience magnified itself. Before she could respond to the extension in the annex, the ringing would have stopped and a few moments later Amita would rap at her door. "Telly-fon," the landlady would sing, and halfway through greeting her caller Elaine would hear the phone in the main house clatter into its cradle. She had taken the trouble to buy an answering machine, but it was Amita who screened her calls. If by some chance the machine's green light was flashing when she came home, the caller frequently turned out to be a friend of Amita's who had ignored Elaine's businesslike message ("Amita is not home. If you wish to reach Elaine Prentiss, please leave your number after you hear the tone") or who had not understood it.

IIII She tried very hard not to be guilty of bad manners herself, returning the phone to its stand instantly if Amita was talking with someone, always being careful when she depressed the cradle switch that the disconnect would be soundless. But one morning, at the height of the desert summer, she lifted the receiver to silence and had actually begun to dial before she realized she had broken in on a pause in a serious conversation.

"It is most burdensome for you," she heard Amita say. "Yet it is a burden you must be schooling yourself to bear, possibly to be feeling gladness for."

Elaine held her breath. The telephone was tight in her hands, poised halfway between her ear and the cradle so that, while she was not exactly eavesdropping, she was nevertheless able to hear what was being said.

"I can't find anything to be glad about," said a woman's voice.

"You must think how long is eternity," Amita said gently. "You must not be being a servant only to this present life."

Elaine hung up carefully. Death, she thought. They were talking about death.

She had thought Amita too frivolous, too preoccupied with trees and lawns and gardens, to concern herself with matters of human life and death, and for the first time she perceived the woman in a sympathetic light. Until now, she had often spoken scornfully of Amita and her habits—made fun of her to the girls from the office when they went on weekends to Montclair Plaza to window shop or eat frozen yogurt—especially to Becca Livingston, her supervisor.

"Oh, God, yes. India," Becca would say. "Aren't you just sick to death of that stupid country? All the Public Television junk that drags on, episode after episode, with handsome brown men always running afoul of constipated Brit women. All those E. M. Forster movies."

"With handsome Brit women running afoul of constipated brown men," Elaine would say, to make Becca laugh.

"Any-who," Becca said. "Deliver me from ladies who wear bed-spreads and throw themselves on funeral pyres and stick pasties between their eyes, and from men with bad teeth, who smell of curry and gin. Not for me. No, thank you very much."

Today, Becca was pouring iced tea from a plastic pitcher. She was being conciliatory, taking her cue from Elaine and, possibly, from a temperature in the low hundreds. "Still, they're interesting people spiritually. Gods and goddesses for this, that and the other. And sex; lots of holy and explicit sex."

"I wouldn't know," Elaine said.

"Not to mention infinity," Becca said. "The inviting endlessness of the Universe. We Westerners are brought up to go straight ahead through life, cradle to grave and pray for the best. But your basic Hindus—nothing comes to a stop for them. Existence is like one enormous mill-wheel, and the river that turns it never runs dry." She stopped. "I should write that one down," she said.

|||| Becca liked to read Elaine's fortune from Tarot cards, and once in a while she cast the *I Ching*, using three Liberty-head dimes. "I don't know why it doesn't work with Roosevelt dimes," Becca said. "I just can't get readings that aren't contradictory." Sometimes she brought out the Ouija board and prompted Elaine to ask questions of her guide, an androgynous presence named Vatah. "What is Elaine's word for the year?" Becca asked at the first Ouija seance. The planchette moved through the arched alphabet to answer "B-E-L-I-E-F." "In what?" asked Elaine. "S-E-L-F," said Vatah. How to account for that? With her fingers on the pointer, Elaine was certain she was not willing the choices of alphabet, but the pale wood, shaped like a leaf fallen from the tree of her life,

moved and spelled and answered. The planchette had a circular cutout, large enough to display one of the Ouija letters, and it was inset with a tiny magnifying glass like an eye focused on Elaine's future. All her fortunes told her that she would face one major setback, but that if she were patient—and if she believed in herself—she would achieve her life's desire.

Becca herself claimed to be psychic, and was full of gossip about the occult and the supernatural. Elaine was never sure if she should trust the things Becca told her; perhaps they were only stories she made up while she was on the freeways, driving from town to town to read the account books of small-businessmen.

Once Elaine asked, "Do you really think everyone has had a past existence?"

"Oh, yes." Becca was positive. "How else to explain people's irrational fears, or the déjà vu phenomenon, or that queer sense that the things we're doing are being guided by forces outside our will? My friend Heather? You remember: the skinny brunette we had dinner with in that Chinese restaurant in Riverside? She's terrified of earthquakes."

"Isn't everybody?"

"No, I mean really, pathologically afraid of them. It isn't normal, the way she reacts. She has a breakdown; she just curls up in a ball and weeps for days. Any-who, I took her back through her previous incarnations and, sure as you're born, she'd been killed in an earthquake in Peru, three hundred years ago. Enough said."

"You took her back?" Elaine was amazed.

"It's no big deal," Becca said. "You just have to let go, let yourself be carried back across the past. It's just one kind of self-hypnotism. Like to try it?"

So one day Elaine had positioned herself comfortably on Becca's couch, while Becca put a tape in the machine. She closed her eyes and relaxed, listening to a man's voice explain the procedure. She was to think of nothing, to open herself to the universe, to float upon the currents of time. Becca sat near her in a butterfly chair; Elaine could hear her friend's breathing, like a soft, celestial breeze that played through the interstices of the man's hypnotic words.

Not much happened. There were moments in those spaces between words that might have been glimpses of either past or future, silences filled with echo or premonition. There were moments when the words might have belonged to other places—her childhood Sunday School, the garden outside the annex windows, a music room. Finally, after what seemed a long and mindless time, Elaine heard herself say, "I wonder what Amita would think about this."

"Oh, Amita," Becca said.

"I do think I could begin to like her. If only she would sleep later on the weekends."

She kept her eyes closed. She heard Becca move against the canvas and the frame of the chair creak.

"I have the feeling you're not taking this seriously," Becca said. She got up and stopped the tape in midsentence.

"I'm sorry," Elaine said. "I don't know why I'm so distracted."

ⅢⅢ She missed her father. After a year had passed, she wrote to invite him for a visit—invited both parents, in fact, confident that her mother would decline. "There's a wall between mother and me," she told Becca. "A wall even love can never climb over."

"I'll bet that goes way back," Becca said. "Probably to some empress who slaughtered her children. Or an old patriarchal tribe that snuffed its daughters at birth."

"I think I was just too much responsibility for her. I came along while she still wanted a career."

"That's one way of looking at it," Becca said.

Her father arrived on a March afternoon at the Ontario airport. Standing at the arrival gate, a tamed and warmish Santa Ana wind blowing her hair across her face, Elaine was not surprised to feel impatience when the flight from Cedar Rapids was held out of the gate by an enormous UPS airplane that crawled slowly across the apron; a year was the longest separation from her father she had ever endured. When his plane was at last parked, she watched nervously—what if he'd missed his connection?—and was relieved when he emerged from the doorway and came down the steps, a magazine under his arm, a sporty driving cap perched on his head.

But as he walked toward her she was heartsick. His step seemed slower, his face was drawn and lined; even his smile was thinner than she remembered. It was ten years since his cancer surgery; had the doctors failed him? When he saw her and waved, she could scarcely lift her hand, and then she touched it to her mouth in a gesture of sad recognition.

"Daddy."

They hugged; she could feel his shoulder blades as if they were stripped bare under his suit jacket. He smelled of talcum and stale malt. When he kissed her cheek, his beard was harsh on her skin.

"I had to change planes in Phoenix," he said. "I've never seen mountains like that. When we were coming down, I thought they were slag heaps, like up near Superior."

"You look wonderful," she lied. "I'm glad you could get away."

"Not much doing in March," he said. "Can't get into the fields yet—not that I'm that active. Next year I think I'll rent all the land out to Paul Tobler."

"How's Mom?"

He grinned at her. "Tough," he said. His gums had drawn away from his teeth, and the teeth were the color of stucco.

Elaine took his arm and steered him into the terminal.

"Your bags are through here," she said.

"Only got one," he said. "I travel light."

She thought he had lost his balance, for he suddenly fell against her. My God, she thought, he *is* sick, he's having some kind of attack, and she tried to embrace him, to keep him from falling. But then she realized something was happening to her own equilibrium.

The cement floor under her feet was rocking; the air of the terminal echoed with shrieks and shouts; people dropped to their knees between the rows of seats. She looked anxiously at her father.

"The hell," he said.

Before she could say "It's an earthquake," one of the windows between the waiting room and the arrival gates shattered and fell. The sound of the breaking was like a chord, but without the tremulous echo that trails real music. Shards of heavy glass sprayed through the room, making lighter notes where they struck.

All she could do was hold on to her father; she put her free hand up to cover her eyes and hugged him against her, thinking the movement under and around them would stop at any moment and they could breathe with relief and make jokes about the event. But it went on, the shuddering and the excited voices, far longer than the tremor that had once given her pause in the shower at the annex—went on for ten seconds, twenty seconds, more seconds than she was prepared to count.

When it was finally finished, she felt dazed. The voices in the terminal fell to an ordinary hubbub, people picked themselves up from their crouching, a few children were sobbing. She looked at her father. The expression on his face was sardonic.

"I imagine you're used to this," he said.

She shook her head. "Never," she said.

And then she saw that there was a vivid trickle of blood down the back of the hand that held his magazine. She gasped.

"Look at you," she said. "My God."

He looked down. "Must have been a piece of that big window," he said. "I didn't even feel it." He took a handkerchief from his back pocket and wrapped it around the cut. "It's piddly," he said. He winked at her. "Let's go tell those baggage handlers to shake a leg."

By the time they left the terminal, it was dusk. The wind had died, the air was balmy, palpable. Here and there in the expanse of the parking lot were flashing headlights, and the relentless pulse of car alarms shaken into life by the earthquake. Elaine carried her father's bag—a blue Samsonite case that belonged to Mother—and led the way down a long aisle of cars.

"Doesn't feel like March," her father said. "Balmy. I see why you like California, earthquakes and all."

"That's only the third or fourth I've felt in all the time I've been out here. And it was the worst."

"Mother Nature wanted to initiate me," he said. "Show this Iowa farmer you can't take the land for granted." He took off his cap and wiped at his forehead with the back of his hand. "I could use a nap," he said.

Elaine thought how thin his hair was; how bald he had gotten since she had last seen him.

‖‖ Her father's hand healed in a few days, and the aftershocks from the tremor that wounded him gradually subsided in strength and frequency. For the first week the shocks were surprisingly violent, shaking her apartment with a noise and a shudder like a truck hitting the side of the building. Books fell; dishes rattled. If it happened while she was home from work, her father raised an eyebrow in her direction. Did he think she had some private foreknowledge, some wisdom she kept from him?

"Those things aren't unusual," Becca said. "Mystics know. Animals have premonitions. Did you know that the day your father flew in, hours before the five-point-five, coyotes gathered in a clearing on the side of Mt. Baldy and howled together?"

"I wish they'd howled loud enough so I could have heard them"

"But don't you just love quakes?" Becca said. "That energy, that elemental force?"

This was a conversation they'd had at work; Elaine had walked away. How could one possibly respond to that sort of enthusiasm?

"I was with friends," Amita said when Elaine introduced her father on that Sunday afternoon. "We were making gossip, drinking tea, and then we saw a mountain fall down."

"Rockslide," her father said. Amita nodded and bowed.

As for Father, he took a solemn interest in the neighborhood fault patterns—a subject to which Elaine had never paid much attention. They were between the San Andreas and San Jacinto faults, she told him. That was as much as she knew. "The side of the San Andreas that will someday be desirable beachfront," Becca liked to say.

After scrupulous attention to the television, her father announced to Elaine that in fact they were perched on top of a smaller east-west fault known as the Cucamonga, and it was this one that lay at the center of what he took to calling "his" earthquake.

"Years from now," he said, "you'll remember my earthquake and think of it as the time the airport fell on Father."

His plan was to stay the month—long enough that she was afraid entertaining him might become a problem. She had made a tourist list: Universal Studios, the L.A. County and Norton Simon museums, the gardens at the Huntington, the Queen Mary. None of those places engaged him, and so they did not go to them. He wanted to see where she worked, made flattering remarks to her colleagues, rode with her on one of her auditing daytrips. He spent hours sitting under the blue-and-white umbrella in Amita's back yard, "watching flowers grow"—though in fact he mostly dozed in the shade. One Sunday Elaine coaxed him to Santa Anita and watched him lose seventeen dollars on the horses.

"Big spender," he said to her. "But I can't take it with me."

It surprised her that her father was so easy a guest. She was relieved not to squander her vacation time, and yet the feeling nagged at her—she was frightened by her father's lethargy.

"Nothing special," he said when she asked if anything was wrong. "Your old dad's maybe getting past the gallivanting stage."

When she could, she left work midafternoon, and they sat together in Amita's green and flowered yard with iced tea and sugar cookies—listening to the mocking bird that regularly held forth from the live oak, breathing the heady scent of rambler roses that had begun to open into the unseasonable warmth. From time to time Amita joined them, and then they drank spiced tea from translucent cups and talked about the world and its differences from one culture to the next.

"In India are farmers too," Amita said. "What now I am hearing people call 'aquaculture,' it is the ancient way of my father and grandfather. Rice. Beans. All lifting to the sunlight from mud and wet."

"There's another word," Elaine's father said. He put up one hand, as if to keep the women from interrupting. "I've read about it. It's getting to be fashionable." His eyes darted from one face to the other, as if the word might be read there. "Hydroponics," he said. "That's what they call it now, but it's the same thing."

"Full circle," Elaine said.

"Like the serpent which swallows its tail." Amita looked at Elaine's father and reached for his teacup. "Do you wish me to read your fortune?"

Elaine's father grinned. "I've heard that's what everybody does in California."

"Only *some* bodies," Amita said solemnly. "But you must hold the cup so—" Left-handed, she held her own teacup by its handle and lifted it from the saucer. "—and be moving it in a circle, three times, leftward. Yes?" She looked at Elaine. "Leftward?"

"Counter-clockwise?" Elaine said.

"Just so."

Elaine's father imitated their hostess; he winked at Elaine.

"Now to put the cup down, this way, so, in its own dish." Amita inverted her cup over the saucer and set it there. The man did the same; some of the dregs of pale tea seeped out from under the edge of the cup. Amita reached across the table and rotated his cup three times more—Elaine counted—and tilted it up to look inside.

"What's the verdict?" Elaine's father said.

Amita tipped the thin cup to show him a cluster of tea leaf shreds at the bottom rim, under the handle.

"Once more a circle, but this one only slightly open, not yet being closed."

"Which means?"

"Perhaps some thing soon to be finished," Amita said.

"Of course," Elaine said. "Daddy's visit. His plane leaves in a week."

"Maybe it means the end of the world," he said. "Another one of your quakes."

"Also success," said Amita. "The circle as it is closing is the sign of achievement. Yes? 'Achievement'?"

"Ah," Elaine's father said.

But Elaine felt suddenly annoyed. She wished Becca were here; Becca would have done the same ritual, but she would have explained it as she went and Elaine would have put more trust in the outcome. "What about the stars?" she said. "You should ask my father his sign."

"Libra," her father said.

"Astrological science," Amita said. "Are you believing in such?"

"Could be," he said. "I don't want to shut my mind." He looked over at Elaine and winked again. "I guess that if stars control planets, and planets influence moons, and the moon affects tides here on Earth, then it would be foolish of me not to concede that they might push around my hundred-and-fifty pounds pretty easy."

"I am not so familiar with Zodiac things," Amita said.

"It's O.K.," Elaine's father said. "I've had enough hocus-pocus for one day."

"You should talk to Becca," Elaine said, but what she was now thinking of was how little he weighed—his casual acknowledgement of how slight he had become—and how different he was from the strapping man whose presence had guarded her childhood.

"I am seeing eternity in the eyes of your father," Amita told her early one evening of the last week of his visit. The three of them had taken tea, and the man was napping in the white chair set under the bird-of-paradise blossoms. "It is making me humble."

She whispered, so she would not wake him, but the words sent a chill through Elaine, a coldness sharper than the mere onset of dark.

\\\\ On the night before her father's departure she lay awake and wondered how ill he might really be: his cheeks so hollowed, his skin almost gray. The next morning in the terminal, her father walked warily and quickly under the new glass. At the departure gate, he motioned for her to sit beside him on the heavy bench and told her what she had known and been afraid to confront. The wind was hot on her face and took her breath—it was as if each word her father uttered brought her nearer the suffocation of dread.

"They never got all of it," he said. "They never do. It's the same cancer they wrestled with ten years ago. My young doctor thinks it started farther back than that, way back in the fifties or sixties, from the chemicals we used on the crops. Herbicides or pesticides—who knows which? It might be like that Agent Orange stuff we sprayed on our own troops in the jungles. You know how careless we were in the old days, how we didn't know any better. Nobody ever warned the farmers, and if they had, we're a stubborn bunch. What farmer would have listened?"

He embraced her and kissed her.

"That's why I came out to California," he said. "To see you all grown up and living your own life. To tell you we probably shouldn't plan to get together again. Leastwise not on this side of the border."

Elaine sat without words, his thin hands enclosing both of hers, his life—pulse and warmth and the small tremblings of his love for her—touching hers for probably the last time.

He grinned at her. "I don't mean Mexico," he said.

How could she laugh with him? She wanted to beg him to stay, not go back to her mother who, she knew, would never be patient with him, or gentle, or generously attentive. She wanted to keep him here, thousands of miles from the land and the life that had murdered him.

Instead, she leaned her head against his shoulder and gazed silently through the bars of the waiting area: at the sun shimmering off the white tarmac, at the baggage handlers laughing together under the silver belly of the jetliner that would take her father from her.

"Why is she the way she is?" she said.

"Your mother?" She felt a movement of his shoulder that was either shrug or sigh. "I think she just expected a better shake from life."

"Then why didn't she leave you?"

He laughed. "'What fools these mortals be,'" he said.

He sat straighter, obliging Elaine to lift her head. "I took good care of her," he said. "She was never cold, never hungry."

"And you took care of me," Elaine said.

"I tried. God knows I tried."

"Do you remember the day you killed the rooster?"

His brow furrowed.

"I was six or seven. That was back when Mom was trying to raise chickens, and you and I were walking across the yard when this huge red rooster came after me. He was pecking at me, at my ankles. I was terrified. I was bare-legged, and every time the rooster pecked me I'd see a new spot of blood appear."

"And I wrung its neck," he said. "Did I?"

"Yes. You do remember. You reached down and grabbed its neck and just swung it in the air once. It took a half-second." And the sound it made, she could still hear; the awful breaking of the rooster's neck—something tearing: thick paper, or a cloth becoming rags. "Then you just tossed it onto the ground."

"It didn't please your mother."

"Oh, Daddy," she said. She flung her arms around his shoulders and hugged. "I thought you were perfect."

The gate was open, the other passengers making a queue, and her father stood up to join them.

"It's funny," he said, "that you remember me killing something."

He kissed her on the forehead and gave up his ticket to the attendant. Then, when he was halfway across the tarmac, he stopped and came back to where Elaine stood trying not to weep. He put up one hand as if in farewell, but he didn't touch her.

"Thanks for the earthquake," he said.

Ⅲ A few weeks after, she had dinner with Becca and told about her father's fortune as revealed in his teacup.

"What's Amita doing with tea leaves?" Becca wanted to know. "That's not a Hindu thing."

"I don't know. She just offered to tell his fortune."

"Well, it's obvious," Becca said. "The circle is completion, a death image, the end of a life."

"But Amita said the circle could also mean success."

Becca gave her a pitying smile. "Don't you know? If the reader offers the reading, the prophecy is actually always bad."

"Oh, God," Elaine said.

When she came home from that very dinner, she found recorded on her answering machine the news she dreaded most: her mother's terse "Your father's gone; the funeral's Saturday morning." It was too late to place a call to Iowa, so she undressed herself in a kind of solemn trance and went to bed. Amita had forgotten to turn out the yard lights; the room glowed with pinkish light and unusual shadows, as if that day's sun would not quite set. She slept brokenly, and late the next morning she woke with sharp cramps in her legs. The pain was in the calves, at the back of the legs, and she gritted her teeth as she kneaded the muscles and tried to relax herself. Salt, was it, that made cramps happen? Lack of salt? She thought she had read that somewhere, and resolved to take better care with her diet.

To make her discomfort worse, she heard voices—many voices—outside her bedroom window. The voices were close and clear, the rhythm of them like the rhythm of Amita's speech, so that Elaine was not surprised after she hurriedly put on her robe and looked outside to find the backyard populated by black-haired women in saris, and brown-skinned men in white shirts and ties and dark business suits. There were perhaps a dozen people, some carrying tall tumblers of iced tea, some with shorter glasses she took to contain whiskey or colored gin. They stood in knots of three and four in front of a large canvas propped against the back fence—the canvas an enormous painted landscape that displayed snow-capped mountains rising from a green, tropical valley into a turquoise sky.

I have solitude without privacy, she reminded herself. She wanted to slide the aluminum window-frame open, to shout at Amita and her guests, *My father is dead.* But then she remembered the compassionate tone of Amita's voice as she had consoled the unknown woman at the other end of the overheard phone connection, and her anger softened. The impulse to complain left her; she limped into the bathroom to shower and begin her first full day of grief.

After she dressed and made coffee, the cramps were gone, but now the pain had consolidated itself in her right foot, in the heel, so that she favored it by limping on the ball of that foot. She called a travel agency to arrange her flight home, and by the time she had packed, and phoned Becca to tell her she would be away from work for a few days, the pain in her right foot was so severe that she almost fell when she stepped outside to empty the trash. All she wanted was to drag herself back into the apartment, pour a small glass of wine, and prop herself up in bed with a book until it was time to leave for the airport. But as she was carrying the wastebasket into the annex, Amita appeared at the back door of the main house.

"I am having a nice cup of tea," Amita announced. "Please to join with me? Perhaps from your father's visit we are at last truly acquaintances?"

Her sentences curved upward like questions pleading to be answered. There was that about Amita's speech—the inimitable lilt of it that turned English into unresolved melodies.

"I'd like to," Elaine said, "except that I'm having a lot of trouble getting around." She turned so that Amita could see her face and—she hoped—the agony written upon it. "My foot," she said. "It's very painful. I don't know if I've sprained it or what."

"You are not feeling well?" Amita descended the two steps from the back door and took Elaine's arm. She was dressed as she had been earlier, in a vivid blue sari and pale-leather sandals; a spot of cosmetic red was vivid on her brow. "I will help you walking," she said. "Come."

"Really, no," Elaine said, but her protest was futile. Amita was supporting her up the steps and into the main house.

"What is?" Amita said. "Did you fall?"

"I don't know. It's like a shooting pain in my right foot; it starts in the arch and stabs into the heel."

"Shooting?" Amita said. "That is serious business, shooting."

"It *feels* serious," Elaine said. She let herself be led to an upholstered chair and sank into it. The chair faced an ornate coffee table upon which Amita's tea service was set out: the delicately-flowered teapot, sugar and creamer, the shallow bowl with lemon wedges, two paper-thin cups and saucers—all arranged on an oval silver tray. The table was low, of dark wood, exotically carved into a relief of elephants and palm-leaf backgrounds, and it looked as if it might also be a cabinet of some kind.

"You had company earlier," Elaine said. "Very distinguished-looking ladies and gentlemen."

"Oh, yes. It is Doctor Chatterjee, my painter friend. He is arrived home from a visit to India and Nepal. He is showing off to us in my flower garden his new work. Stately mountains. He and his wife, and I with my late husband, we have been closest friends from India and from California. Kamal and Bharati Chatterjee."

"I didn't know about your husband—that you were married."

"Oh, he is long dead." Amita laid her right hand over her breast. "The heart," she said. "He had no pain. As for myself, I have the tending of the trees, the grasses, the flowers."

"Death is very much on *my* mind," Elaine said, "because my father has just died. My mother telephoned." She tried—her foot was throbbing—to make herself more comfortable in the chair.

"I am sorry to hear. I had thought it, meeting him, looking into the deep well of his eyes. But the death is no matter," Amita said. It was as if the older woman were scolding her. "Because of death, the soul is hastened on its path through the Creation. It achieves—" She stopped. "I cannot say the word for it."

"Rebecca would agree that the soul lives on. A friend of mine."

"Yes, she is correct. You will grieve for your father's body; that is proper—but also you will rejoice for the soul which leaves him."

"I wish I understood that."

"A dear American friend of my own, she recently has lost her daughter in a motorcar accident. I am trying very hard to wish her to be at peace. She cannot be convinced."

"Americans are skeptics," Elaine said. "An American wants to know exactly where the soul is going, and which airline it's taking."

"I am no wise person," Amita said, "being like you merely a woman. But if you ask me: What is the farthest destination of the soul's journey? My reply is: Its farthest destination is to the city of enlightenment, the place where the labor of each soul is accomplished and is of highest imaginable good." She poured steaming tea into Elaine's cup. "Please," she said, "share with me this lovely tea."

Elaine took the cup and saucer and brought them to her lap. The light from the front window glowed in the teacup; the liquid was the color of sunsets she had seen regularly since she moved West.

"It is from my native Calcutta, this tea. Sometimes it is called 'Mogul's Dream.'"

"But how does the soul know when its work—its labor is accomplished?" Elaine pursued. "How does the person—the person in whom the soul lives—how does she know?"

"She will know," Amita said. She sipped from her cup, her eyes fixed on Elaine. The red spot on Amita's forehead seemed to Elaine to be a center, an artifice like the bright object a hypnotist might use to keep the attention of the person being mesmerized. "You will know," Amita repeated.

"How?"

"You see: the soul has lived many lives. Many, many lives. In each life the soul is carrying out some part of its entire mission. In each life it is accomplishing some part of its long journey to find the sublime." She clapped her hands together once. "That is the word I could not recall before. *Sublime*."

Elaine sat utterly without movement, her eyes fixed on the color between Amita's eyes. I am in California, she reminded herself. I am sitting in an ordinary house in California—one of the states of the United States, just as Iowa is.

|||| "To achieve the sublime, it is a serious endeavor," Amita said. "It cannot be attained in one lifetime only, nor even in two or three, for the sublime is a very far distant place. This is why the soul—which is making what you Americans may call a 'deal' with God, saying to God, 'I will make the sublime my destiny'—this is why the soul must cross the bridges of several lives in order to carry out the arrangement agreed upon. You understand 'deal'? It was my husband's word. In some religions, the people say the soul has twelve lives before the deal is finished, but it is not my particular belief."

"Is it a happier place—this next life?"

Amita smiled. "This is depending," she said.

"On what?"

"On many things. For my poor husband, I am sure the bridge has led him to a better universe—a better deal. He is now godlike, as he always wished. He was a man of strong opinion, a positive man. 'Do you wish to argue?' he would say, 'or do you wish the truth?' He is perhaps a rock, or a tree of teak. He is something which cannot be bent, I am sure."

"Do we all have many lives?"

Amita smiled. "Child, you have had many more lives than one," she said. "And your father especially more. Do please be drinking your tea."

"Yes," Elaine said. She tasted the liquid in the cup. It was warm and smelled of perfume; it left a bitter aftertaste. She realized she must have grimaced, for Amita appeared surprised.

"You don't like?" she said.

"I'm sorry. It's different from what we all drank outside. Not a taste I expected."

Amita opened the carved wooden door of the table and reached inside. She brought out a green bottle, uncapped it, and poured a small amount of clear liquid into Elaine's tea.

"Simply gin," Amita said. "It will make the Mogul's Dream perhaps more palatable for you. Also it will be relaxing the body." She poured a bit into her own teacup, then put the bottle away.

Elaine tasted her drink; the odor of the gin mingled with the other, and it did seem to cancel out the novel bitterness of the tea.

"My friend Rebecca," Elaine said, "she often talks of the travels of the soul. She claims she can lead me through my former lives."

"Yes, if you wish to go, then you must go," Amita said. "Have you tried already?"

"I lay on her couch and listened to a tape recording."

"And the voice of the record was carrying you back?"

"I'm not sure," Elaine said.

She tried to recapture the afternoon at Becca's house, before her father's visit and her mother's message blotted it out. There was a sunporch behind Becca, a brilliant cube of light, like an aquarium she swam in—the butterfly chair a giant sea creature, a ray; the room swimming too, the furniture mimicking a topography of the floor of the ocean, and Becca's sleek gray cat moving across the figured carpet as silently as a marine shadow. The voice from the tape machine was measured and deep, almost a whisper, urging her—not backward in time so much as downward—and she had experienced an odd sense of dissolving in this room of Becca's, putting herself back together in another room, another time. Too much television foolishness, her mother would have said, and yet now she remembered that for a few moments she had indeed been moving among unfamiliar people in a familiar place. There were gaslights; she could smell the heat of the flames. The walls were paneled. She was dressed in unaccustomed clothing that rustled. She could not quite manage to see anyone's face. "I don't think I tried hard enough."

"It is not so very easy," Amita said. "It is like what you would in other places call—I do not know the word; it is what prevents a still object from moving."

"Inertia."

Amita clapped her hands happily. "Justly so. Inertia. Inert, yes? You know its meaning? The soul is resident in the body, it needs not to be moving except at the birth and death, at the beginning and end, of a human life. And the body, you see, the body makes claim upon the soul; the body is not wishing the soul to travel, for the soul is what gives body the spark of living; the body is being fearful the soul will not return, lest the body die."

"Like my father's," Elaine said. She drank the last of the spiked tea and set the delicate cup in its saucer. "I have to fly home."

"And so you should do, should you not?"

"Except that I'm practically an invalid," Elaine said. "I can hardly walk with the pain in my foot and ankle."

"Ah," Amita said. "Ah, yes."

"Rebecca would tell me it's psychosomatic—that it's all in my head, my fancy—but I say what difference does it make? I still can't get around."

Amita poured both tea and gin into their cups, sliding Elaine's toward her, sipping from her own, her bright black eyes fixed on Elaine, the mark on her brow taking the afternoon light and transforming it into a vermillion as pure as the color of blood. Elaine drank. A truck rumbled past the windows and the liquid in the cups trembled.

"Your father, he was very young," Amita said.

"Not even sixty. But he was a farmer; he handled those chemicals—weed-killers, insecticides—all his life." She shrugged, thinking she could not exactly explain to Amita the significance of such chemistry. "It's cancer," she said. "He told me when he was here."

"In his soul's next life," Amita said gently, "there will be no poisons. The poisons are done for him."

"I hope in my soul's next life there will be no pains in the legs," Elaine said.

But Amita did not smile. "What is true of body is always true of body," she said. "I do not mean to be saying a mystery; I mean that whenever the soul journeys, the body is being fearful. Your pain is a manifesting of that fear. The feet, they are the future. They are the means of taking you into the tomorrow, and so that is where body has chosen to put the pain. But you must be respectful to your father, despite discomfort."

"I can't bring him back," Elaine said.

"The spirit does not look back," Amita said, "of course. But so much is clear: You are obliged to go to him. It is in the pact the soul has made. If it should be otherwise, then body would not try to deceive you with the pain in your foot." She smiled and lifted her cup. "Go. As soon as your airplane is in the sky, body will surrender and your foot will not be hurting you."

And it was true. By two o'clock the following morning, when she arrived at her parents' house and let herself in the front door with the key she always carried—and even though she was met by her mother standing on the hall stairs, insisting that her father had died peacefully and, never mind, he would not have recognized her—her foot felt fine.

|||| She stayed three days. On the third day, after the funeral service, she drove her mother home from the cemetery. The two women were silent the whole way. Outside the car the undulating fields showed corn-green to the horizons; the only trees were lines and groves of windbreak pine or poplar along the west and north boundaries of empty farmyards. The air had a clarity and a luminescence that magnified distance, and because there were neither forests nor mountains, nothing concealed the passages of the weather over this place.

Inside the house where she had been a child, she sat for a while in the dim parlor with its lace curtains and gold-framed paintings and the baby grand piano that had not been tuned in years. Mourners—mostly family friends from towns nearby—stood or posed stiffly on the edges of needlepoint chair seats; they sipped tea and coffee from cups that had belonged to her father's maternal great-grandmother. There were small white cakes on white paper doilies, brought by one of the neighbors. The conversations were subdued and the atmosphere, Elaine thought, strained.

"We never use this room," she murmured to her mother. "It smells musty."

"I didn't have time to straighten up the living room," her mother said crossly. "And I didn't have the will. I had to make do."

Elaine looked away and bent her head over the teacup in her lap. It was an ordinary tea from ordinary teabags—nothing like Amita's. And this was an occasion when Elaine would certainly have welcomed the gin. Now she overheard her mother describing her father's last days: the morphine, the hallucinations, the awful end. When had his soul slipped away to resume its travels? she wondered. At one secret, flickering instant, in the agony between the sleep of the drug and the sleep of the body's death?

"Do you like California, dear?"

Startled, Elaine turned toward a small woman in a black cloche and black dress. "I'm sorry," she said. "My mind was wandering."

"Isn't that where you're living now? California?"

"Yes. Yes, I like it a lot."

"I'm Margaret Adams," the woman said. "You went to school with my Beatrice."

"Oh, yes." *You have to be crazy to think something like that could happen.* Elaine smiled and pressed the woman's hand. "Forgive me. I think Mother expects me to help her."

She went to the kitchen. Her mother was taking a tray of tiny, crustless sandwiches out of the refrigerator.

"Remember when Daddy took me to the place where the space-ship landed? Out behind the school?"

"Your father was an extremely gullible man," her mother said. She peeled aside the sheet of waxed paper that covered the sand-wiches. "Look at these," she said. "The church auxiliary sent them; what do you bet they're leftovers from last Wednesday's hen-party?" She picked up the tray and carried it to the parlor.

Elaine followed. Mostly it was women who had stayed to nibble the trimmed sandwiches and talk in hushed voices about the service. She tried to imagine the presence of Amita in sari and sandals, the red mark bright on her forehead, her sweet smile radiant among the mourners.

"I thought maybe I'd drive out there," Elaine said.

"Suit yourself," her mother said.

Elaine set her tea aside and left the room, acknowledging as she went the few mourners she knew, the eyes and mouths that ex-pressed condolence. Not a single face said: *joy.* No one said: *fare well.*

ꟷ The road that led to Andersen's field was familiar and still un-paved, but she scarcely recognized the neighborhood of the old school. The school itself had been torn down. Houses were every-where, ranch houses with small yards and tiny attached garages. The development had a single cement access road, off the end of which, starlike, the houses clustered along three short sidestreets ending in cul-de-sacs. It encroached on most of the old hayfield.

For a few minutes Elaine was lost, but once she had left the rented car and walked behind the houses to discover the wonderful arc of goldenrod, what had originally happened there flowed back into her mind with all the pure force of a vision. She saw her child self in the center of the curious landing site, standing beside her fa-ther, holding hard to his upper arm as if she feared she would be blown away by the winds of another world, another atmosphere.

"Look at this," her father had said. "Imagine the size of it." Then he had drawn her hand down his arm until his own fingers gripped hers and led her to the blackened perimeter of the circle. "You take the inside track," he told her, "and I'll take the outside."

Still holding hands, the two of them had walked the ring, counterclockwise, her father outside the circle, herself inside, the path of bent and blackened grass making a distance of a yard or so between them. Periodically, there would be a place within the ring where the grass was burned shorter and the earth itself had changed color, and here her father would stop for a moment, their joined hands so far extended above that place that she could feel the stretch of the muscles under her arm.

"Hotspot," her father had said. "This was where the exhaust shot down from the engines. Imagine the heat."

They found seven such spots; at each her father made her pause, and at each he marveled. Driving home in the pickup, he had lectured her. "Old Shakespeare had it right: 'More things in heaven and earth' than we dream of. Maybe yours'll be the generation that sees these things for real—not just the scars they leave behind."

"Maybe," she had said. What had she believed at the time, and what ought she have told Beatrice Adams? Whatever she should have said then, today she would have to say, "How dare I not believe?" Anything less would betray her father, herself, all the traffic of the world's souls on the crowded paths meandering toward eternity.

"Sometimes they take people away with them," her father had said. "Take them right into space to find out what makes humans tick. And sometimes the people never come back."

"Do you believe that's true?"

"I don't know, honey. Those are just the stories."

"Maybe the people are liars," she said. "Or crazy." She had kept quiet after that, pondering the matter. Why would people make up such a thing? And what about those who supposedly never returned?

"Maybe they're just lonely," her father said.

On this adult visit she knelt in the curved field of goldenrod and began gathering the bright flowers, pulling the stalks out of the ground. The earth smelled like mildew; she wondered if its smell was unique because of the intense heat it had once absorbed. She brought the roots of one of the plants up to her face. Something intense, acid, filled her nostrils, like ammonia or lye or strong vinegar or all of those, mingled and indistinguishable. Nothing at all like the death-smell of earth at her father's graveside.

The day her father first learned of his cancer—it was hardly a year after they had walked their fascinated circle—she had come alone to this place. She had sat in the center of the ring and wept for Daddy, though she was scarcely thinking of death at thirteen years old, had not yet even begun to confront the possibility that the cancer would kill him. She had only sat and wept, a part of her mind wishing the UFO would return to fetch her, take her wherever the people who never came back had been taken; another part weighing her love and concern for her father, trying to make sense of the news he had brought home to his family. Finally she had gone even further, to the deepest part of her mind, to grapple with the question of what happens when someone dies—where do they go, and is it the same place where they came from?—and she heard herself complaining out loud, "Wherever I was before I was born, why didn't you leave me there?"

All at once her father's arms were around her, and he was lifting her up, saying, "Because we wanted you. Because we love you."

She remembered that at first she had thought the voice, and the arms lifting her off the ground, were God's—a confusion Amita might understand—and when she realized that her father had followed her here, she had begun crying all over again.

She took a different road back to the cemetery, crossing the wooden viaduct over the abandoned Illinois Central tracks, the long stalks of goldenrod heavy with harsh perfume on the seat beside her. Elaine marveled that at the funeral she had not been able to cry for her father's sake. She felt not much of anything—certainly not loss, not regret, not fear—and for a few minutes she sat in the car at the

Prentiss plot and surveyed the empty scene. The mounded earth that hid her father's physical remains was smothered in the flowers from the church. What was important about her father was no longer accessible to her; certainly it was not buried under this decorated earth.

She got out of the car and carried the armful of goldenrod to the grave. She arranged the stalks in a circle, on top of the nursery flowers, knowing how foolish her action would look to anyone watching—these weeds, piled on these cultivated blossoms—but saying to herself that everyone chose a different measure for grief. Her mother's was bitterness; hers was only a version of her father's willingness to believe in things he could not see.

"Safe journey," she whispered over the swollen earth. "Remember this place."

In the car, she looked back only once. Perhaps she might have done or said something more appropriate—surely the soul in its travels could not in any conventional sense "remember"—though even in the dusk the wreath of goldenrod blazed behind her like a landmark. She drove away from it as fast as she dared on gravel— home first for her bags, and then on to the airport, California, the unsettled edge of this world.

Hard Times

When I was twelve the war was still in its first
year and Jimmy Barraclough, who had been our paperboy for as
long as I could remember, enlisted in the navy and went off to fight.

"How could that happen?" my mother said to my father. "He
can't be more than sixteen if he's a day."

My father shrugged. He was hidden behind the *Evening Express*,
probably reading yesterday's Red Sox totals for the third time—he
also read them in the Boston Post and the Portland *Press Herald*,
both morning papers, as if he thought his re-readings could multi-
ply the Sox's success when they won, undo their failure when they
lost—and the shrug was not seen but telegraphed in the movement
of the newsprint.

"Only a child," my mother said. She looked at me, sadly, and
reached out to brush my hair away from my eyes.

"He looks old enough," my father said. "That's all a recruiter
cares about."

My father had been in the First World War; he enlisted in the
army out of college and was sent to officer candidate school at
Plattsburg. His view of Jimmy's enlistment was doubly brusque, first
because he had some experience of wartime, and second because he
thought my mother was too sentimental to exercise good judgment
in such a matter.

"I think it's a shame," my mother said.

My father lowered the newspaper to look at her. I never got used to that look; it combined aggravation and pity and scorn, and though I had seen it many times before, it always shocked me. When I was very young it had frightened me because it seemed to say that there was no more affection between them, and I wondered what might become of me, left alone in a hard world by loveless parents. Now that I was older, the fear had only turned to confusion. My mother seemed to displease my father, but he did not become angry or abusive; he simply looked at her, so.

"Well, it is a shame," she repeated. "What if he's killed?"

"He won't be killed." My father disappeared behind the *Express*.

"I hope not." She kissed me gently on the brow. "Think of his poor mother then."

||| Even though Jimmy Barraclough had no mother—she had "run off" with a man she worked with in the payroll department of the Scoggin textile mill, Jimmy told me—I shared my own mother's hope that he would survive the war. I felt I owed him a lot, for though he was nearly four years older he was a sixth grade classmate of mine, and I was one of the few younger boys whose presence he tolerated. Jimmy was waiting to be sixteen so that he could legally drop out of school, and I think my size—I was tall for my age—had something to do with his tolerance. Everyone else made him seem out of place, a giant among pygmies, and he must have felt singled out and oafish in that Edison School classroom presided over by Mrs. Florence Hardy.

In matters of true wisdom, matters unrelated to arithmetic and Palmer Method penmanship, Jimmy far outdistanced me. He had taught me to swear; he had introduced me to the vocabulary of human anatomy, particularly the female; he had taught me snappy comebacks—if somebody said, "Got a match?" you might say, "Yeah, my feet and your breath"—what my father would have called "smart remarks," worth a cuff across the face if he ever heard them.

Once Jimmy had actually shared a cigarette with me—a Lucky Strike—and, though I could not then appreciate the pleasure of inhaling, the dark green Luckies pack with its red-disc bull's-eye symbolized for me the world adults lived in and enjoyed. For all her compassion, my mother would have been horrified to know how much, and for what, I admired Jimmy Barraclough.

At the end of April, when Jimmy lied about his age and went away to the navy, I took over his paper route. The inheritance was unexpected. True, I had helped him—or he had let me follow him on the route—many times, especially on Fridays and Saturdays, collection days, and I think it was not only that my arithmetic skills were useful to him, but that I could be more patient with his slower-paying customers. All but one—a Mrs. Ouellette, who lived on the first floor of a yellow tenement house on Riverside Avenue—he seemed relieved for me to attend to.

There was no Mr. Ouellette. Mrs. Ouellette was a divorced woman, small and plain, whose apartment smelled of something spoiled. She had at least two small children—we saw them or heard them whenever we knocked at her door; they were forever bawling—and she wore a pink housecoat and pink bedroom slippers coming apart at the seams. Rarely did she have the money to pay Jimmy and me. Sometimes she would fetch her purse and make a show of looking through it for the thirty cents she needed, but more often than not she would simply look helpless and ask us to come back another day.

"Come back Sunday," she would say. "I'll have it for you then."

She must have known that Sunday was the most awkward day for Jimmy or me to call—though for a long time, call we did. Eventually, Jimmy seemed to write her off. "Never mind old Ouellette," he'd say. "I'll collect on my way home from the Y." The YMCA was on the third floor of the Masonic Building, but the basement was occupied by Scoggin Square Billiards and Bowling, and that's what Jimmy meant when he referred to the Y. It had five pocket-pool tables, one three-cushion billiards table, four candlepin alleys, and it was the high school hangout, the place where "the bad boys," as my mother referred to them, played Baby Eight—a nickel on the three and five, a dime on the eight. Sentimental like my mother, I used to worry that he might be distracted enough to stop delivering to her, but he kept her on his books, and then I imagined that some of my own patience had rubbed off on him.

|||| I already had a sort of job, stopping by the Western Union office in the Hotel Belmont after school, delivering whatever telegrams had come in that day, but I was paid only a dime for each telegram and I could never count on a tip unless I brought especially good news to somebody. Taking over Jimmy's paper route gave me new status at home, and the extra money was a large part of that status. My father was a schoolteacher—he had gone to Amherst and gotten his master's in history at Harvard, and for a year when he and my mother were first married he had taught at a famous prep school in New Hampshire—but now he was practically unemployed. He did substitute teaching in the local high school, but mostly he kept the books for Tony Apollonio, a Greek who owned two novelty stores—we called them "fruit stores"—and operated a small trucking business between Boston and Portland. He was no trained accountant, my father, but he had a head for figures, a neat hand, and a polite but abiding interest in dollars and cents. I supposed he was good at his job for Apollonio. When I was younger, if I visited him on a Wednesday or Friday, days when he worked on the books, it seemed to me he was happy—that he was more accessible to me, more relaxed with me, than at home.

My mother was a telephone operator all through the 1930s and 40s. She never worked full time, except in the summer when the regular operators took their vacations, but she worked frequently and probably earned as much as my father did. I was terribly proud of her. Sometimes when she was working the day shift I would stop at the telephone office just before five o'clock and walk home with her. She let me sit in a high, caned chair beside her, watching her

work until her relief arrived, and I would admire her competence—
how she responded to the rows of pink and white lights on the board
in front of her, drawing from their storage holes the snakey cords
with brass plugs and punching them into the holes under the lights.
She asked for numbers in an exaggerated, telephone-operator
voice—"Number puh-leeze"—and when she was making a toll call
she recited numbers to other operators in Portland or Boston or
New York in such a way as to deny any mis-hearing: "I'm calling
thuh-REE, NI-yun, NI-yun, Jay-as-in-James." If I ever had to call
home from school, I would mimic my mother, telling the operator
"one, FI-yuv, thuh-REE, M-as-in-Mary," and feeling a kinship that
is impossible in modern times. "Is that you, Stevie?" one of them
would say. "Your mother has to work till six today, so she wants you
to go straight home."

IIII With Jimmy Barraclough's paper route, of course I inherited
Mrs. Ouellette, and I was determined from the start that I would not
permit the kind of postponement of payment Jimmy had been willing to tolerate. After all, I told myself to justify my determination,
Mr. Bradbury, the town's newspaper distributor, gave no extensions
to me. I would be exactly as hard with Mrs. Ouellette as Mr. Bradbury was hard with me.

For a few weeks I heeded my own advice and was as persistent as
I knew how to be in collecting Mrs. Ouellette's weekly thirty cents.
If she didn't have the money on Friday, the usual collection day, I
stopped again on Saturday, and if on Saturday she put me off, I was
on her porch, knocking on her screen door, on the following Monday. I think my doggedness shamed her; she always blushed and
made clumsy apologies when she finally brought out her purse and
gave me money. "I'm awfully sorry," she would say. "I don't want
you to think I'm a piker." I would duck my head and mumble that I
didn't think anything bad about her. "Sometimes my check is late,"
she'd say. "Sometimes I don't get to the bank to deposit it before
Friday comes." I didn't know what might be the source of her

checks, or if indeed there were checks, but I began to imagine Mrs. Ouellette might be a widow, not a divorcée.

This possibility softened my attitude toward her later on—widowhood being acceptably tragic, free of the taint divorce carried in that small New England town—and after a couple of months I returned to Jimmy Barraclough's pattern. If Mrs. Ouellette had no money one Friday, I let the matter go and hoped she would pay me the next. Sometimes she did. More often when she came to the door she looked at me sheepishly—the blue of her eyes was pale, like ice, or like the coarse crepe ribbon my mother bought to decorate our parlor when the telephone operators had a baby shower—and put me off again. "I don't know what's wrong with the mail," she would say. "My check's late again."

Through all of my visits the two little Ouellette kids were in the kitchen, crawling on the linoleum floor or tugging at Mrs. Ouellette's ratty-looking housecoat; their faces were always dirty, and even if they weren't bawling there would still be a greenish smear of snot shining under their noses. The kitchen was too warm and smelled of kerosene from a heater in the corner; something was always cooking on top of the gas stove—soup, I thought, or some kind of fishy-smelling chowder. Mrs. Ouellette herself looked tired and sad to me. She was never really dressed; if she wasn't in the housecoat, she was in an old blue men's bathrobe that was out at the elbows, and her hair looked as if it hadn't been washed or combed in weeks. Now, looking back, I realize she was a prettier woman than I gave her credit for at the time—even-featured, with melting blue eyes and a sweet, generous mouth—but in that first full year of the war I believe I simply wasn't wise enough to see past her weariness. To a twelve-year-old, appearances are everything.

\\\\ Fairly early in my administration of Jimmy's paper route I noticed that Mrs. Ouellette was pregnant. Even despite the looseness and chenille coarseness of the pink housecoat, the swell of her stomach became more and more obvious, so that by summer's end she could not have hidden the fact of the child she carried even if she wanted to. I knew it was wrong for women without husbands to have babies —never mind whether the women were widowed or divorced—but it didn't occur to me to condemn her. I only felt sorry for her, picturing a third runny-nosed child crawling on the kitchen floor and imagining the stink of dirty diapers added to the unpleasant atmosphere of her tenement rooms. All the more reason—or so I must have thought—not to press for the weekly thirty cents she owed me.

It was not entirely one-sided, this leniency between us. As time went on, Mrs. Ouellette changed in gestures and actions toward me. She was less apologetic about her failure to pay for the newspaper, more sociable and outgoing toward me when I knocked at her door. Sometimes she offered me lemonade or Moxie or, once in a while, iced coffee—which I always refused because coffee was a drink for adults. We sat at the kitchen table, the two of us—the Ouellette children squalling around us—as if we were at an afternoon tea party, and we talked about the men in our lives. She told me about Mr. Ouellette, who was not dead, and about his abandonment of her just before their second child was born, and I talked at some length about the difficulty of living up to my father's expectations of me. Probably I was boring company for her, but she never said so.

It must have been in the course of these Friday afternoons in Mrs. Ouellette's kitchen that I began to see that she was not as plain as I had thought. Perhaps it was the pregnancy that helped transform her, or it may have been the further sympathy I felt for her being rejected by her husband. In any case, her face seemed different—the features livelier, the eyes brighter—during our discussions. It might have been our subject matter; I had begun to wonder about the relations between married couples—how they seemed to leave each other in the lurch at crucial moments of their lives—and I remember one day confessing to Mrs. Ouellette my fears about my parents. She seemed amused by me.

"They sound pretty normal to me," she said. "If that's the worst he gives her—that dirty look—you're in luck."

"I wouldn't want to live by myself," I said.

"No, you wouldn't," she said. "It's no fun, unless you have something to look forward to."

That was the one time she touched me: reached out one hand—it seemed terribly small, the fingers pale and delicate, not a strong hand at all—and brushed the forelock of hair out of my eyes the way my mother sometimes did.

"Hope," she said to me. "We live on it, even when there's nothing and no one else."

IIII Jimmy Barraclough had been gone only a little more than four months—it was September of 1942—when the telegram came saying he'd been killed in the Pacific. I delivered it.

It wasn't the first telegram from the War Department I'd seen and handled. I'd brought missing-in-action messages to three or four families since the start of the war, and a couple of wounded-in-actions, and I'd even had an earlier killed-in-action that I delivered to a house on Ridgeway Avenue, a neighborhood where some of the wealthy mill executives lived. But until the telegram about Jimmy, I hadn't personally known the people affected. Also, I'd always put the bad news into the hands of the mothers of the soldiers and sailors—the fathers were at work in the afternoons, and in Scoggin the mothers didn't begin to do men's jobs in the textile mills or the shoe factory or at the Navy Yard in Kittery until later in the war—so that if I wasn't exactly comfortable with their moaning and weeping, at least I knew what to expect, and I didn't stay around any longer than I had to. Once they'd signed for the telegram, I was away, leaving them alone with their grief.

Because Jimmy's mother had gone off with another man, the address on the telegram didn't include her name. The news came to "Mr. Frank Barraclough, c/o Miller," Miller being the last name of the woman Jimmy's dad had moved in with after Jimmy went off to enlist.

Frank Barraclough was a local hero. When he graduated from

high school he'd had a tryout with the Red Sox, signed a contract
with them for a bonus that was rumored to have been a thousand
dollars, and actually played in the minor leagues for a couple of Sox
farm teams in the late 1920s. In his last year with the Sox, he played
for their Pawtucket farm team, but halfway through the season he
was hit in the face by a pitch. After that, he was a changed man. He'd
been a sensational shortstop—my father told me all this as we sat
outside Apollonio's store during his lunch hour, on one of the rare
occasions when he and I found ourselves interested in the same
topic—and he was famous for his ability to go to his right and make
miracle throws to first without planting his feet. "Fancy" was his
nickname; he was a cinch to be called up to the majors the following year, my father said, "if Fate hadn't intervened."

"Fancy Frank" Barraclough played ball for Robertson's Ready-
Mix Concrete & Cinder Block Company—"Robertson's Raiders,"
for short—in the Scoggin Twilight League. He was close to forty,
old for baseball—though this was wartime and even the major
league rosters included players nearly as old as Frank Barraclough—
and shortstop was no longer his position. He was in left field that
year, batted sixth in the lineup, and had already told the sports editor of the *Scoggin Tribune* that he was giving up baseball at the end
of the season. "I don't see the ball like I want," he was quoted as saying. "It looks kind of fuzzy to me around home plate." But he was
still a popular player in the league; he had a strong arm, so oppos-
ing baserunners were cautious on fly balls hit to left, and though he
struck out more often than not, when he connected he had more
than his share of home runs—big, booming drives that had been
known to clear the Johnson's Chevrolet scoreboard in dead center
field, 415 feet away.

ⅢⅢ It was the middle of the afternoon, the Tuesday after Labor
Day—the first day of the new school year—when I stopped at the
Western Union office to see if there were telegrams to deliver.
There were two: the one for Frank Barraclough and the other for

Mr. Gowen, who owned a jewelry store on School Street. I delivered the Gowen telegram first—it was from his sister, telling him what time her train from Boston was arriving in North Berwick the next day—because I knew what the Barraclough message was. I wanted to postpone as long as I could—which turned out to be a mistake, because postponing gave me a lot of time to think about Jimmy being dead.

It was the first time I had confronted the death of someone close to me. A couple of years earlier Billy Roy had been crushed and killed by a freight elevator at the mill. I knew who Billy was, and I went to his funeral, but only because he was the older brother of René Roy, a classmate of mine. Jimmy was different: he had been a friend, and his dying raised a multitude of questions. How had he died? was one of them. And was there a body, or had he gone down to the bottom of the Pacific Ocean with his ship, never to be brought home, like the men on the *Arizona?* If there was a body, and the navy sent it to Jimmy's father, would there be a church funeral, and would the casket be open for all of us to look at Jimmy's corpse, and would I be able to bear to see it? I wondered too if Jimmy had done anything heroic, as if heroism—earning a medal—would justify the loss of his life. By the time I got to the Miller house on Kilby Street, I was crying; I had to wipe the tears off my cheeks with the back of my hand before I rang the doorbell.

It was nearly five o'clock, and when Frank Barraclough came to the door he was already wearing his Twilight League uniform—pale gray and pinstriped, with the words *Ready-Mix* across the front of the blouse in dark red script.

"Telegram," I said. My voice cracked on the word. I held out the yellow envelope with its glassine window, and Jimmy's father took it from me.

"Thanks, kid," he said. "Sit tight for a second and I'll get you something."

I never knew what he planned to give me for a tip, a dime or a quarter or what. As he moved down the hall away from me—number 3, the same as Jimmy Foxx's, on the back of his jersey—he was opening the envelope, and right away he saw what the telegram said. I heard him curse, saw him stumble and put out his left hand to steady himself against the nearest wall.

"You'd better scram, kid." He said the words hoarsely, but not unkindly. He didn't turn around to look at me—didn't let me see his face—and I scrammed.

IIII Until Jimmy's death I had thought of myself as the caretaker of his paper route, working and profiting from it only until his return from the battlefields of World War Two. Now that it was truly an inheritance, I began to feel the full weight of the responsibility the route carried with it, and I began to see some of the work I ought to do if I was to make it mine.

For one thing, I decided I should enlarge the route, add new customers, treat it as a living, growing enterprise. Jimmy had left me with eighty-six customers, and I still had the same eighty-six. Now, on weekends, I knocked on the doors of people I didn't already deliver to, selling them on the idea that—especially with a war on—they needed the day's news brought to them regularly and on time. I even called at the Lemieux Funeral Home, never mind my timidness at banging the brass knocker and following old Mr. Lemieux along a carpeted hallway past something called a Slumber Room, where a pale gray-haired woman—a dead woman—lay face up in a casket of glossy dark wood. It was my second view of a corpse, but this one was a stranger; the sight didn't bother me, and in any case it was incidental to my signing up Mr. Lemieux. Within the month I had ninety-nine customers.

My second decision was purely financial. That first Friday after I'd delivered the telegram to Frank Barraclough I told Mrs. Ouellette she would have to begin paying me each week, or I would stop delivering her paper. I said I was sorry, but circumstances had changed. I told her about Jimmy being killed in action in the Pacific.

"I don't believe it," she said. Her expression didn't change; she simply looked straight at me, her blue gaze solemn and unblinking, her white hands working at the belt of the pink housecoat, and waited for me to unsay what I had just told her.

"It's true," I said. As it happened, the *Evening Express* I held in my hands contained the story—and his picture—of Jimmy Barraclough's death. I opened the paper to his obituary and held it out to her.

She didn't look at it. She struck the paper down with her right hand, tearing the page almost in half, and ran out of the kitchen.

I sat down in one of the kitchen chairs and waited for her to return. One of the Ouellette kids was on the floor in front of the stove, nose running and mouth open, looking as startled as I felt, and then he started to cry. I didn't know what to do. When Mrs. Ouellette stood up to leave the room, the front of the housecoat had parted and I'd been able to see she wasn't wearing anything underneath— her skin was creamy white and I could see the swell where she carried the new baby, and the hair, like cornsilk, where her thighs came together. I was dizzy with ignorance; I had scarcely any notion of what was happening here, except I knew I had witnessed something I had no right to see.

I was sitting, confused, trying to refold the torn newspaper, when she came back into the kitchen. The child went quiet when she appeared. Mrs. Ouellette was calm; there was no sign of agitation on her face; it didn't look as if she'd been crying. The pink housecoat was closed and the belt tied. She took the newspaper out of my hands and held it against her chest.

"I'm awfully sorry," she said, "but my check is late again."

"Well—" I said. I had no idea what I was going to say to her.

"I know you want to be a good businessman," she said, "but I wonder if you could give me a few days grace. Just till Monday. Just this one last time."

IIII It was an eventful month, that September of 1942.

It was the month when my father was offered—and accepted—

a permanent job at Scoggin High School, teaching history and civics, which meant that he was able to stop keeping the books for Tony Apollonio's fruit store. His change of fortune pleased my mother, who was forever wary of anyone who spoke English with an accent—not only the Greek Apollonios, but the town's large, blue-collar French-Canadian population and, finally, the Edelsteins, an elderly Jewish couple who lived across the street from us.

It was the month I left Edison School and moved up to seventh grade at Emerson. The change from grammar school to junior high was important to me; it enhanced my opinion of myself, made me self-important in a way that Jimmy Barraclough might have appreciated, even if he couldn't have expressed it.

It was the month of Jimmy's funeral, a simple ceremony that took place in the Congregational Church on Main Street without the dead sailor's presence. His ship, a destroyer, had gone down in the Coral Sea with few survivors, so there was no body, no casket, no object to be mourned. Two strangers, uniformed naval officers with white caps tucked under their arms and uniforms that carried cords and stripes and jewelries of gold and silver, sat in a front pew while the minister praised Jimmy and "this young man's impatient desire" to die for his country. Frank Barraclough sat in another front pew, far from the officers, and listened to this praise with his head lowered; he looked like a stranger—in street clothes, with no name or number on his blue suitcoat—and I noticed the gray of his sideburns and the bald spot forming at the crown of his head. I had thought perhaps here was an occasion at which I would see Jimmy's mother for the first time, but she seemed not to be in the church. The one woman who was at the service was Mrs. Ouellette; it was the first and last time I ever saw her dressed up.

And it was the month, September of 1942, that I lost her as a customer.

|||| I know now that there's a lot of paraphernalia associated with death, especially death of an unnatural sort. Ambulances and doc-

tors, police with their cars and their blatting radios, ordinary cars that belong to curious neighbors and other gawkers, and people—lots of people standing around in groups of two and three, talking in subdued voices, watching every movement around the scene of the dying.

A couple of days after Jimmy's funeral, that was what I saw when I arrived at Mrs. Ouellette's. The street was a chaos, with cars parked every which way and uniformed policemen—state troopers as well as locals—trying to get the curious to go on about their business. Red and white lights were flashing from the tops of the cars and the one ambulance parked nearest the porch steps. The door to Mrs. Ouellette's flat was open; I could see people moving around inside, in her kitchen, but I couldn't get close enough to see what they were doing. One of the front windows was broken out, and shards of glass were spilled all over the porch. Up on the third floor some stupid little brat was hanging over the railing, trying to look down, and his mother was hauling him back by his belt before he fell. While I was watching, one of the ambulance men came out of the flat carrying something wrapped in a brown blanket. He put it inside the back of the ambulance; then he went into the kitchen again and came out with a second blanket that also went into the ambulance. Finally he and his partner carried a blanket between them and loaded it after the others. Then they got into the cab of the ambulance and drove away, the siren making slow, soft whirring noises to warn people to move. There was no way I could get close enough to deliver Mrs. Ouellette's paper, even if I'd wanted to, so I decided to finish my route and come back later.

Nobody had told me Mrs. Ouellette was dead, but I knew she was, and so were her two poor little dirty kids—they were all under those blankets loaded into the ambulance. I didn't know why or how; I think I knew it had something to do with Jimmy Barraclough being killed in action in the Pacific, but I couldn't have explained the connection if you'd asked me at the time. All I was really sure of was that it was a shame, this business of dying for something that had no size or weight or shape: for democracy, if that's what Jimmy died for;

for love, if that was Mrs. Ouellette's reason—which is what Doc Ross was saying when I got back to the tenement.

"Some people are too young to die for love," I heard him say. He didn't know I was there in the kitchen, and the man with him, the Scoggin chief of police—I recognized him from the picture on fliers he'd passed around for the coming election—raised one eyebrow and gave a slight nod in my direction. Doc Ross was our family doctor—J. Watson Ross was the name on his office door, but nobody ever called him anything but Doc—and when he made house calls he carried a small black valise filled with pills, wooden spatulas and gauze bandages, a rubber hammer, and his stethoscope. "Pink pills for pale people," he would say when he opened a vial and poured a few of its pills into a tiny white envelope.

Now he turned to look at me. Everyone else was gone; the ambulance men, the police directing traffic, the lookers-on—they'd all vanished. It was just the three of us in Mrs. Ouellette's dingy kitchen, the kerosene heater throwing orange shadows against the walls in the corner where it stood, the door of the gas oven wide open. There was more glass on the linoleum inside the door, a dirty white towel tossed under the table; the lace curtains stirred in the breeze that blew in through the broken window.

"What are you doing here, boy?" Doc Ross said.

"She was my customer," I said.

"Customer?" He took a step toward me, squinting at me in the half-light of the room. "What kind of customer?"

"On my paper route."

I think he recognized me then, for he smiled, and then he laughed—a short bark of a laugh. "Better she yours," he said, "than you hers."

"Yes, sir," I said, though his words had made no sense to me.

"What do you know about this business?" the police chief asked me.

"Nothing, sir."

"Nothing?"

I hesitated. "Is she dead?" I said. "Are they all dead?"

"All three," the chief said. "And the one she was carrying."

Doc Ross put out one hand as if to stop the chief of police from talking. "Do you know who the man is that made her pregnant?" he asked me.

"No, sir."

"No idea at all?"

"No, sir," I said. "No idea."

He gave me a long look, then shrugged and straightened up and put his hands in the pockets of his suitcoat. "I don't guess there's anything else to be done here," he said to the chief.

"Guess not," the chief said. He bent down to turn out the kerosene flame, went over to the gas stove and checked all the knobs to be sure they were off, closed the oven door, carefully, so it didn't bang shut. "You'd better skedaddle," he said to me. "Your folks'll be waiting supper."

\\\\ I tried to tell my parents what I had seen—the deaths, the broken glass, the police and Doc Ross—but my mother stole my thunder.

"I was on the switchboard when the calls started coming," she said. "It was about three o'clock. First it was Mr. Wiggin, from the flat just above Mrs. Ouellette, calling for an ambulance. He was the one who broke all the glass. First he had to smash the windowpane in the kitchen door, so he could reach in and turn the lock. Then when he got inside the kitchen the gas smell was so strong he had to use a chair to break out the window."

"He could have just opened the window," my father said. The evening paper was folded lengthwise beside his plate; he'd seemed so interested in it, I was surprised he'd been listening to my mother.

"He was in a hurry," she said. "I imagine he really thought that if he could let in fresh air—if he could do it soon enough—he could save the poor woman's life."

My father shrugged without looking up.

"Then it was Todd Emery, at the fire station, calling Doctor Ross," my mother went on, "and then, later on, it was the doctor calling from the flat. He wanted police to come, to make people move out of the street. 'Get these damned ghouls out of my hair,' I heard him say."

"What's a ghoul?" I wanted to know.

"Somebody who enjoys the company of dead people," my father said. "Are you enjoying this?" he asked my mother.

"There was a dirty towel on the kitchen floor," I said.

"It was against the door. She didn't want any of the gas to leak away," my mother said. "She wanted it all for herself—and for her little ones." Her voice trailed off; I thought she was going to cry.

"Dot," my father said—my mother's Christian name was Dorothy—and I knew my father had pronounced it that way as a warning, though the tone of his voice was as gentle as it was firm.

My mother stood up as if she were about to clear away the supper dishes, but for a moment she paused behind my chair, her hands resting lightly on my shoulders. "How terrible," she said, "to be poor and all alone."

My father opened the paper and gave her a sharp look above its pages. "That's enough," he said.

I understood why my mother was excited by her inside information about the deaths of Mrs. Ouellette and the children, and in some imperfect way I understood how her intimacy with the facts could upset my father, for whom history needed to be distanced—reported in the papers—before it was worth his attention.

But I didn't get to tell what happened just after the police chief told me not to keep my mother and father waiting supper for me—how I already had my left foot on the bike pedal, about to swing myself up to the seat and ride home, when Doc Ross called my name.

"Stevie," he said. "Just a minute." He came down the steps toward me. "She owe you money?"

"Yes, sir."

"How much?"

"Three weeks," I said.

"How much is that?"

"Ninety cents."

He took a dollar bill out of his wallet and gave it to me. "Keep the change," he said.

"Yes, sir. Thank you."

He looked up at the police chief, who was just locking the door to the dead woman's flat. "Now she's square with the world," he said.

Florida

The outlet to the sea passes directly under the balcony of the Florida highrise where Fowler and his fiancée and his fiancée's two daughters have come to spend the New Year's week. Channel markers—green squares on the right, red-edged triangles on the left—lead the way to open water, and all morning, starting at seven-thirty or so, powerboats have made their way past the hotel.

Today is their first full day on the island, where the idea is that the four of them will meld into a new family, and Fowler is only beginning to adjust to the unrealness—of the resort, of the group dynamic. Last night at dinner in one of the pricey resort restaurants, where the Christmas decorations are still up and a green-jacketed waiter behind the buffet table picked his nose and wiped his upper lip with the back of his hand, Fowler and the woman agreed that this was not their kind of place. The other children are bratty, the adults smug, the staff condescending. When he thinks about it, he supposes others would consider him just as smug and find his own youngsters equally bratty. He says to himself: *We are all on this island together*—as if they are castaways, waiting for a rescue of some yet-to-be-determined kind. In short, a part of his adjustment to life with a new family is social.

The rest of it is natural. Past his balcony drift sea birds of various sorts: gulls, of course, and cormorants; a blue heron or two; escadrilles of pelicans. Their shadows break across the backdrop of pale blue sky, an interruption of light where he sits reading the morning paper. "The moaning paper," the woman calls it, teasing him for his interest in the world's events. Directly below him is a green lawn that has for some reason been patched with squares of sod, the patchwork in the shape of a rough oval. Fowler wonders what was removed. A tree? A putting green? A garden? The woman suggests it is the place where unhappy guests are buried and coaxes him to "loosen up."

IIII The second day at the resort they walk along the beach, two miles of it, and look for shells. The day is overcast, the wind onshore and warm; the beach sand is not quite white, the sky is not quite blue. Everything is subdued, muted, softened. There are tidelines of shells by the millions, laid out in three irregular paths by tides of various heights. The daughters scurry from one shell-path to another, gathering the shells for their color, for their shape, for qualities that remind them of things from their ordinarily landlocked lives—gas stations, perfumed soaps. Occasionally they encounter adults with tight-woven baskets: shell-shop owners, Fowler imagines, who sit cross-legged before recent and especially rich shell-troves piled by the Gulf waters. Their hands are quick, their eyes expert; they fill their baskets slowly but wisely.

By low tide the shopkeepers are gone, the tourist families have casually broken the shell jetsam under the weight of their comings and goings. Contemplating the beach and the shell gatherers, Fowler wonders if the higher and lower tidelines have something to do with the moon's phases, the way the patterns of sexuality between himself and the woman seem to have an ebb and flow disconnected from simple desire, from ordinary wanting. There are days when his hunger for her seems limitless and endless, as if satiety is a dream to be pursued at all hours and never achieved. On other days, the very idea of lovemaking seems an irrelevancy—something that exists for the pleasure of men whose lives are otherwise empty of purpose.

That same night, because he cannot sleep and has gone out to the balcony to sip a nightcap of Glenlivet neat, he hears his adjacent neighbors *in flagrante*. They are on their own balcony, only a few feet away from where he sits. He can hear the difficulty of their breathing, the frenzy of their bodies on the weatherproof carpeting, the broken words and phrases they say to each other. He imagines he even hears the explosion of their consumated encounter and, in its aftermath, the blissful silence of their little death. He wonders do he and his woman sound like that when they wrestle in the bed upstairs, and do the daughters hear—and if they do, what do they think? When the woman was first married, did she love her husband as she now loves him? And what numberless passionate words of theirs were broken under the force of young lovemaking?

On the other balcony, the invisible woman laughs—a bar of sweet music, a night birdsong, that intrudes to cancel his jealousy. He hears the sliding door between living room and balcony drawn shut. Unearthly quiet follows. The wind continues onshore; it rustles the morning newspaper, still on the floor where he left it, and carries on its cool back the distant hum of a powerboat engine. Fowler feels isolated, a mariner out of his element, a true loner.

|||| Perhaps Fowler and the woman drink too much. In the mornings they send the daughters downstairs to the pool—the older daughter, twelve, has made friends with a boy whose parents are German tourists; every day before nine the boy, tall and blond and solemn, knocks at their door to fetch her and her sister—and more often than not Fowler and the woman open a bottle of wine and sit on the balcony overlooking the Gulf. Some mornings the woman runs on the hard-packed edge of the beach and comes back glowing, her cheeks flushed, her skin damp with sweating. Often they make love when she returns; at least they kiss. Then they open the wine. It seems to Fowler that the atmosphere around them, the self-created ambience of this time and place and behavior, is a necessary part of their accommodation to each other.

There is no deep, psychological reason for Fowler's drinking—

or so he has persuaded himself. He does it only out of habit. He has been a long time divorced, and during his single years he went back to sailing, the avocation of his youth. Once his budget recovered from the cash settlement he made with his wife, he bought a nineteen-foot, gaff-rigged sloop, wooden hulled, painted deep green with white trim. He renamed her *Kestrel*—he is surprised to realize he can no longer remember what she was called when he bought her—and sailed her out of Yarmouth, Maine. The boat was his weekend escape from the demands of his growing software business, a getaway from plain and simple boredom. It was during the *Kestrel* years that he ran with a drinking crowd: younger men and women, many of them rich, who summered in New England. They sailed away their days and drank away their nights. Fowler, a generation older, fancied himself their mascot, their familiar, a figure of curiosity and, possibly, of obsolete wisdom. Not, please God, their guru. In any event, he drank with them ashore, and alone on his boat he kept a small supply of the single-malt Scotch he still fancies. He was not an alcoholic; he simply drank to appear gregarious. Though *Kestrel* is long-since sold, the drinking lingers on. It has nothing to do with his ex-wife.

He cannot speak for the woman. The two of them, by agreement, never talk about their past spouses: he has never even learned the ex-husband's name. Yet for all the tacit anonymity of her marriage, Fowler suspects the woman drinks out of guilt and shame and a sense that she is somehow responsible for its recent failure. Her past—he has begun to gain only the barest idea of its dimensions— seems to haunt her. Sometimes he wakes in the small hours of the morning to find himself alone in their bed, a baffled light from downstairs showing on the walls of the stairwell, the remote murmur of the woman's voice sounding like a radio left on in a distant room. It is, he supposes, her ex-husband she is on the telephone with, still trying after the first six months of divorce to thrash out some arcane leftover of their wedded lives—a hopeless quest for expiation, Fowler thinks, better forgotten than dwelt upon.

When the woman returns to the bed she lies awake for a long time; Fowler hears her sigh, whisper to herself as if continuing a conversation. Relationships—with him, with her ex—obsess her. The therapist she has been seeing tells her to be wary of love, cautious about considering another marriage. Her postdivorce involvement with Fowler may only be "transitional"; it is a matter of statistics, the therapist says, how many such affairs turn out not to be permanent. When she comes home from the Professional Building on Wednesday afternoons and reports each new caution to Fowler, he shrugs, says something like, "Well, we have to weather it," and pours the wine. He loves the woman, wants what they share to "work," but he cannot deny that the therapist's warnings electrify the air with tension and doubt. "He says I shouldn't make any commitments for at least two years," she reports. Fowler suggests that perhaps for her the two-year period actually began long before her divorce was granted; perhaps her two years are already up.

They sometimes quarrel. Fowler deplores the woman's connection to her former husband; the woman criticizes Fowler for his jealousy. Invariably the quarrels conclude in threat, one of them threatening to leave the other. It is as if the worst that each can do is condemn the partner to a solitary life. And yet, because the condemnation is two-edged, reconciliation is built into it. "If one of us is alone," they agree, "we are both alone." Then they kiss, make love, drink wine.

\|\|\| New Year's Eve, sitting in the turbulent warmth of a Jacuzzi near the edge of the pool where the daughters swim, Fowler and the woman make friends with the couple in the unit next to theirs—the couple he has heard making love. They are British, their names are Lilian and Lloyd—Fowler calls his counterpart "Lloyd of London"—and they work in the United States for a European airline whose name Fowler forgets. Lilian is a tiny blonde with no breasts and an aristocratic nose; Lloyd is a robust man with sandy hair and a gray mustache that is a parody of British-colonel pomposity. They own a Morgan two-seater—Fowler has seen it parked outside the resort restaurant: a low, narrow, tan-colored machine with a Royal Auto Club medallion on its grille.

On this first occasion the four of them are drinking champagne, while the warm night wind brings them the far-off music of a steel band. The daughters are asleep—or watching television—and a third bottle of Pol Roger has just been opened for the adults. It is a get-acquainted session: the two women are chatting at one corner of the Jacuzzi, the men are in charge of the champagne in the corner nearest the bar. Lloyd and Lilian are not married either. She is the widow of a Dutch publisher killed—ironically, given her employment—in a plane crash. Lloyd seems immensely to enjoy talking about himself, and Fowler soon learns that the vintage Morgan is a signal of Lloyd's interests.

"When I was in my teens," Lloyd says, "my dream was to be a racecar driver. This was in the early fifties, and it was about then that Mercedes got back into racing and started winning everything, and so of course I wanted to drive for them. The stories about their cars and drivers had a mythological force to them. 'The gray ghost'; Moss and Fangio and Jenkinson . . ."

Fowler nods, though the names mean nothing to him.

"My father despised my ambition," Lloyd says. "He was a motorcar magnate himself, rather high up in the Morris Group, and for him the racecourse ambitions of Mercedes-Benz were only fascism disguised. That silver race car was anathema, and the idea that his own son wished to drive such a machine—he couldn't abide the thought of it.

"What happened, of course, was that in 1955—when I was twenty-two, and I'd barely begun to make a modest reputation for myself as a driver in Britain—Mercedes got out of racing. They'd won everything in sight, there'd been a fatal accident at LeMans involving one of their cars, there didn't seem much point in risking more lives for what was essentially no contest and therefore no sport. That was the story, anyway."

"You must have felt," Fowler says, "the way I felt in 1945, when the war ended before I was old enough to join the U. S. Navy." He feels obliged to listen to Lloyd's life story, but cannot resist the attempt to intrude his own.

"No doubt," Lloyd agrees. "In any case, I was thwarted. I drove Jaguars for a while—perhaps you remember the XK-120? It was a machine I was mightily fond of. I suppose I believed if I distinguished myself as an independent I'd be an attractive prospect for the Jaguar team. That never happened, either—story of failure, eh?"

"Best-laid plans," Fowler says.

"Exactly. Anyway, I came to the States, early sixties, just before your president was murdered in Texas. Did a bit of racing in the dear XK—Lime Rock, Sebring, places like that. Then one afternoon at Ontario—California, not Canada—I caught a wheel in the soft shoulder, lost control and flipped the car. Stupid. Smashed my right wrist, totaled the car. End of career."

"Were you afraid to drive afterward?"

"Not, actually." Lloyd refills Fowler's glass and his own, sets the bottle back in its bed of ice. "But even after the wrist healed, I hadn't nearly my previous strength; could hold the spanner, but couldn't unthread the bolt—that sort of thing. It seemed to me that if I couldn't even work on my own machine, then what was the point? Thus am I what you see before you: a bureaucrat driven from his dream."

"And you own the Morgan," Fowler says. "That tan two-seater I've seen around the place."

"Right you are. It belonged to the pater. He was kind enough to leave it to me—that, and a little money, and no good will whatsoever." Lloyd sips his champagne. "Perhaps I forgot to mention that I disliked my late father."

A startling burst of noise—laughter, shouting, the racket of party horns from a balcony over their heads—announces midnight and the new year: 1995. Fowler kisses the woman; Lloyd kisses Lilian. Fowler and Lilian kiss tentatively, like the strangers they are to each other, while the kiss shared by Lloyd and the woman—Fowler watches over Lilian's shoulder—is so chaste as to appear downright cold.

After this ritual, Lloyd raises his champagne glass toward Fowler. Fowler raises his own; the glasses clink. Despite the occasion and the distant melody of "Auld Lang Syne" essayed on steel drums, what the two men are toasting seems perfectly unclear to him.

IIII Later in the week Fowler and the woman bump into Lloyd of London and his Lilian at a bar on the northern tip of the island. The daughters have gone shelling with their friends—Fowler thinks it is wonderful of the woman to manage so successfully for their adult pleasures not to be interfered with. The afternoon is cool; the fog which obscured everything during the early morning has been mostly dissipated by an offshore breeze, and a single white sail is visible on the near horizon. Fowler has been watching it tack southward, wondering idly at the boat's dimensions, her equipment, her skipper. It occurs to him that he doesn't know if the *Kestrel* still carries the name *Kestrel*, or what waters she sails in now, or if the lawyer he sold her to still owns her. There are times when Fowler's past seems inaccessible even to his own memory, and today is one of those times.

"It looks like a desirable sort of life," Lloyd says, having seen where Fowler's attention is. "Skimming the waves. Master of your fate. 'Alone on a wide, wide sea.'"

"Can be," Fowler says. "Buy you a drink?"

"Whiskey-soda," Lloyd says. "Lilian tells me you're a sailor yourself. Her source is impeccable."

"I haven't done much lately. I had a wooden boat I sold a few years back. Before that, I owned an Aquarius—a twenty-three-footer, fiberglass." Fowler orders drinks. Lilian and the woman have drifted to a table across the room, and the light coming in the windows glares off the expanse of lacquered floor that separates women from men. He is tempted to complain that if his own father hadn't spent the family money on drink and risk, he would have been able to afford a bigger boat. "I never acquired anything larger," is what Fowler says. "The best I can manage nowadays is to read a couple of sailing magazines."

He has almost forgotten the Aquarius, *Water Sign* by name. A dozen years ago, the last summer of his marriage, he trailered her to Little Current, on Manitoulin Island, and spent a month in Georgian Bay, giving his son sailing lessons. The boy was still in his teens, towheaded and wiry, restless on the green edge of life where childhood meets manhood—mother still the only woman in his life, a beautiful and formative woman who vied for the boy by setting her love of horses against Fowler's fondness for boats. As if pleasure were the true reality, Fowler thinks now; as if leisure alone gave life its meaning, its spine, and so they spent great blocks of time traveling to places where leisure and pleasure were to be found out. Sometimes he saw his whole married existence as a succession of trailerings—boats to blue water, mares to snobbish horse shows. Not that Fowler underrated the value of his son's work in the ring; not that he hadn't appreciated the boy's guts in taking the jumps astride thirteen-hundred pounds of beautiful dumb animal; not that he hadn't been supportive of the boy, laying out a course in the meadow behind the house, painting the green and red stripes on the oxers, encouraging practice and raising the poles ever higher.

"'English pleasure,'" Fowler says to Lloyd, shaking his head in wonder as he tells those old days.

"Genuine oxymoron," Lloyd says, and smiles into his drink.

But sailing, Fowler wants to say; that's the thing, that's the real sporting pleasure. That September day on Lake Huron, putting out from Little Current at dawn, his son at the tiller, his wife in the stern, her brown hair loose in the breeze, a white scarf around her neck—that morning, he must have been almost happy; how could he have been otherwise? The blessing of a warm sun in a sky nearly cloudless, the kiss of the wind, the rhythm of gentle waves breaking under the bow. Paradise, he thinks now. He felt pride for the skills he had taught his son—though it was no easy matter to have kept his patience with blood of his blood, bone of his bone—and he felt comfort in the presence of his wife, her trust in her men evidenced by her relaxed preoccupation with some new best seller.

Early that afternoon they made for a small island and anchored in a cove on its lee side. The wife brought out a woven basket of sandwiches and red wine; the boy swam ashore and returned with a handful of day lilies for the three of them to eat as a salad, the bitter petals red and orange and almost-yellow. The fiberglass and fittings turned hot in the sunlight, the water lapped at the hull, the *Water Sign* lolled against her anchor-chain. It was like a dream of dreams, the green shoreline shimmering in the heat, the sky whiter than the lowered sail. The wife dozed over her book, the boy sat in the bow and practiced knots, Fowler smoked and watched while a school of minnows changed directions in nervous unison. Time seemed unimportant.

In fact, time escaped him, and only the realization that the wind had shifted brought it back. He threw the cigarette over, woke his wife, put the boy to work setting sail. It was late afternoon; the wind was colder, the light altered to a harshness unlike the sun's. When the *Water Sign* emerged from the idyll of the cove, the surface of the bay had changed from swell to chop and the northwest horizon displayed an ominous gray-violet cloud bank. In less than a half-hour the storm was on them, had caught them uncomfortably distant from port.

The boy was at the tiller. At first Fowler imagined he could turn the adventure into a test, an initiation. "Get us home," he told his son. "It's on your shoulders." He remembered the determination on the boy's face, and his own pride in the boy's willingness for responsibility. But everything went wrong: the boat carried too much sail for the growing force of the wind, the waves deepened—Fowler estimated twelve to fifteen feet from crest to trough, the *Water Sign* plunging and bucking, barely under control. It was the first time Fowler had ever been truly frightened on a boat, and the fear was that he would fail his wife and son. Here was an unplanned initiation. It was one thing to sail alone, with photos and mementos of family tacked to a bulkhead; it was something entirely other for the family to be real and at risk through his own carelessness. Love was at issue: the easy love of signs set against the difficult love reality seemed to demand.

"Plato forever," Lloyd says.

"Something like that." Fowler remembers the cold return to Little Current—taking the tiller, wrestling the boat against wind and water, trying to turn his son's resentment into crewmanship. He remembers reassuring his wife, who clutched the soaked novel against her orange life jacket with one hand and hung on to the rail with the other. He remembers, finally, long after dark, his relief when Little Current's channel lights appeared. *Red Right Returning*, he remembers thinking, like a novice sailor. *Red Right Returning*.

"My son never forgave me for taking the tiller away from him," Fowler says.

"Battlefield conditions," Lloyd says. "Mitigating circumstances."

"I'm looking forward to daughters," Fowler says.

"Indeed," Lloyd says. "Captain and fresh crew—so to speak." His speech is beginning to slur.

"Exactly," Fowler says. Across the room the woman and Lilian, wine glasses before them, laugh together. Women could live quite nicely without men, Fowler thinks. The reverse is plainly impossible.

"I wonder," Lloyd says, "if you miss your wife—your ex-wife. Do you sometimes think fondly of her? Do you from time to time say to yourself, *mea culpa*, and feel that if you could start over with her, the marriage might yet be retrieved?"

Fowler ponders. It is so many years, he almost cannot conjure her face. "Do you?" he says.

"Indeed," Lloyd says. "Indeed, I do. There are days—God, there are weeks—when I eat, drink, and sleep the love I discarded. And make no mistake: I did toss it away."

"But there are other days . . . ?"

Lloyd signals the waitress for a new round of drinks.

"Ah," he says, "all the other days, I think—if I think of her at all—I think what a bitch she was."

Fowler nods. "Likewise," he says.

"We seem to have come to this artificial tropic for similar reasons," Lloyd says. "New partner, new adjustments, threshold of a new life. Do you reckon it's done us any good?"

"Yes," Fowler says. "I reckon it has."

The two men sit in silence. The women's conversation on the other side of the room comes to them as a music, something like distant birdsong, the words unintelligible but soothing. Fowler thinks he is happy, not unlike the last morning on board the *Water Sign*, and—perhaps it's the drink—he feels a need to define the happiness.

"With *her*," meaning the woman, "I feel entirely differently. Loving her, caring for the daughters, fretting about the way her ex-husband badgers her—I feel I know what I'm doing because now life has importance. What I do—it not only matters, it's . . . it's *effectual*. Know what I mean?"

"Oh, yes," Lloyd says. He takes a drink from the fresh whiskey and soda. "Yes, indeed I do know."

\\\\ The next morning is Sunday. When Fowler wakes up, the bed beside him is empty, sunlight is streaming down the hallway from the daughters' room and the digital clock on the nightstand reads nearly ten o'clock. From downstairs comes the subdued sound of television talk—though he cannot make out the words, Fowler thinks he recognizes the cadences of a news voice from one of the networks—and the aroma of fresh coffee.

He has not meant to sleep so late, but now he remembers that the night has not gone well, that between the drinking he has done and the intermittent intrusion of a brisk onshore wind through the palms outside the bedroom window, he was awake more than he was asleep. And even in the interludes when he slept, his dreams were unsettling—though of course he can't recapitulate them this morning. He has a dim memory of waking the woman, of a conversation, of making love, unless that was a chapter from one of the forgotten dreams.

He gets up, goes to the bathroom, puts on the running suit the woman has given him as an engagement present. It is a soft, comfortable article of clothing, remarkable for its absence of color, and he wears it whenever he is late or feeling too lazy to get dressed. In his bare feet he descends the stairs to the living room, where he finds the woman doing her nails before the television screen. He sees that the program is not a news show after all, but one of the so-called "infomercials" that have begun to clutter the weekends. The voice of the commentator has deceived him.

"Sorry," he says. "You should have rolled me out."

"It's O.K.," the woman says. She stays involved with her nail filing. "We didn't have anything planned."

He pours a cup of coffee for himself from the pewter pot supplied by the resort. He finds an envelope of sugar, tears it open and pours half into the coffee.

"The girls are at the pool," the woman says.

"What else is new?" He sits in the bamboo chair opposite her. "Shall I walk out and get the *Times?*"

"Why don't you?" she says. "Maybe this week's crossword won't be so cutesy."

"Right."

He goes upstairs to put on tennis shoes and find his key to the unit. He gets a five-dollar bill out of his wallet and tucks it into a pocket of the running suit bottoms.

"Don't buy it at the pharmacy," the woman tells him. "Go to that little general store across from the gate."

"Whatever you say." Fowler takes a quick swallow from his coffee cup. Then he leaves, locking the door after him, and trots down the stairs to ground level.

As he is crossing the parking lot, he glances toward the pool, and there, sure enough, are the daughters—the younger in her flowered one-piece, her sister in the yellow bikini that makes her seem older than she is. He waves, but they don't see him. He is about to shout their names when he notices Lloyd of London is with them, sitting on the edge of the pool with his feet in the water. The daughters are laughing with him; he appears—from the movement of his hands and the animation of his features—to be telling them a story. Maybe he is telling them what it's like to drive a racecar, Fowler thinks wryly.

When he jogs back from the store, the *Times* under his arm and change jingling in his pocket, Lloyd is gone. The daughters are alone in the pool, shrieking and splashing in a game of badminton. It occurs to Fowler, not without an unexpected shadow of the kind of guiltiness he used to feel with his son, that he has spent too little time with the girls. He decides—an impulse he will forever consider to have been lucky—to change direction and join them. He strolls across the pavement toward them; halfway there, he waves to them but isn't noticed.

Finally he is close enough for the daughters to be aware of him. They stop splashing and contemplate his arrival.

"Hi," he says.

He draws one of the resort's plastic chairs close to the edge of the pool and sits in it, the *Times* a substantial weight across his thighs.

The daughters exchange glances, the older one, looking at twelve like a miniature version of the kind of model Fowler has noticed in the pages of the fashion magazines the woman reads, cocking an eyebrow, the younger stepping back to lean against the pool's aluminum ladder.

"Do we have to go back to the room?" the older girl asks. "Is it lunch time?"

"No, no. I just thought I'd say hello. See what you were up to."

The daughters wait for him to say more. The eight-year-old is as plump as her sister is thin, Fowler notices. Both have long blond hair slicked over their ears, and an aura of chlorine and warm moistness envelops them.

"The four of us haven't been together much lately," Fowler says, "so I came over."

"That *was* the whole idea of Florida," the older daughter says.

"You guys are always off somewhere," the younger says.

"I guess maybe that's the way your mother wanted it," he says. "We should do something about that."

"Probably we should," the older daughter agrees. She slaps her badminton paddle, bright orange, against the water. "Let's play," she tells her sister.

"I saw you were talking with Lloyd," Fowler says. He tries not to make it an accusation, though it comes out sounding like one.

"Yes," the eight-year-old says.

"Actually, he was talking with *us*," her sister says. "He tells funny stories."

"And he has that accent," says the younger. "It's English."

The two girls look at each other, the older one frowning. For a moment or two the silence around them is marred only by the whine of a powerboat engine and the abstracted slap of the older daughter's paddle against the surface of the pool.

"He's our dad," says the eight-year-old.

The older girl rolls her eyes. "You promised you *wouldn't*," she says to her sister.

Fowler leans forward at the edge of the plastic chairseat. The newsprint feels cool under his elbows, and the smell of it—paper, ink, whatever it is—seems unusually strong, as if his senses have suddenly been sharpened. He is surprised at his equanimity while he absorbs this new information.

"Really?" he says.

"Yes," confirms the older girl, "he really, truly is. It was Mom's idea."

"She wanted Daddy to like you," says the younger.

"And does he?" Fowler asks.

"Oh, yes," says the eight-year-old.

The older daughter is nodding. "It's true," she says. "He does like you."

Fowler gathers up the *Times* and hugs it against his chest as he stands. "That's good news," he says. "I'm glad I passed the test."

"He says you seem to be a sensible chap."

"Daddy calls people 'chaps,'" says the younger daughter.

"Well," Fowler says, "it gets better and better." He raises one hand in an awkward kind of salute to the two girls. "I'll see you later," he says. "Your mother's waiting for the paper."

The stairs leading up to their unit are unadorned concrete, damp and smelling of mildew, and Fowler feels the chill of his climb with a particular intensity. Again it is as if the revelation that Lloyd is the woman's ex-husband has ground his senses to a keener edge: the noises of the island—birdsong, the crackle of tires on the sandy pavement, the rustle of wind through palm fronds—all resound in the stairwell as if through a loudspeaker.

Unlocking the door of the unit, stepping into the efficiency kitchen, for a moment Fowler thinks he will confront the woman with what the daughters have let slip, but when he sees her—cross-legged on the chaise in front of the now-blank television, buffing her nails, a look of serious concentration on her face—he chooses to postpone. He lays the paper before her at the foot of the chaise.

"All the news that fits," he says.

The woman smiles up at him. "Thanks," she says, and begins rummaging through the sections.

"I saw Lloyd out by the pool," he tells her.

"Oh?" She finds the magazine section and thumbs through it until she finds the crossword page.

"He was holding forth for the daughters," Fowler reports. "There was no sign of Lilian."

"I wonder where she was." The woman holds the paper out to him. "You start," she says.

\\\\ On their last night at the resort, the man and woman have dinner at the island's most expensive restaurant, a place of dim lighting and candlelight, warm gold decor accented with a subtle trim of dark wood. The daughters are taking care of themselves—that is, the twelve-year-old is ostensibly in charge of the eight-year-old, though in fact the younger daughter is in bed before the man and woman have left for dinner. The plan is for the car to be loaded tomorrow morning before breakfast, the four of them to be on the road by eight-thirty at the latest.

Fowler is not fond of this place—it is the sort of restaurant where the maître d' tells you your table is "not quite ready," even though you can plainly see that all the tables are set up and most of them are empty—and besides, he is understandably preoccupied. The two of them order martinis in the lounge, this being the point of tables "not quite ready," and soon enough are ushered into the restaurant proper. They are seated by a window overlooking the water, which glows from a light that may or may not be the moon's. The waiter puts a match to a candle nestled in a crystal chimney and pours ice water for them. They drink their drinks and hold hands across the table while they wait to be shown menus.

"Should we call the daughters?" Fowler wonders. "Make sure they're O.K.?"

"They're fine," the woman says. "Not to worry."

"I'm not used to daughters," he says, for perhaps the hundredth time since he has known her.

"Look," the woman says. "Lloyd and Lilian are here."

He glances in the direction the woman indicates. Lloyd has just held Lilian's chair for her. Looking up, he sees Fowler and the woman and lifts his hand in a small acknowledgement. Lilian waves; the woman waves back.

"They're everywhere," Fowler says.

"I like them," the woman says. "I especially enjoy Lilian. I like that wonderful accent of hers."

"It's the same as his," Fowler says.

"Not quite," the woman replies. "He's West Country."

Fowler finishes his drink and signals the waiter for another. "Did I mention how surprised I was to see Lloyd with the daughters," Fowler says. "I didn't think he knew who they belonged to."

"It's a small world here," the woman says.

Fowler hesitates. His mind has been making a summary of the week just past—the coincidences, the serendipity of the meeting at the pool, the too-convenient absences of the daughters. Even the painfully formal New Year's kiss the woman shared with Lloyd has taken on a fresh significance since his poolside conversation with the daughters. But should he make much of what he now knows?

"Perhaps too small," is what he says.

"I hear what you're saying."

"Do you?"

The woman takes her hand away. "Don't let's quarrel about it," she says. "The girls told me what they said to you. Perhaps they're too honest for us grownups, but what's said is said."

Fowler turns the stem of the empty martini glass between a thumb and forefinger.

"I used to imagine having it out with your ex—a confrontation," he says. "Especially after those long phone calls of yours. I always imagined he was abusing you about the past, blaming you for the divorce."

"Sometimes he was. But he also fretted about the girls—about what kind of stepfather you'd turn out to be." Now she takes both of Fowler's hands in hers, and he believes he will never in all his life forget the wonderful coolness of her touch at that moment. "Please don't be upset."

"It was a shocker, you know."

"I couldn't think of another way to settle things," she says. "Honestly. And I couldn't bear to be on the phone with him, week after week for the rest of my life with you."

"I'll get over it. The daughters said Lloyd approves of me."

"He even *likes* you."

"I'm a 'sensible chap.'"

"Something like that."

The second martini arrives. Fowler plays with the twist of lemon that clings to the edge of the glass, nudges it over the rim into the drink. He realizes he can't simply let it pass, this arrangement; if this is an ending, it fails to satisfy him.

"Excuse me for a minute," he says.

"Wait." As Fowler pushes himself away from the table—the martini, the tasteful low candle, the gold-rimmed plates—the woman reaches out to catch his sleeve. "Please," she says.

"No," he says. "It's all right."

He pulls free and strides across the room toward Lloyd and Lilian. He hasn't the slightest idea what he will say, what he will do; he knows only that the subterfuge of this week has caught up with him.

Lloyd stands to meet him, but presently there is an awkwardness brought about by the arrival of the waiter, carrying Lloyd's whiskey and a red drink for Lilian that Fowler imagines to be Campari. Fowler's moment is undercut: if he genuinely wishes to make a scene, the waiter is in the way.

"Well met," Lloyd is saying. He offers his right hand, the whiskey and soda in his left. When Fowler declines to shake his hand, he says to Lilian, "Darling, why don't you girls catch up on the day while we men discuss our travel plans."

Lilian gathers up her drink and scurries away.

"You have some tall explaining," Fowler says.

Lloyd doesn't flinch. "So she's told you."

"The daughters did. It was after I'd seen the three of you poolside."

Lloyd smiles, perhaps looks rueful. "They do grow more charming," he says. "They're still the happiest product of the marriage."

Fowler waits. There is a disturbance of cutlery from the direction of the kitchen, the discreet reappearance of the waiter, a fragment of the subdued conversation begun between Lilian and the woman.

"I'd rather it had happened differently," Lloyd says. "I'd far rather have remained anonymous, motored away in the morning, left everyone to live happily ever afterward. I was careless." He shakes his head. "Betrayed by a father's affections."

"This *act*," Fowler says. "Why was it necessary at all?"

"The children: the obvious reasons."

"But we get along very well. We're becoming a new family."

"'Bonding,' I believe they call it."

"Better than that. Respect. Friendship. Love."

"Without benefit of matrimony," Lloyd says.

"That will come," Fowler says, "and soon enough." He turns the chair Lilian has vacated, its legs scraping the parquet floor with a sound like a broken cry, and sits facing Lloyd across the table. "You won't be surprised to know that I've imagined meeting you. Meeting Mister Ex."

"Ditto here," Lloyd says.

"Every time I hear her on the phone to you—I never really hear the words; just the tone of her voice: pleading, angry, hurt—I think how I want to face you, tell you to let up, get the hell out of her life. Our lives."

"Perfectly reasonable."

"This isn't how I pictured it." In the back of Fowler's mind the imaginary meeting plays itself: confrontation, voices raised, perhaps not a fistfight but certainly an aura of tension, of not knowing what might happen next between the two men.

"Something on the edge of violence," Lloyd says. He turns the whiskey glass, considers the pale mixture it holds. "I must say it was a relief not to be knocked down when you came to the table. That was the way I'd dramatized our eventual encounter."

Fowler sits back. "Bottom line," he says. "Are you letting go? Or will I see you lurking behind the potted palm of every place we go?"

"Dear chap," Lloyd says. He pauses, takes a swallow of whiskey. "I trust that you and I have been genuinely honest in our conversations, that everything we've told each other has been God's truth. It might be the case that if I should have devoted as much energy to my marriage as once upon a time I gave to my Jaguars, you might never have had the pleasure of this woman's company, but in the actual instance, everything I've said about my former wife—the love of her, the hate of her—is unvarnished gospel. Possibly that's the great virtue of being incognito: if one gives up his identity, then there's nothing to be hidden."

"I'm sure I haven't tried to conceal anything."

"And I am equally sure. You have my blessing—which is, after all's done, the crux of this holiday occasion."

Again Fowler waits. Across the room the two women have their heads together—what new conspiracy, he wonders, then dismisses the thought—and the waiter fidgets between the In and Out doors to the restaurant kitchen.

"I expect sooner or later I'll return to the U.K.," Lloyd says. "My inheritance includes a flat in London and a cottage in Cornwall, as well as the Morgan you've admired. Whatever I thought of him, it would be a shame to flout my father's posthumous generosity."

"It would," Fowler agrees.

"I do expect my visitation rights to be honored."

"Of course."

"And you must promise to forgive your fiancée her part in this week's curious adventure."

"I shall."

Lloyd makes an open gesture, arms wide, palms up. "Then there's an end on it," he says.

"Buy you a drink?"

"I think you should return to your beloved," Lloyd says. He extends his hand and this time Fowler takes it. "Tell Lilian I've put in for another Campari."

\\\\\ At the end of their dinner, looking across the room, the four of them bathed in the restaurant's warm gold of candlelight and varnished oak, Fowler lifts the stemmed glass: to Lloyd and Lilian, but especially to Lloyd. It is nothing like the New Year's Eve toast; this time he believes he knows what he is drinking to.

"I know what you're thinking," the woman says. "Please don't."

"You did let him kiss you."

"Oh, really," she says. "It was New Year's Eve."

"And what about Lilian?"

She looks away from him for a moment. "All right," she says. "I admit it: I was curious about her."

"And?"

"I told you. I like her."

"The first night we were here," he says, "I heard them making love."

She looks at him and shakes her head, very slowly, almost as if she is pitying his trying to make her care. "You shouldn't have listened," she says.

Fowler shrugs. He supposes he needed to say something flip, something teasing, because he cannot now find it in himself either to be angry with her or jealous of her strategies. Glass still raised, what shall he propose? *Happy New Year? Safe Journey?* "Comrades in arms," is the toast that comes to mind. He thinks he has said the words under his breath, but the woman hears.

"That's nice," she says. "It's a kind of pun."

Or it is more than that—an accommodation, a reluctant, necessary truce. Back at the unit, where the daughters are sound asleep, Fowler and the woman open a last cold bottle of wine and carry their glasses from room to room, shushing each other while they gather up the small odds and ends not to be overlooked in tomorrow's packing.

Grief

\\\

There's a house, halfway down our block toward the center of town, that went on the market in June, not too long after old Mrs. Addison died. We looked at it, Sam and I, but it was too rich for our blood—or, for a long time, for anybody's blood, which probably explains why it stayed unsold till the middle of October. It was a knockout of a place, Chicago brick with a slate-shingled roof and dormers sharply pitched; we walked through it in early fall, when the maples were only just beginning to yellow and Sam was getting restless.

"It won't cost anything to have a look-see," she said.

That was O.K. with me, even though I'd heard from the Addisons' next-door neighbor what the asking price was. Suzanne was just a year and a half at the time, and I knew Sam was close to the edge of cabin fever. We're late-blooming parents; I'm forty-two, Sam—Sandra, though she's gone by Sam ever since I met her—is thirty-nine, and even though we were thrilled when Sam got pregnant, there's no getting around the stress of caring for a kid when you're a lot older than the norm. Anyway, she needed a break; something to take her mind off mothering.

I called the realtor, Alvin Clifford of Clifford & Ransom—it happens I know him personally because I've done most of his job printing over the last ten years or so—and in we went, Suzanne already half asleep in her mother's arms because it was nap time.

As I said, the house was a knockout. There wasn't much to the outside: a narrow lot and no front yard to speak of, but there was a good-sized backyard, all fenced in by chain-link, with a weeping willow and a couple of silver maples and a row of tall poplars along the back lot line. As for the inside—Lord, it was nice. Maggie Addison had lived alone for the last dozen years, after Raymond died, and it didn't look as if she'd ever used more than two or three rooms in the whole place: the kitchen, naturally, and this one downstairs bedroom off the back hall—probably a servant's room once upon a time—and a cozy sitting room with a couple of leather chairs and a writing table with a green-shaded lamp and a pair of glass-door bookcases that locked with a hollow brass key. The rest of the place smelled like it hadn't been occupied since day one; it wasn't a bad smell— just a kind of closed-up mustiness. All the furniture was still in the house, and of course that helps a house show better. Al Clifford told me the Addison children—there was a lawyer son and two married daughters—wanted to sell the furniture separately, but he'd persuaded them to leave things be until the house had a buyer.

Sam did plenty of exclaiming, oohing and aahing over almost everything that met her eye, and old Al was tickled pink.

"It's a pleasure to show a house to a party that understands its fine points," is what he said to us—though I'm sure he knew the place was miles outside our range.

"I hear they're asking one-fifty," I said to him.

"But they'll listen to offers," Al said. "That price isn't etched in stone."

So on we went. There was a foyer—a kind of vestibule, my grandmother would've called it—and a big front hall with a lavatory tucked under the stairs that led up to the second floor, and a good-sized dining room with a gilt chandelier, and the kitchen and sitting room, and a huge parlor with an oriental carpet underfoot and a baby-grand Baldwin piano in one corner. Upstairs were four bedrooms and two baths, and sliding doors—triple-glazed—that opened onto the porch roof so you could spread a towel and take the sun in July and August. There was an attic—I climbed two-thirds of the way up the stairs and poked my head into it—and a full base-ment that we didn't visit, where Al said the furnace had been con-verted from coal to heating oil and ought to be replaced.

"You can't expect a house this age not to have at least one draw-back," he told me. He said he thought the place had been built in the early 1880s, and some upstairs remodeling done in the 1970s.

The whole tour took about an hour, and at the end of it we stood out on the curb for five or ten minutes, reciting a list of the virtues inside before I finally shook Al's hand and thanked him for show-ing us around.

When we were walking home, Sam said, "We'd have the big bedroom with the patio doors, don't you think?"

"Likely," I said.

"And Suzanne could have her own room directly across the hall from us. The one with the blue wallpaper."

Suzanne woke up then, whimpering, and had to be fed as soon as we got home.

|||| The house sold in mid-October. I hadn't heard any rumors about the pending sale—neither had Sam—but one Thursday morning a yellow Mayflower van from out of state lumbered down the street and pulled up in front of the Addison place. It was a clear day, for-tunately; rain would've thrown a real monkey wrench into things, because some of the furniture that was still in the house had to be put out on the sidewalk and the little bit of front lawn to make room for what was going in. It was clear some kind of deal had been struck: a lot of Mrs. Addison's pieces seemed to be staying. One thing that didn't get left was a big old oak sideboard Sam would have killed to own if I'd just given her a weapon.

"Go on down there," I told her. "Make an offer." She didn't.

When the movers had got everything unloaded to the house, they wrestled the sideboard into the van, along with the clawfooted dining room table, also oak, and eight oak chairs, and a mahogany

Governor Winthrop desk with attached hutch, and the two leather chairs we'd last seen in the downstairs sitting room. The show was all over by noon, and the van gone back to wherever it came from.

The people who'd bought the house—it was a couple named Keller, I found out later from Al Clifford—were in their late twenties and had no kids, but they owned a pair of boxer dogs. They arrived in the wee hours of the next morning. No fanfare, no hoopla. Just that when I got up to make coffee on Friday, here was a dark red Jaguar sedan sitting in the driveway beside the house. I couldn't make out the license tag from my pantry window—that afternoon I walked right up to the car and discovered it was one of those fancy British registration plates with the big silver numbers and letters raised against a black background—but even from a distance I could tell it was some expensive machine. A twelve-cylinder engine, if you can imagine.

"How many miles to the gallon do you suppose he gets?" I asked my pressman a couple of days later.

"How many gallons to the mile, is more like it," he said.

IIII The first time I saw Fred Keller's two boxers, Mrs. Keller—Karen —was walking them. I didn't at the time know the Kellers were named Fred and Karen; then I only knew they owned a pair of beautiful dogs, and Mrs. Keller had them leashed and out for a stroll, her all dolled up in a bright red car coat with black collar- and pocket-trim.

I was across the street, having a few words with Corey Shaw— Shaw Dairies; we print their milk cartons, with the company logo and, lately, the photo of the missing child of the month—when she waltzed past, and Corey broke off what he was saying in the middle of a sentence.

"Will you look at that," he said. "How those dogs are put together."

You have to know that Karen Keller was an extremely attractive young woman, with long blondish hair and the kind of delicate features you see in magazine ads for cosmetics, but you also have to know that Corey Shaw is an avid duck hunter, and a member of the National Rifle Association, and the owner of a prize-winning golden retriever that he dotes on—by which I mean to say that he was genuinely admiring the boxers. He was not making an oblique reference to the charms of the woman walking them.

The two of us watched the dogs. They were just a bit of a handful for the woman, trotting along at a pace that forced her into an almost-run, keeping their leads taut as they led her down the street. They wore choke-chain collars, so it was clear that she could have brought them to heel anytime she wanted, but it was equally clear that she was enjoying the exercise.

Corey called out to her. "Nice animals," he said.

She turned her head to look at him, and she smiled. "Thanks," she said.

I'm sure you've seen boxer dogs. They're a breed that moves lightly, rhythmically, like a human athlete wearing an expensive shoe that's perfectly cushioned for his weight, and their muscles shiver under the skin as they move so that the whole animal seems made of motion and brute strength. And they're a handsome beast, with short, square muzzles—not the pushed-in faces of bulldogs, but the square-jawed faces of, say, a marine guard. These two could have been twins, live bookends, they were so much alike—pale brown in color, a couple of feet tall at the shoulder, graceful and fearsome.

"Imagine them hunting," Corey said.

I couldn't, but I knew he could. I could tell from the wistful way he watched the two dogs that he was thinking with some little touch of envy about his golden retriever, also a beautiful animal, but one whose only talent was to fetch wild game that had already been brought to ground.

|||| The second time I saw the Keller boxers, they hunted. It was a few days after my conversation with Corey—the day after Halloween, to be exact—and Sam was out in the front yard with the baby, putting those white styrofoam cones over her cut-back rose-

bushes. There'd already been a day or two of the snow squalls that sweep down from the tip of Lake Michigan, but so far we'd lucked out and hadn't had a really hard freeze. Suzanne was all bundled up in her new green snowsuit with the pointy hood, and she had on matching orange boots and orange mittens. She wasn't much of a walker yet, having only been at it for a couple of months, so while her mother was covering the roses, Suzanne was toddling around after her, sometimes falling into her, once in a while losing her balance and sitting down, hard, on the dead grass and looking surprised. It was a sight, I'll tell you. If Buster Keaton was still alive, he could've taken lessons in double-take from baby Suzanne. All the while, Sam was talking to her—about the weather, about the flowers that'd blossom in the spring, about you-name-it—the way mothers do.

And then here came the boxers.

They were loose, which surprised me; no master or mistress trotting behind them with leashes in hand, no sign of the Mr. or Mrs. watching from the brick house—just a decorator's panel truck that was parked out front more often than not lately. Our town has an ordinance that says dogs have to be tied up or on a lead, and it's pretty rigidly enforced. I wondered if the Kellers had been told about it, and I made a mental note to myself to stop by and let them know. Being friendly to the newcomers. Meantime, I began to get an uneasy feeling about the dogs' freedom, so I left the living room window and walked out through the screened porch to the driveway, where I could take in the whole neighborhood.

The two boxers stopped when they heard the porch door slam and stood, stock-still and side by side, looking in my direction. Heads cocked. Ears pricked up. Alert twins.

Sam stopped what she was doing when she saw me.

"Coming to help?" she said. "Better put on a jacket."

"I was keeping on eye on them," I said. I gestured toward the dogs. They were on the sidewalk in front of Billy Hanley's, the big yellow house across the street from us, still motionless, interested.

Sam turned, seeing them for the first time. "Lord," she said, "don't they look ominous."

Just about the time she said this, the boxers began moving again—only they weren't any longer moving in unison. Instead, one of them went to my left, up over the Hanleys' lawn, while the other headed to the right, along the sidewalk and out into the street between us. I swear I could feel the hair stand up on the back of my neck.

"Take the baby inside," I said.

"Just let me cover these last three bushes," Sam said.

"Take her inside. I mean it."

My tone of voice must have got through to her. She scooped little Suzanne up in her arms and hurried toward the porch. I held the door open for her, closed it after her. She put the baby down and stood behind the screen to see what was happening.

The dogs had stopped again. One twin was on Billy Hanley's lawn, directly across the street from me; the other twin was at the foot of my lawn. From the one, to me, to the other, you could have drawn an exact right angle, ninety degrees down to the minute and second. It was scary: they'd put me in a crossfire. Animal intelligence. A perfect hunting team.

"Come inside, honey," Sam said. I thought I caught a tremble in her voice.

Baby Suzanne was slapping at the screen with one tiny palm. "Doggie," she was saying, "doggie," real cute.

I went inside.

|||| The third time I saw the two boxers, they killed Hanley's little black and white rat terrier. I was at the window by chance, and here came the hunters, unleashed, unaccompanied. The terrier was tied up in its front yard—but I don't think it would have had the chance of a snowball you-know-where even if it had been free. Their method of attack was predictable: the pair splitting up, surrounding the poor pup the way I had imagined they might surround baby Suzanne. When they went in for the kill, they went simultaneously,

as if they had a way of communicating with each other. I raced outside, but don't ask me what I thought I could do for the terrier. Looking back, I can imagine the boxers turning their interest toward me, with bad consequences, to say the least. By the time I crossed the street, the smaller dog was dead—shredded, is more like it—and one of the boxers, the one on the right flank, was trotting away with the carcass in its bloody jaws. It was a sight to see.

Billy emerged about then, standing outside his front door, looking puzzled. He saw me and put his hands wide in a questioning gesture.

"What's the racket?" he said. "Where's Buster?"

I told him. He didn't believe me at first, but we went over and studied Buster's bloodied collar together. Billy picked it up, turned it over in his hands, shook his head.

"Poor little bugger," he said.

"We should call the police," I said.

"No," Billy said. "Let's talk to those folks. Then we'll call the cops."

But after we'd rung the front doorbell of the brick house, and then used the doorknocker when we thought perhaps the bell was out of order, it was clear nobody was home. So then we went back to Billy's house and phoned the police. Billy offered me a beer, and the two of us sat in his front room, waiting for the law.

While we were sitting with our beers, the dogs came back, shoulder to shoulder, trotting down the sidewalk as if they owned it. I saw them first.

"There they are," I told Billy. "The both of them, big as life."

Billy got up and went over to the bay window and sat on the green plush pillow of the windowseat. "Christ," he said, "either one of them'd make ten of Buster. They must weigh sixty pounds apiece."

I watched over Billy's shoulder. I couldn't see any blood on their muzzles. I figured they'd swallowed poor Buster down and licked their chops clean. They were squarely in front of the house, at the end of the Hanley driveway, when the police car pulled up and

stopped. There were two officers; I could see the one in the passenger seat peering out at the house number. The dogs had come to
a halt, standing between the car and the house, studying the car with
their ears tipped forward, their muzzles moving, snakelike, as if they
were reaching for scent. When the door opened on the passenger
side, one of the boxers took a step or two toward the car. The door
went shut.

Billy looked back at me and nudged me with his elbow.

"Spooky," he said.

"Those guys don't know what to do," I said.

Billy shook his head. "And you would?" he said.

It was an impasse. The two policeman sat in the car and had a
conversation; the driver leaned across his partner and surveyed
Billy's house, as if he were verifying the number of it. The two dogs
held their ground, waiting for some adventure to come out of the
car. After about ten minutes, the police car drove away.

"I'll be goddamned," Billy said.

Once the car was gone, the dogs went away as well. The next day
we learned that the police had eventually found the Kellers at home,
had sold them license tags and instructed them in the finer points of
the local leash laws. Billy was told that Mrs. Keller was upset to hear
what had happened to Buster, and a few days later he got a check for
a hundred dollars in the mail.

"That's some consolation," Billy told me. "Buster was just a plain
old mutt we rescued from the pound."

The Kellers told the authorities they didn't know their dogs had
the run of the town. They'd been letting them out into the fenced
backyard, never realizing the chain-link was so easy to jump over.

|||| Things were quiet after that. The snows came: a big storm at the
end of November, and a couple of smaller snowfalls in December.
The print shop did a better than average business in holiday cards,
the plain ones with the standard Season's Greetings, and the fancy
ones you could get with your own photographs on them. We did up

a batch for the Kellers—Fred and Karen kneeling in front of the fireplace with their boxers, red ribbon-bows around the dogs' necks, the two humans looking like nothing so much as proud parents. Christmas came and went, and New Year's. At the end of January, Sam and I celebrated baby Suzanne's birthday with a chocolate cake and butter pecan ice cream. You ought to have seen Suzanne trying to blow out the two candles.

||| In early February there was a thaw to beat all thaws—days so warm it brought the snow right down to bare lawn, and after four or five days of temperatures as high as fifty you began to think the trees might bud and get killed off when the weather turned normal again. Sam fretted about that, and about her precious rosebushes thinking it was already spring. I did my best to distract her; I brought home a seed catalog we'd printed—four-color, vegetable pictures so real you could have eaten them off the page, if I do say so—and bought her a pad of blue-lined graph paper so she could map out this year's garden. It worked, after a fashion. She leafed through it and got all excited about the farming prospects. "Let's call Clarice and Billy," she said. And I said, "Sure." There's a vacant lot between us and the next street over; Sam and Clarice Hanley cultivate it together—with mixed results, I might say, last year having been the year the sweet corn flamed; "flamed" was the experts' way of describing corn plants that turned a sudden orangey-brown just as the ears were starting to mature. Too much nitrogen in the soil, or too little—I can't remember which. I didn't hear any rumor that real farmers were troubled by it, which at the time is what I told Sam, and then ducked.

We all planned to get together the next afternoon, at the cocktail hour. I'm not a drinker, but I will say yes to a Manhattan or a Rob Roy if I know I'm not going to have to do any driving, and Sam the same. To be on the safe side we called the Shaws and got Corey's middle daughter, Marta, to babysit so we could let our hair down and know baby Suzanne was in good hands.

By four o'clock next day, when Marta's dad dropped her off, the thaw was done with and winter had made a comeback. The temperature was down in the high twenties, the sun was gone, and right around noon snow had started—no wind, but a slow and steady fall of big flakes that filled in the grassy places and turned the bare streets and sidewalks white in no time. Billy and Clarice walked across to our porch door; by the time I'd collected their coats and brought them a drink, I glanced out the living room window and noticed that their tracks were already covered over.

We were having a fine time. Suzanne was outdoors, letting Marta drag her around the yard on the old Flexible Flyer we'd bought at a garage sale last fall. Billy was holding forth in the living room with a war story—we were both navy; he was Seabees in Nam while I was keeping America safe behind a quartermaster's desk at Great Lakes—and the girls were out in the kitchen, supposedly making up some fresh dip, but more likely dipping into the cooking sherry and arguing about whether leaf lettuce or tomatoes was the better salad crop for the coming year.

Why is it the worst things happen when you're most relaxed and your head's empty of everything serious? I've asked myself that a hundred times. I've gone over that afternoon in my mind: what we did, what we said. If we hadn't been drinking, would that have changed the day? Did we do something that made us bad parents? No, says my common sense; we weren't drunk, or careless or incompetent. We just weren't there.

That was it: we weren't there, and so we were helpless. I heard a commotion under the window, a noise like the rumble of a train coming from far off, and yelling and crying like—God, I can't tell you, except when I heard it, it burst my heart. One minute we were laughing and planning gardens, the next minute I was headed for the front door and practically ran over Marta coming in. I grabbed her by the shoulders—to stop her, to stop myself from whatever it was I thought I was going to do. "What is it?" I said. She was out of breath, she didn't even look like herself, and when she didn't say anything I shook her, hard. "What?" I said. I was yelling at the poor kid. "Tell me what!" Then I just shoved past her to the door and outside. I could hear Marta crying in the hallway behind me. I could hear Sam asking her questions, and the answer was Suzanne's name. Baby Suzanne! Sam's voice trailed me down the steps and floated on the outside air like echo.

The snow was still falling, those big, slow flakes with no wind behind them at all, and it was dead quiet—so quiet you could hear the snowflakes landing all around, like an endless sighing. There was no sign of the baby. I listened as hard as I could, but I couldn't hear anything else: just the snow, soft as cotton. I looked around under the windows where I'd heard the racket. The sled was there, tipped on its side; the clothesline I'd knotted at each end of the steering bar was looped into a loose figure-eight in front of it. Close to the house you could see where the snow was disturbed, like there'd been a struggle, but who was struggling with who?

Farther out from the sled I found one of baby Suzanne's orange mittens, and that was when I saw what looked like animal tracks, two sets of them. One set came up the slope of our lawn from the direction of the Hanleys; the other followed the edge of our front walk. Dogs, I said to myself, and it had to be the Kellers' boxer dogs. The two sets of tracks met beside the sled at a right angle—no surprise, I thought: that's how they do it. The question now was: What would I do? There was a trail in the snow, a jumble of pawprints and something dragged, that led off up the street in the direction of the power plant, but at the rate the snow was coming down it wouldn't be long before everything was covered up.

I ran out into the silence of the middle of the street and looked up it and down it. I don't know what I expected to see—some sign of life, any kind of life—but there was nothing anywhere, and the snow was coming down so heavy I could hardly make out the stop sign at the end of the block.

I was scared by then; I mean, scared to death. When I headed back inside the house, Sam was standing halfway down the front steps, hanging on to the wrought iron railing as if she'd fall over without it.

"Where's the baby?" she said. "Where's Suzanne?"

"I don't know. I've got to talk to Marta."

"She's hysterical," Sam said. "She's useless."

So am I, I wanted to say, but instead I said, "You should have a coat on." She gave me a wild look. "I think it was dogs" I said. "I think they carried her off."

"No," Sam said. "No." She shut her eyes and closed both fists around the railing. "No," she said again.

"It doesn't do any good to keep saying 'no,'" I told her, and I kind of herded her inside. "You call the police. I'll try to talk to Marta."

Marta's sat for us before, and she's always impressed me as a level-headed kid, absolutely to be trusted. She's not boy-crazy, so you know you can leave her in the evening and not come home to find her making out on the couch with some no-neck football star. The fact is, she's one of the plainer sort, maybe a little overweight, but all the more likable for not being some pea-brained beauty queen.

She was in the dining room and Clarice was sitting beside her, trying to calm her down. Clarice had poured a couple fingers of whiskey in a tumbler, and she was trying to get Marta to drink it. "It'll make you feel better," she was saying. "Come on; just take a swallow."

"Marta? What happened?" I said.

I said it as gently as I could, not wanting to set her off into hysterics, but she started in again anyway, choking on her sobs as if she couldn't catch her breath.

"Stop it," I told her. "Tell me exactly what you saw."

IIII As it turned out, Marta had seen exactly nothing; she wasn't there either. She'd come inside "just for a minute" to use the downstairs bathroom, and when she went back out Suzanne was gone. She came racing inside to get me, which is how we'd bumped into each other in the hall.

Sam had called the police and she'd called the Shaws to come get Marta. I tried to send her to bed.

"I'd go crazy," she said. "I can't"

"You don't have to sleep," I said. "I'll call you when we find her. There's nothing you can do, so you might as well take a pill and lie down and try to rest."

Clarice seconded the motion, and the two women went off upstairs. I didn't know what I was going to do next, but I couldn't let Sam think I didn't have a plan.

|||| What we did was organize a posse—Billy, Corey, and me—armed and dangerous and going out after the dogs. We were some trio, slogging through the snow, following a trail that was getting fainter and fainter as the flakes came down, smaller now, but just as steady. Billy was in his old Pendleton parka with the elbows worn through, a 12-gauge shotgun in the crook of his right arm, his pockets bulging with shells. Corey was in his red-plaid mackinaw and orange Day-Glo hunting cap, carrying his thirty-aught-six, new at Christmas; he was sulking because I'd talked him into leaving Galahad, his retriever, locked in his Bronco in front of our house—my argument being that I didn't think we'd want to shoot Galahad by mistake when we were aiming at the boxers.

And me. What I was armed with was a pellet gun I'd bought ten or twelve years ago to terrorize the local rabbit population. It looked real enough; I'd figured when I picked it out that I could probably scare an intruder with it—if there was enough light, and if the intruder had the courtesy to hang around to be seen, and if I had the guts to challenge him. At least it was more than an air rifle; you could pump it up to increase the velocity of the pellets. "Six pumps will kill a cow" was the gun maker's slogan.

I know that when you're in shock you're supposed to be numb, your brain on hold, your sense of time in suspension, but all the time we were walking up Lafayette Street in the direction of the power plant, all the crazy thoughts in the world were ramming around in my head, and I swear my senses were sorting through every little thing around me. You take the silence—I mean, it was still, with no sound except the snow underfoot and the noise we made breathing, but here I was trying to compare this stillness with other stillnesses in my life. I thought about going into the shop at night, when the day's jobs were done and all the presses and folders and binders were shut down, and how, because you expected noise in a print shop, the silence was twice as pronounced. I thought about times Sam and I had gone on vacations to the Upper Peninsula, and how the first couple of mornings the silence was uncanny because we weren't used to it; we were still waiting for the noises of in-town traffic. And I was analyzing the quality of the silence in relation to its environment, how I could tell—I swear I could—when the temperature dropped another degree or two because the creak of the snow under our boots went to a different pitch.

And smell, too. The closer we got to the power plant, the stronger the smell of the engine oil that lubricated the turbines, and the headier the ozone their spinning made. "Smell it?" I said to the others. "Smell the plant?" No, they said. They couldn't smell you-know-what.

And dogs; I thought about dogs. How I hated them. How I could not imagine Corey's—or anyone else's—fondness for them. The dogs you read about in the newspapers, that kill for the fun of it: smaller animals, helpless small children. Predators like the Kellers' boxers. Pit bulls, and the whole gamut of German dogs—the Alsatians that eat babies out of baby carriages, the Dobermans and Weimaraners and Rottweilers trained to murder on command because the rich are afraid of the poor. And all of them, those murderous animals, made kennel-club pretty with their bobbed tails and their cropped ears up in rollers like society dames.

Fucking dogs, I kept saying to myself as we crossed the Grand Trunk tracks into open ground where the trail grew fainter and fainter. Fucking beautiful killer dogs, man's best fucking friend. I worked myself into a state, I'll say. I reached down and grabbed a handful of new snow and rubbed it over my cheeks and brow and the back of my hackles-up neck.

All this crazy, aimless mental dance—the sharpened edge to my senses, the perception of who we were and what we would have looked like to a curious observer, my subjective list of the world's evil canines—all this was in the back of my mind as we tried to track the two boxers. But always at the front of my mind, coloring everything else, was the image of baby Suzanne: was she all right, would we find her, how could I have prevented this horror. Every so often I'd get a flash of her already dead, her snowsuit ripped to tatters, blood all over the snow, her face unrecognizable and parts of her—hands, feet—missing, devoured by the rapacious dogs. Just a flash, no more, because the instant it appeared I'd push it aside, think of something else, put a new picture on the screen of my imagination. But Suzanne dead kept coming back, the time in between these visions getting shorter and shorter; I kept putting up new alternatives, my brain like a printing press turning out impressions but not keeping up. And what was going through Sam's mind? At least I was moving, at least I had the illusion of action. Sam was stuck at home, surrounded by well-meaning women intensifying her misery.

"We've lost it," Corey said. He put up his hand and we all stopped. The plant loomed ahead, the halogen bulbs that outlined it muted by weather, the top of its stack lost in the storm and the steam from its cooling tower barely visible in the whiteness of snow. "I don't see any track at all."

I couldn't either. Wherever Suzanne was, there was nothing left to lead the way to her. They got away with it, was what went through my head—as if the two boxers had carried out a premeditated crime, as if they were as smart as humans.

"Let's split up," Billy said. "I'll go around the plant to the right; you two go left. We'll meet by the containment pool on the other side."

And that's what we did. I knew Billy was sending me in partnership with Corey because he thought my pellet gun was too puny to be effective by itself, but what difference did it make? When we met beside the pool, its mists pinkish with halogen light, it was only to announce to each other that we'd seen nothing.

"Let's go on a little farther," I said. "Maybe we'll get lucky and pick up the trail again."

"Hell, there's too much snow," Billy said. "You could walk all the way to Gary, you wouldn't pick it up."

"Just a mile or two," I said.

"I know how you feel," Corey said, "but use your head."

That was when the police finally showed up—the same two officers Billy and I had seen the day the boxers laid siege to them in their car. They asked us a lot of questions, and then they lectured us for taking the law into our own hands. I held back; I didn't lose my temper, or call them names, or question their competence. I just turned away and shut up. When they drove off, I let Billy and Corey lead the way home. It was a lot colder now, and full dark, and the snow seemed to be letting up. Our own old tracks were almost as clear as day in the beam of Corey's flashlight.

That was the worst day of my life, the worst day of Sam's, the worst day that ever was in the world.

||| The Kellers are people of taste; I could see that, looking around at the changes they'd made in the old Addison house, which I hadn't seen the inside of since Sam and I walked through it with Al Clifford. I didn't necessarily approve of what they'd done. They'd turned the dining room into a living room, and vice-versa, so that where the big oak sideboard had been was a fancy music wall: tape decks, tuner and amplifier, disc changer, speakers big enough for a church. Corey's got the same sort of music system, state-of-the-art, enough decibels to break your neighbors' windows if you wanted to. There were carved-wood doors, dark finished, that you could close to conceal all the modern equipment except the speakers, so the electronics wouldn't clash with the room's decor. Sam's dragged me around to enough auctions and antique barns so I knew the furni-

ture was Eastlake, or maybe imitation Eastlake—upholstered chairs and sofas with elegant carved backs, pieces that look as if they'd be uncomfortable but aren't. They do make you sit straighter than you're used to, but I suppose the furniture was appropriate: it made the occasion look as formal as it was supposed to be. I didn't see the rest of the house, except I noticed lots of touches: old fox-hunting prints on the walls, little decorative crystal and china pieces all around, reminding you that this was a house without children.

There were six of us: the chief of police, in uniform, and a plain-clothes officer with him to take notes; the county medical examiner—we print his invoice forms and a coated-stock advertising flier he passes out to his private patients; the p.r. director from the power company; Karen and Fred Keller; and me. Sam was home in bed, sedated, cried out. Clarice Shaw was with her, mostly answering the telephone.

All of us were sitting with coffee in china cups you could almost see through, trying not to spill; there was a cherrywood coffee table close by, with a plate of cookies and a stack of cocktail napkins with the initial K in the corner. The medical examiner, Henry Watt, had been doing all the talking—how this was similar to an inquest, but it wasn't really an inquest by any legal definition of the word, and we were just all here to try to get at the true facts of the matter before us. A friendly exploration of what we think happened. He stressed the word friendly.

They'd found baby Suzanne the morning after Billy and Corey and I lost the trail this side of the power plant. The power people dragged the containment pool, and that was where they found her. Her snowsuit was in tatters and she had cuts and bruises all over her, but there weren't any actual dog bites. Doc Watt said she'd drowned, which meant to me that all the while those damned dogs were dragging her, she was alive. And Corey and Billy and I had stood near her with all our stupid arsenal, had looked out over the misty water and been ignorant.

I dreaded this meeting. The details—the "true facts," so far as we already knew them—were what did us in: Sam in bed, me hung over because, proud of it or not, I got as drunk as I've ever got after I'd gone down to the funeral home to look at the body. Pray to God you never have to say to some stranger in a strange room, "Yes, that's my baby." I wanted to be dead too.

Well, we put our coffee cups down and started talking. I went first. I said I didn't much care what the rest of them decided about facts; my little girl was dead and that was the only fact that mattered to Sam and me. What I wanted now was for those dogs to be put down—not so much because they'd killed Suzanne, but because I didn't think the authorities should wait for somebody else's child to be killed.

"You'll forgive me," Fred Keller said, "but the fact is that your daughter drowned. She wasn't killed by my dogs."

Of course I didn't know Keller—had never met him before this night—but I hated him and his tweeds and his good taste, and I hated the way he talked about Suzanne, cool and indifferent, all this fucking objectivity in his voice.

"Well, Fred," said the police chief, "strictly speaking you're correct, but we did find dog saliva on the child's clothing, so indirectly—"

Keller interrupted. "That saliva could have been from anybody's dog," he said.

"We can do tests for that," Doc Watt said.

"Then you'd better do them," Keller said, "before anybody goes off half-cocked about murdering my dogs."

That was about the end of it. Everybody agreed the boxers would be locked up at the pound, and the tests would be done, and if the saliva on Suzanne's snowsuit matched the boxers', they'd have to be put down.

"How do you feel about that?" Doc Watt asked me.

I told him I was a hell of a ways past feeling, and then I came home to pour myself a drink.

IIII The printing business stays strong. A lot of evenings I work late at the shop; there's always something to do. Shaw Dairies changes the picture on their milk cartons every month or so, and every time they do I try to figure some way to hold the dot pattern so the ink doesn't make the kids' faces into caricatures. I catch myself staring at those cartons for Shaw's 2%. I know the child's picture is too small and too blurry to be useful, but it gives the parents hope, and it postpones their real grief.

The Kellers' dogs were put down, and nothing changed. But grief—grief transforms the whole world. I want to talk about the transformation with Sam, except I don't know how to bring it up. I want to explain why I bought a gun—not like the kid's pellet gun I carried when Corey and Billy and I went looking for Suzanne in the snow, but a shiny .32-caliber revolver with real bullets in the cylinder, a gun small enough so I can almost cover it with my hand. Sam, if she'd listen to me, would say that I'm not myself, that she doesn't know me anymore. When I stood at the glass showcase in Paulsen's Hardware, looking down at the dozen or so handguns old Tom Paulsen had on display, I'd half persuaded myself I needed protection for the nights I was staying late at work, but in my heart I knew better.

I want to tell Sam how the word—*grief*—doesn't look to me as if it's spelled right, and I keep wanting to recite the old rule about *i* before *e*, in case I've got the letters transposed. In the old days of the Linotype, I want to say to her, the days when you had to hand-set the banners, you were always reading words backward as well as frontward, but that was easy and different. Now when I get gloomy and print the word and stare at it a while, *grief* looks to me like the purest gibberish. Then when I come home from the shop I find Sam at the kitchen table, the room dark except for that little light on the panel at the back of the stove. She's always smoking a cigarette, looking off into space as if she hadn't heard me come in. We don't talk. I wish she'd get hold of herself, maybe go back to schoolteaching, which is what she did before she got pregnant with Suzanne, but I don't dare break in on her. I think she feels the same as I do, only she's fastened onto something else, something private and not like words.

We don't sleep much, either one of us. I'll wake up at two or three or four in the morning and look over at Sam. I'll see the small glitter in her eyes, the reflection from the streetlight outside our bedroom window, and I know she's just staring at the ceiling, regretting, hurting. Usually that's when I'll decide to go for a walk. I get up and put my clothes on and sit on the edge of the bed to lace my shoes. I tell Sam—I always whisper, don't ask me why—that I won't be gone for long, and then I go downstairs to the kitchen. Sometimes I start the coffee; most times I don't. I dress for whatever the weather's doing, and then I take down my new revolver from the back of the cupboard over the refrigerator. I make sure the safety is on—I decided I had to keep the gun loaded—and slide it into my pocket.

You can guess where I walk to. I might set out at first in the opposite direction, up Lafayette toward the power plant, or take a turn around the block, or if it's late enough go all the way to the city bus stop and buy a morning paper from the kid who's just starting out on his route, but sooner or later I end up across the street from the house Sam and I wanted but couldn't afford. I stand there. I watch. The Jag is in the drive. The only light inside the house comes pale and curtained from the bathroom window under the middle dormer. I see the layout of the rooms in my mind's eye, just as when Al Clifford showed us through—the foyer, the front stairway, the bathroom door half open and a narrow shaft of light falling across the upstairs hall. I imagine Karen and Fred Keller asleep in the big bedroom with the sliding doors, the moonglow making soft shadows on the bedclothes, a nightstand. I picture a fancy antique nightstand, with a digital clock showing spindly red numbers, so if they wake up in the dark—maybe they'll hear the creak of one of the old floorboards—they'll know what time their time has come.

A Simple Elegy

\\\

Magnus is dying. He is a great man, a composer, who has lived boldly into his eighty-third year, but the cancer secret inside him has long since revealed itself. Magnus is hollow, an appearance, something memorable but lost. The surgeons have given him up. The medical staff have disconnected the life-support; they have sent Magnus home to be in a familiar place, though they expect he will die in the unfamiliar ambulance. Everyone is resigned. The wife sits at the window and watches the light play under the shade trees. The son sits with his guilt, and thinks he has been afraid for years that his father might outlive him. He thinks how much he has resented Magnus—the old man's talent, vitality, knowledge, a shadow across the young man's career.

"He'll live forever," he has told the young woman he lives with. "That old fool won't ever let go."

"Nobody lets go," the woman says. "But nobody holds on, either." She is scarcely thirty years old, and the son wonders how she arrived at the tone of what she knows. Anyway, the old man won't live forever after all. He'll die in the ambulance; the doctors have said so.

\\\ Magnus doesn't die.

He is carried up to the front bedroom, where the light is broken by the restless crown of the maple and played through the bay window onto the room's pale walls. He is propped against the eider pillows; the muslin sheet that bears his wife's monogram is drawn up to his chin. He is asked if he wants anything.

"Open a window," Magnus murmurs.

His son does so. The air in the room shifts, a rippling motion; the lace curtain billows inward like white wings. The summer afternoon smells clean, and the high trill of the cicada is an edge around whatever is said at Magnus's bedside.

"Good," he whispers. His wife bows her head to him. "Good," he insists.

The wife, the son, a doctor, a nurse—the four of them wait to be instructed, but Magnus is asleep.

"He may have anything he wants," the doctor says. "Any drug. Any visitor."

Magnus's oldest friend, a man of the same age, a sculptor, has come to bid Magnus goodbye. He is a tall, formal gentleman with gray eyes and white hair, and he carries a cane whose head is carved, from ivory, into the shape of a human fist.

"He'll be so pleased to see you," Magnus's wife says.

She leads the friend up to Magnus's bedroom, the son following, the nurse positioned outside the door to remind all of them how little time they have. The friend sits at the bedside.

"How are you feeling?" the friend asks.

Magnus's answer is less than a whisper. The friend, his hands holding the fist of the cane, leans forward until his ear is only a few inches from Magnus's mouth. The weak whisper is repeated; the friend nods and says, "I guess that's right." He sits up. "That's right," he says again.

Nothing more is said in the room.

Later, as the friend is descending the front staircase, he tells Magnus's wife, "Magnus says he won't see Halley's Comet again."

He stops at the foot of the stairs.

"We both saw it when we were ten years old." He puts his arm around Magnus's wife and hugs her. "Dear old Magnus," he says. "My God, this is the saddest day of my life."

IIII "It's uncanny," the son tells his mother. "That he can sleep through his awful pain, and I can't fall off for the life of me."

It is two in the morning. The cold supper brought by neighbors has been eaten, the dishes done up by the son's young woman. Magnus has been looked in on. Wife and son have embraced each other, standing in the upstairs hall, weeping tears that have to do with loss and conclusion and, for the son, perverse triumph. The full-length hall mirror has framed their emotions; the son imagined himself an outsider, a witness to this scene, and was horrified at the cruelty of his imagination, its refusal to pretend he is not an outsider shamming sorrow. What he saw in the glass was a man preening. How do I look?

"The doctor left pills for your father. Perhaps you should take one."

"What are they?"

"Something for sleeping."

He gets up and kisses his mother on the cheek. She is nearly eighty herself, shrunken, her skin like the craze of an old painting. He hardly knows her eyes; they are transformed by Magnus's ordeal.

"I will," he says. Whatever they are, he thinks, if I took all of them I might still be first to go. The only way he'll die is if they tell him he outlived me. "I'm so tired, I can't think straight."

IIII The son has one dream.

He is at a party, apparently in his Boston apartment. The living room is crowded, people are dancing in extremely close circumstances, drinks are raised. The light in the room is smoky; the shadows it throws are in hectic motion. He makes his way in and out of the crowd with marvelous ease. The guests all seem to know him, though none of them, so far as he can recall later, have faces. He is in fact going to the door, as if to welcome some new arrival.

When he opens the door he sees his father and a woman who

may or may not be his mother. Both of them are extraordinarily young, possibly in their thirties. Magnus is as handsome as early photographs have shown him. The woman beside him is a true beauty. Neither speaks, neither moves. The son thinks he might as well be looking at a portrait.

He wakes up knowing Magnus is dead, and for a long time he lies in the dark, trembling, absolutely unable to control the terror that eats at his stomach, his heart.

"What is it?" says the young woman. She is beside him in bed, raised on one elbow, the dim light from the motel bathroom revealing her hair, the left side of her face, her bare shoulders, and the outline of her small breasts. "What's the matter?"

ⵏⵏ The next day, when the front bedroom is empty and the funeral plans are settled, he sits with the young woman in the lounge of the Holiday Inn. He orders whiskey, and tells her as much as he can remember about the dream.

"His dying really did move you, didn't it?" she says. "I thought you were above it."

"The power of fear," he says. "That's what moved me."

She looks at him sadly.

"Or love," she says. "In return for his."

What can he answer to that? How can she think that?

ⵏⵏ The following afternoon the church is filled, the odor of flowers swims on the tides of light through the stained-glass windows, seven on each side, though this is a Protestant church. The names of donors —Yankee names, biblical names—are etched into one clear, rectangular pane at the bottom of each window. The gold-colored pipes of the organ cover the walls behind the oak pulpit and the choir loft. Magnus's wife, his son, his son's young woman, and his few surviving friends are seated in the front pews. The coffin is at the left, below the pulpit; a piano is at the right—the two objects like complementary pieces of furniture, polished and glowing with dark beauty.

It is an odd ceremony. No music plays, no prayers are said. At one o'clock precisely the murmur of voices in the church dies out, the minister folds his hands at the edge of the pulpit, and the sculptor—with the assistance of someone sitting beside him—gets to his feet and turns slowly to face the mourners.

"What I regret," he begins, "is not only the passing of my friend Magnus, but the loss of my ability properly to remember him. I am an artist whose art has forsaken him, a sculptor whose hands are traitor to my craft. These hands will no longer manage my tools; their answer to my deepest need is only unbearable pain."

The sculptor's voice is thin and difficult to hear. Magnus's son wants to say "Speak up," but he prevents himself out of respect not for his father or his father's friends, but out of a sense of social propriety.

"If it were not for my age, I would make a monument to Magnus, larger than life and more lasting." The old sculptor turns to face the coffin. "Forgive me, dear Magnus. I have nothing left me but inspiration. I am as dead, my friend, as you."

The young woman seats herself at the piano.

"Here is the last music Magnus wrote, and a lyric he dictated to me over the last five days of his life," she says. "He called it 'A Simple Elegy for Speaking and Touching.'"

There isn't much to it, the son thinks. The melody is uncomplicated; the treble obbligato the young woman plays reminds him of the cicada outside the dying man's window, insistent and coarse; the left hand makes figures like the wind in the silver maple. And the words—the words are the same old stuff of beauty that decays, of colors that turn brown and gray, of loves that are transient. Pleasure becomes pain, light darkness, life death. Only memory endures for a while, the ardent remembrance of promises and caresses.

My God, thinks the son, who would have believed that even on his deathbed a pretty woman could inspire him? My woman. Mine.

|||| When it is the son's turn he stands so quickly that for a moment he fears he will stagger and fall, but he holds the back of the pew until the vertigo passes. The young woman's sweet voice has distracted him; jealousy and anger are a curtain woven between himself and his speech. He has lain awake all night, contriving the words he will say. He fancies himself a poet, and he has imagined that he will move the mourners to the truth about his father—what was good and what was not, what was genuine and what was false, what was admirable and what was base. Images swim in his head; words blossom in his throat; he is conscious of all eyes watching him.

"My father," he says, and the word chokes him. "My father is not in this box."

When he faints—from the smothering odor of the flowers, the heat kindled in the church by the afternoon sunlight, or the intimation of some hidden weakness—it is his old mother on one side and the young woman on the other who catch him and keep him from harming himself.

Remembered
Names
\\\\\

Kelly met Jim Stiles in Portland, Maine, on a Friday in mid-September of the year she turned forty. The bookstore where she worked had scheduled a signing for that afternoon, by a romance author whose jacket photos made her appear thirty-ish, but who in fact arrived looking twenty years older and wearing makeup that showed alarming crazes at the corners of her eyes and mouth.

Stiles came in when the store was about to close, just before five o'clock. He was a tall man, older, and Kelly remembered having seen him before. Yesterday he had come in much earlier—over Gwen's lunch hour—and stood around for a while reading among the store's display of magazines. He hadn't bought anything. Today he carried a copy of the guest author's novel to the register and asked Kelly if she had read it.

"I'm afraid it's not the kind of thing I read," she said, and felt immediately disloyal to Gwen, the shop's owner.

"It's not usually *my* kind of thing either," he admitted. "I thought it might be fun to have a book autographed by a romance author."

"Oh, dear," she said. "Miss Craven—" Rosamond Craven was the author's pen name. "—left about a half-hour ago."

"Your poster said three to five."

"Not a lot of people came in for autographs. Miss Craven gave up early."

"So," he said. He backtracked to the display table and replaced the book on a small stack of other copies.

"I *am* sorry," she said.

"It's all right. People might have gotten the wrong idea about me, owning a book like that."

"You've been in here before," Kelly said. "Yesterday, wasn't it?"

He cocked his head. "You kept an eye on me," he said.

She blushed and extended her hand. "I'm Kelly," she said. "Kelly Avery."

He took the hand. "Jim Stiles. Your first name is a last name."

"And vice-versa," she said.

〣 He told her he was a lawyer, his home was in Virginia, and he was in town for his third conference this year—he had been in Denver and Salt Lake City before his firm decided at the last minute to send him to Maine to take notes at an Environmental Law seminar. Kelly said she had just gotten back to work from her first vacation in three years—a week with friends on Nantucket, where the weather had been unseasonably warm and she had finally been able to wear her new swimsuit. He said that a woman named Eloise, who was at the seminar representing the Maine Yankee nuclear power people, had lost the diamond out of her engagement ring, and he wondered did Kelly think—being literary—that the woman's husband would read the loss as symbolic? She asked if this was his first visit to Maine; he told her no, that he'd been born and raised here, up the road in Scoggin, but he'd been away from the hometown for more than forty years. Then she found out that his father had died two years ago, and now he had no relatives in Maine except a couple of cousins whose addresses he hadn't kept track of.

All this while she went about the routine of closing the store: locking the back door, turning off the lights over the magazine display, returning the Craven novels to their carton so Gwen could decide how many to keep in stock, how many to send back to the publisher. Stiles followed her to make the talking easier; he handed her the novels while she packed them; he commented on the charm of this little bookshop and wanted to know if it did a decent business.

Finally, when everything inside the store seemed in order and Kelly was at the front door, the small orange and black sign turned so the word *closed* faced out, Stiles asked if she would be here tomorrow.

"It's Saturday," she said. "I have Saturdays off."

"I wondered," he said. "It's my last day in Maine."

"That's too bad." She motioned him outside, then followed and locked the door behind them both. "But you shouldn't mind," she said. "The summer's really over."

They walked down Congress Street together, headed toward the Old Port—a touristy, gentrified part of town. It had not been a successful tourist season; the summer had been unusually cool and the rainfall frequent. Kelly had moved here a little more than four years earlier, right after Tom Avery died, and in each successive summer more shops and restaurants had closed, more For Lease signs went up in blank windows from Monument Square to the waterfront. She kept track of the signs, in spite of herself. Answering the question about the bookshop, she had fibbed, telling Stiles business was better than ever. Tell that to Rosamond Craven, or whatever her real name was.

"I dread tomorrow," Stiles said.

The remark startled her, coming as it did out of nowhere. For a little while they had been walking in silence, past shops active or empty, past sidewalk cafés, past little clusters of blue pigeons scavenging the brick walkways. She assumed that he was saying he dreaded leaving his home state, going back to his law office—or perhaps that he didn't like flying.

"I have to make a visit to my father's grave," he went on. "It's not something I'm looking forward to. I thought you might care to come with me."

Kelly had been in cemeteries before, and not only with her parents on Memorial Days when they visited the graves of Kelly's grandparents and left carnations and glads and mums at the base of the family tombstone. Of course she had been at Tom's funeral, though she had not made a habit since then of paying her respects—of being attentive to his memory as if there might be a heavenly reunion that awaited husbands and wives at the end of this life. When she was in college there had been nights with fraternity boys, necking in cars parked behind the mausoleum on Colvin Street; there had even been times when she lay in damp graveyard grass while a boy kissed her mouth and neck and breasts, his hand under her skirt like a curious small animal, and times when she had gone on to do for the boy the selfish thing he asked because the agony of his own pleasure excited her and made her reckless. But this invitation was different. She was more than grown up now, Jim Stiles seemed a respectable older gentleman, and there was surely no impropriety in a visit to a father's grave—never mind whose father he had been.

"Wouldn't I be intruding?" she said.

"It's nothing sentimental," he told her. "I'm not taking flowers or paying my filial respects. The monument people are supposed to have put in his headstone, and I thought I'd check up on them while I'm here."

"In that case," Kelly said.

Stiles squeezed her elbow. "Wonderful," he said.

ꟿ Her fortieth birthday had brought Kelly to a level of restlessness she hadn't known since her graduation from Syracuse—the restlessness possibly made more intense because she was a widow and lived with a much younger man named Warren, a painter in his middle twenties. This evening when she arrived at the apartment, Warren was out—jogging along the Marginal Way, perhaps, or hanging out with Jeremy, his photographer friend, at a tavern on York Street, or sitting near the ferry slip, perhaps on the deck at DeMillo's, to watch the arrival of the *Scotia Princess* from Halifax. For an artist, Warren spent precious little time in his studio; Kelly wondered at his lack of interest in a vocation he seemed deliberately to have chosen for himself, and, lately, at his lack of interest in her. He was often away from her, sometimes gone all night. If she should move out of his life, he might not even care—though where in the world did she think she'd go?

Tonight she ate alone, nibbling at a salad left over from yesterday, sipping iced tea, watching the ritual unpleasantness of the news on television. She did up her few dishes and cleaned off the kitchen counter. She went to bed and read a small collection of imaginary letters sent between imaginary lovers, then she turned out the light.

It was barely nine-thirty, and for a long time she lay in the dark, thinking about Jim Stiles. Was he married, she wondered; was he engaged; was he divorced or a widower, left alone, like her, after expectations of a lifelong partnership? It was marvelous that for all their small talk, she knew none of the answers to those questions. What was she thinking of, accepting a date with this stranger? He might be a serial killer, and if he didn't do her in, dear Gwen probably would. Yet she felt a pull toward Stiles that defied convention; she wondered if it had something to do with their destination—if the ordinary commerce between a man and a woman was this time enhanced by the fact of a visit to the dead.

Next morning when she woke up, Warren was in the kitchen; she could hear him filling the coffee maker with water and grinding the beans, could hear the hot water burbling through the machine. She looked at the clock—eight-thirty, late for her; she had promised to meet Stiles at the bookstore at ten—and swung her feet to the blue carpet beside the bed. She slipped into her robe, knotted the belt across her stomach—the small pressure of the knot made her think of Stiles, of risk—and went to the kitchen. Warren looked up from the sink, where he was rinsing his coffee cup from yesterday. Kelly had never seen him actually wash a dish.

"Hi," he said. "Coffee's not quite ready."

"I'm late," she said. "I'll settle for tomato juice."

He poured it for her, handed her the glass, kissed her on the brow as if there were no difficulties between them.

"That was a wonderful talk we had last night," he said.

She wondered at his sarcasm. She had no idea when he had come home; whenever it was, he had not shared her bed, nor had they spoken. "Oh?" was all she said. She watched him over the rim of the juice glass, reading his face.

"What you said about the two of us—about going away together, escaping the doldrums." He poured himself a cup of the unfinished coffee; its color was somewhere between brown and orange, like tea. "Asking me what was the one thing I'd never done that I most wanted to do."

"And when was this?" Kelly said.

"Last night, when I came in and sat by you on the bed."

"I don't remember."

He studied her. "I was afraid of that," he said. He sat at the end of the table and made a face over the weak coffee. "I was afraid you might be talking in your sleep."

I never talk in my sleep, she could have said, but didn't. Nor did she ask what he had answered to the question about the thing he most wanted to do.

IIII When Stiles pulled up in front of the bookshop, driving a tomato-red coupe—the same color as the icon of the No Parking sign beside it—Gwen was at the window, sipping from the first of the several mugs of strong coffee that would propel her through the day's sparse business. She held the cup before her as if it hid her from view.

"He's distinguished looking," she told Kelly. "Sort of a Cary Grant type."

"He's very pleasant," Kelly said.

"And he's taking you to a *cemetery?*"

"I told you. He has to visit his father's grave."

"Is this wise of you?"

"Don't try to talk me out of it."

"Does he know about you-know-who?"

"He doesn't need to," Kelly said. Then she was out the shop door and into the red car beside Stiles. She waved to Gwen—a small flutter of her fingers—as the car left the curb.

"I was afraid you might stand me up," Stiles said. "You don't know me from Adam."

"I don't even know Adam," Kelly said.

They were twenty minutes on the Maine Turnpike, and thirty minutes more on a two-lane blacktop that brought them to the town of Scoggin. The seasons were just on the edge of change, the days and nights almost exactly equal in length. A few impatient maples, beginning their turn to yellow and orange, stood out from the pines that grew among them, but the horizon of unruly plaid hillsides was weeks away. It was a gray day, a quilt of clouds pulled flat over the sky, and this morning the clock radio beside the empty bed had proposed rain.

"This used to be a mill town," Stiles said as they drove through— past a shopping mall, a movie complex, a downtown of remodeled storefronts interspersed with churches and banks and filling stations—"but the textile mills moved out in the fifties. South Carolina, I think."

"You grew up here?" Kelly said.

"Born and raised." The car turned at a gray stucco church, crossed a rusting bridge over the river, turned again. Off to the right were brick factory buildings with hundreds of small-paned, white-washed windows; most of the panes were broken out and the buildings themselves wore desolation like a gray film. Beyond the mills the houses looked shabby, the lawns unkempt, the streets too narrow. The people looked shabby as well—small gray men poked rakes at fallen leaves, the yards around them empty of children. Kelly felt relieved to leave the built-up area and be again, for a couple of miles, in open country: fields and stone walls, the gnarled branches of apple orchards with crows waddling up and down the aisles.

"It's just over this rise." He pointed. The car slid over the crest of the hill at a speed that made a surprising catch in the pit of her stomach—"My mother used to call that a 'yes-marm,'" Stiles said, grinning—and not far ahead Kelly saw a house with a high silhouette, pitch-roofed, a tall chimney at each end like handles on a box. It reminded her of a house she and Tom had looked at in Vermont, in the latter days of the marriage when city life was starting to wear on him—their "escape house," he called it—but his health had given out before they were able to make an offer. The Stiles house had the same profile, the same gloominess about it that Tom had argued could be got rid of by tender care and fresh paint. She could see as they came closer that it had a semicircular drive like the Vermont house, and an attached shed converted into a garage. Hydrangea bushes stood, half-bare, at each end of the driveway; an enormous oak tree dominated the front yard.

"Family homestead," he said. "The cemetery's off to the left, up toward that pine grove."

"Your own private cemetery?"

He steered the car into the driveway, parked it facing the converted shed. "We share it with two other families—not that we couldn't have had the whole of the hereafter to ourselves if we'd wanted it. The Stileses used to be people of considerable substance."

"What happened to the substance?"

"I was never sure." He got out of the car, walked around the front of it to open her door for her. "I got various stories when I was growing up. The 1929 crash, the Great Depression, the alcoholism of my father's father. But I think now it might have been some sort of old-family entropy—a gradual material dissolving-away. You choose."

He took Kelly's hand, simply to help her out of the rented car, but she felt an unexpected mix of pleasure and warning that thrilled for an instant, low in her stomach—like the tightened knot of her bathrobe, the scary pleasure of taking a hill too fast.

"This way," he said.

As they left the car a single thread of lightning danced in the distance, and while they were walking up the overgrown path to the graveyard, a tangle of gone-by wild rosebushes on either side, the low grumble of thunder rolled toward them.

"A little Maine weather," Stiles said.

"We won't melt," Kelly said.

The cemetery was a generous rectangle of lawn, an acre or more carved out of the fields, its grass mowed short, the clippings raked into a compost heap just outside the iron-pipe fence painted black. Stiles led her in through a spindly gate. By now the sky to the northwest had begun to spill grayer smudges of cloud toward them. A small wind sprang up and brushed coolness across Kelly's face, and the day turned ominously dark. Kelly shivered.

"You can smell the rain in the air," he said. He held out his hand and she took it. "Dad's grave is over here."

She let herself be led to the corner of the cemetery nearest the weather, past mottled gray-white stones thin as slate that carried other names than Stiles: *Kimball, Willard.* First families now forgotten. She stood beside Stiles—her hand still in his—looking at an ugly granite monument shaped like a chair back, high and narrow, its sides rough-hewn, its face polished mirror-smooth. A single name was carved into the face:

Jameson Patrick Stiles
1899–1990

"That chills me," Stiles said. He let go her hand and walked around to the other side of the monument.

Kelly followed him. The two of them stood reading more names, older dates. This was the actual front of the stone; the father's name was the first to have been cut into the reverse of it.

"My grandparents," he said. "Two other children. My mother."

"Were you and your father close? Is that why seeing his name chills you?"

"It's my name too," he said. "I'm Jameson junior."

She considered this knowledge. She had thought his name was *James*, something more common. Now she tried to imagine how it must feel to see your own uncommon name on a gravestone; in a kind of reflex of concern, she put her hand out to touch his sleeve. As she turned her face up to his, she felt the first dash of cold rain on her skin.

"*Your* first name is a last name too," she said.

He covered her hand with his. "Let's look for that headstone," he said, "and then find some shelter."

The new stone was set into the ground a few yards below the central monument, a simple rectangle of dark blue granite with *Jameson* cut into its face. The face was mirror-smooth and gave back their shadows through the pebbling of the rain. Similar stones were set in a row to left and right: *Alice, Martha, Frank.*

"All right," Stiles said. "Let's get out of the wet."

They ran down the slope together, Stiles slightly ahead, holding her hand, half-pulling her in his wake. Instead of leading her to the car, he led her past it and up the graveled walk to the front door of the house. Once they were under the overhang of the eaves, he released her and fumbled with a ring of keys. The rain was heavy now, wind-driven, the leaves of the oak behind them tossing in the downpour, the rain rattling against the car. Kelly trembled with cold, waiting for Stiles to find the right key.

"I don't know if you're much for antiques," he said. He spoke half over his shoulder, his voice raised against the wind. "But you might like a look at the family past."

〟 Even after the key had turned in the lock, Stiles was obliged to throw his full weight at the front door; only then did the jamb let go with a sound like a small thunder-crack, and the door swing inward, and a pungent, musty smell flow from the closed house into the moist outside air.

"This entrance didn't get much use, even when the house was lived in," Stiles said. "It's too formal. You'll see."

He stepped inside and turned to take her hand. It was fast becoming a habit, this intimacy he had begun by helping her out of the car. But no, she thought—giving him the hand because he was after all her sole guide into a strange place—not really so much habit as *custom*, an indication of the ease he felt in her company. Nothing was wrong with that. He was on an errand to the dead; she had come along to witness for the living.

She found herself being drawn through an entryway: a small square room, really, large enough for a bench and an old-fashioned umbrella stand, wooden hooks on one wall, a coarse mat on the floor. A single rectangular window was set high above the bench, its tiny panes of stained glass colored pale blue and green and yellow around a clear central light that ran with earnest rivulets of the autumn rain.

"Vestibule," Stiles said.

He brought her through an inner doorway, and now the two of them stood in a high-ceilinged front hall. A wide flight of stairs led upward, a brass bouquet of lamps set in its balustrade like an inverted chandelier, the steps rising to a landing, then making a ninety-degree right bend up to the second storey. A Tudor-style window above the landing let the dull gray daylight in.

"It's impressive," she said, noticing how the height of the hall gave a resonance to her voice, and how the rhythm of the storm outside—the front door was still open—filled in around the edges of her words.

"You can see why we preferred to come in through the pantry," he said. He closed the outside door, forcing it with his foot and with the heel of his palm until it latched. "The place is so damned immodest, it practically demands a butler; at the least it needs a downstairs maid."

"Did you grow up here?"

"Oh yes." He crossed the dim hall and went into the room beyond the archway. "The electricity's shut off," he said. "I'm looking for candles, or maybe an old hurricane lamp my grandmother used to keep here in the parlor."

Kelly followed him. The room was furnished, though sparsely. She could make out the shapes of high-backed chairs, a glass-fronted china cupboard, planters whose contents were stiff and leafless. Under her feet she felt carpeting, and in what little light penetrated the windows she could see the design of it, oriental and complicated.

"I was forbidden this room," Stiles said. "It had all the bric-a-brac that filled my grandmother's treasury. A lot of it's gone now. There was a baby grand in that corner; my father sold it. There were ornate pictures on the walls—cherubs and plump naked ladies surrounded by gossamer scarves. God knows who would have bought *them*."

"Did your grandmother raise you? Where was your mother?"

He was kneeling, opening the drawer of a small table beside one of the tall chairs. "Candles," he said.

He stood and handed a candle to Kelly. It was new, still wrapped in cellophane, and the two of them were silent for a moment against the crackle of unwrapping.

"I'll have to find some kind of holder," Stiles said.

"Tell me about being a kid here," she said.

"I hated it. I didn't much like my grandmother."

"She was mean to you?"

He had led her back into the hall, and now he was rummaging in a closet under the stairs. He produced a pair of heavy glass candle-holders and handed one to Kelly. "She was unkind to my mother," he said. "She was indifferent to me, more or less."

"What did she do to your mother?" Kelly said.

He lighted her candle and his own from a book of matches. "Treated her like a servant. Expected her to do all the cooking, the washing, the housecleaning. I didn't think about it at the time. It was the Depression, my father was out of work, we couldn't afford a place of our own. I thought we were a normal family. Now I see how terrible it must have been for my mother—how my father kept his mouth shut and let her be used."

They entered a gloomy room with an ornate chandelier suspended over a table of dark, grained wood. At one end of the room, on a smaller table, a cut-crystal punch bowl gave back the multiplied candlelight; a glass ladle rested inside it, and a dozen or so crystal cups surrounded it.

"Dining room," Stiles said. "That door leads to the butler's pantry, that other one to a den; that frosted-glass window opens into the kitchen."

"Did you really have a butler?"

"Not in my lifetime," he said. She could see the smile at the corners of his mouth, flickering like the yellow candle flame. "I told you: my mother did all the work."

"Is she still alive?"

"No. My father outlived her. He was alone for almost twenty years."

"That's awful," Kelly said.

"I don't think he even noticed," Stiles said.

IIII He insisted that she see the whole house. The rain drummed outside, dull on the roof while they were upstairs, sharper against the downstairs windows that faced the wind, almost like the rattle of sleet. For the first time, Kelly wished she might spend the night here, and she wondered how she could have let the notion cross her mind.

"Most of this other stuff should have been got rid of," Stiles said. They had climbed a staircase, narrow and steep, into the attic, where the rain noise was loudest and he had to speak close to her ear to be heard. Old trunks of leather- or iron-bound wood, bulky cardboard boxes, shelves of books—these filled two rooms whose ceilings came to a peak, and a heady smell of mildew was made sharper by the wet weather. "The things that did get sold usually turn out to be the things I miss."

"Like what?"

"Oh—" He pondered. "There used to be an old banjo-mandolin my uncle played when he was in college, back in the age of the rac-

coon coat. It was a beautiful thing, nickel-plated, the neck embel-
lished with mother-of-pearl inlays. I've never found it, and I've
looked everywhere. Last time I was here I found an old C-melody
saxophone that's pretty worthless. You might know *that* would still
be around."

"You must have had a few happy times in this house," Kelly said,
"in spite of the wicked grandmother."

He lifted his candle as if to get a better look at her face. "Moments of sunshine?" he said. "Unexpected joys?"

"Something like that," Kelly said.

He moved past her to the stairway. "Let's go down." He preceded her down the risky stairs, Kelly keeping a distance that allowed her to hold the candle ahead of her without setting fire to
Stiles. "I was an only child," he said over his shoulder, "so I spent a
lot of time in that attic, inventing worlds for myself. I had a dark-
room. I went into the film processing business when I was twelve."
At the foot of the stairs he stopped and turned to look up at Kelly.

"This was generous of you," he said. "Coming with me on this
nostalgia trip." He took her hand. "This death trip, I mean."

"I like being here," Kelly said. There seemed no harm in re-
sponding to the warmth of his touch. "With you," she added, as if
that admission were harmless as well.

The pressure of his hand increased—not enough to hurt her, but
as if he were ensuring her attention. "Would you like to stay the
night?" he said.

"Yes," she said. "I would." He might have read her mind; she
spoke the words without so much as an instant of thought.

|||| He led her into the room at the foot of the attic stairs—a large
room with a bed in it, a highboy along one wall, a shorter dresser
with a mirror along another, a small bookcase under double windows
where rain streamed down. The available wall space was covered
with framed pictures: faces and family groups, some in rectangular
frames, some in oval, sepia images illuminated by the two candles.

"The ancestors," Stiles said. "Or all we'll admit to."

The bed was unmade, its ticking glossy in the small light and the wide buttons of the mattress a symmetrical pattern of shadows; two pillows were stacked one on the other at the head of the bed. It was, Kelly imagined, a room where someone must have died—perhaps the mother, perhaps the father who hadn't noticed her absence.

Stiles was at the window. He had set his candle down, and now he stood looking out, watching the weather.

"You remember those headstones?" he said. "How uneven they are?"

"Yes," she said. She visualized the polished stones—*Jameson, Alice, Frank, Martha*—and how the ground they were set in was buckled, putting each name in a different plane.

"After my father's funeral I asked the caretaker to straighten them, level them. He said he could, if I insisted, but that they wouldn't stay put. Tree roots—that's what's pushing at them. An old pine; did you notice it?"

"I guess I didn't."

"You can't see it through all this rain," Stiles said. "It's just outside the fence. It's huge—as old as I am." Kelly thought she heard him sigh, though it might have been a gust of wind or a blurred rake of rain across the glass he watched through. "The roots go all over the place."

In her mind's eye Kelly saw the roots of the pine; they reached under the iron fence, encircled and then broke into the vaults where Stiles's dead ancestors reposed, hugged the coffins themselves in a surreal embrace. She leaned into Stiles, resting against him, reaching her arms around his waist. She felt the warmth and solidness of his back, her head in the saddle between his shoulder blades; she could hear the beating of his heart, felt her embrace loosen and tighten with the fall and rise of his breathing. Listening to him talk about death, about family, about roots that she could only relate to the comfortable rootedness of the place where he was born, she felt an enormous sympathy for the man: for his aloneness, for the drift in his life away from Maine. Sympathy she felt—and desire.

The desire was possibly connected to her own drift—the death of her husband letting her loose, the apartment with Warren such a far cry from the escape house in Vermont, the near future so disturbingly unsettled. Whatever it came from, her desire seemed both shocking and natural; it had begun with the first touch of the man's hand and it had hovered on the edge of her consciousness, like an instruction not quite intelligible, as he led her into this house. Now it was mindless. Still in her arms, Stiles turned to her; they kissed. Though she could not afterward recall the exact order of events, she was lifted off her feet and carried to the room's stripped bed. There he began making love to her. His hands peeled her below the waist, his mouth caressed her chilled skin. She lay entirely open. She remembered the sounds she made—broken exclamations, unfinished words, as if by the time she had discovered one response, a fresh one asserted itself, and she could not recite fast enough her body's vocabulary.

"Oh," she said in a voice whose weakness surprised her, "what are we doing?"

He raised himself to look at her, the two candles side by side on the nightstand shading one side of his face.

"Wait," he said.

She sat up. Stiles knelt in front of the highboy and began opening its drawers. From the second drawer he brought out one package—sheets, Kelly could see, still in cellophane wrap, like the candles—and another, pillowcases.

"What in the world—?" she said.

"We ought to do this properly," Stiles told her. "We'll make up the bed; be civilized."

"Those are brand-new."

"My mother's. People gave her sheets and pillowcases and towels and Irish linen handkerchiefs—for birthdays, anniversaries." He tore at the wrappings, crumpled them and flung them aside. "She loved new things," he said. "She couldn't bring herself to soil them."

|||| All along, from the time they had exchanged names at the book-shop yesterday, Kelly had thought of this man as "Stiles." Now, intimate with him on bed linens that were cold and crisp and smelled only faintly of the twenty-odd years they had been put away, she thought it was time to name him with less formality. Of course she could not call him "Jim"—that seemed too common—but "Jameson" seemed right; she felt she had earned "Jameson."

Jameson. His arms cradled her, one hand between her shoulder blades, the other resting lightly, palm down, at the small of her back. His face was against hers; she could feel and hear his breathing, regular and rhythmic, as if desire were only another sort of engine, like the red car's. It was all unlikely, this lovemaking; possibly it was only an intricate, highly emotional dream, and shortly she would wake up, as she had this morning when Warren had tried to appropriate her forgotten sleep for himself.

Meanwhile the rain flowed against the windows of Jameson's parents' bedroom. The sepia faces on the walls were no less still, suspended in their frames, than she was. She felt as if she were floating; any magician could have passed his hoop around her body to show the audience—that wall of ancestors—how no wires suspended her, how illusion was reality. After a half-hour of lying with Jameson—wordless, weightless, motionless, thoughtless—she might as well not have been a person at all; only a scrap of landscape too small for maps, yet too substantial to be left unvisited.

Finally Jameson spoke. "It's stopped raining," he said.

His voice seemed to bring her to life. "Yes," she said, her own voice husky, cobwebby from disuse.

Now they were back to talk, as if the meeting, the courting, the lovemaking, were no more than an interruption to the conversation begun the day before. Yes, Kelly had been married—nearly a dozen years, to Tom Avery. Really she had thought about keeping her maiden name, but wasn't "liberated" enough—if that were really the right word—like some of her friends who hung on to their fathers' names or opted for hyphenation. No, Jameson admitted, he had never married; had had several affairs—"relationships" they were called nowadays; he wanted her to remember that there was a generation, an awkward difference of language, between the two of them—but he had never found a woman he wanted permanence with. How many women? He dared not say. Her Thomas had been a teacher, Kelly told him, at a private school in Manhattan, almost until he died—of lupus; wasn't that a curious thing to cut a young man down? Almost literary? Sunlight was his enemy. He'd worn an enormous wide-brimmed hat whenever he went outside the apartment, had become a kind of neighborhood character. Jameson sympathized; what was worse than to be a young widow, never having had the children or the dream home, or the pleasure of growing old with someone you loved? For himself, he had chosen Virginia as the landscape suited to his deliberate kind of solitude—less rugged than Maine, not so humorless, an accent gentler on the ear, and of course the dreamy blue of the mountains, the green of the meadows, the benign climate. No, she had come to live in Maine because it was a place recalled from her childhood. Summers in Rockland, she remembered; there were family friends on North Haven—wealthy friends, old money, people such as she had never met elsewhere and still in an unserious way envied—and she knew the economy was poor and she could *afford* Maine. It was remarkable how things changed, wasn't it—and how in a way the two of them had changed places, geographies?

All this in the freshly made-up, freshly occupied bed, Jameson holding her, her head on his chest where she could hear his heartbeat slowly resume its normal rate. His heart, her heart: they were simple machineries sustaining ordinary life—not Rosamond Craven's cup of tea. How long they lay talking, Kelly could not have said, except that more and more it was he who listened and she who talked, until after an especially long silence she realized he had fallen asleep, herself still captive in his arms.

When she opened her eyes again candlelight was flickering on the walls and Jameson was watching her, raised on one elbow.

"I'm awake," she said, as if he were accusing her.

"We'd better think about going," he said.

By the time the two of them stood to dress and to fold the sheets and pillowcases into a more or less neat pile at the foot of the bed, one of the two candles—more slender than its mate—had already begun to gutter.

"I'm sorry we can't spend the whole night," he said.

"When is your flight?"

"There's plenty of time." He blew out the consumed candle, picked up the other, kissed her gently on the mouth. "You should wear your hair longer," he said.

She touched the strands at her jaw line. "It used to be long. Warren asked me to cut it." She realized she hadn't told him about Warren. "I live with this man," she said. "Warren. He paints. I should have said something earlier."

"I didn't imagine you lived alone," Jameson said. "Not someone like you."

IIII It was late now, and dark, and the car was racing through the night. Jameson took her hand—his own hand cool and damp, holding hers loosely against the upholstery of the seat and resting it against her thigh. The wind flowed over and around the car with a sound like the background noise of a visit to the beach; the road under the car a tidal rhythm, a drumming she could feel in whatever parts of her touched the seat and the passenger door. But mostly it was speed she was aware of—the car rushing through the dark, the lights of oncoming cars blazing past and leaving little residual dazzles of afterimage on her field of vision, her pulse racing, her thoughts racing, the music from the car radio pounding in her ears. She was conscious of being excited, aroused, hungry all over again for this man she scarcely knew, the desire doing its own racing through her body and mind and—surely—transmitting itself through their joined hands, their entwined fingers, to Jameson. Walking to the car, the rain over, the wind gentled, he had said something about the law firm where he worked, how it had a strong reputation for something he called "oral advocacy." She had giggled. "You must be a senior partner," she'd said.

She shifted in her seat and put her other hand over his. His gaze was straight ahead; the approaching cars lit his features like slow lightning, and each time they were revealed she felt herself surge toward him—her heart, her mind, her foolish blood. She supposed that after a while—seasons, years—she might manage to achieve a balance between her actual life and her imaginary life. Or, more likely, when she went to work Monday morning—flipped the sign in the door so the word *open* faced outward, turned on the slim fluorescent light above the magazine rack, and unlocked the back door in anticipation of the UPS man—it would be as if Friday at five was seamlessly joined to Monday morning at ten, as if there had been no visit with Jameson Stiles to the home of the dead.

When the car came to a stop in front of the place she shared with Warren, the curtains at the apartment window were half drawn. Only the nightlight—the table lamp with the square, green-glass shade she'd found one Sunday at a shop in Lisbon Falls—was on in the living room. The sensation of being at rest unsettled her; the silence of it rang in her ears, the burden of separating from Jameson tightened her neck muscles and made her mouth dry. Around the car, its vivid red surfaces looking at this hour almost black, the pavements were still wet; they reflected the orange incandescence from a streetlight at the end of the block. Jameson looked straight ahead. His features were partly shadowed, partly aglow as if from some subtle fire inside him—but that was her, Kelly, already weaving the fantasy she would share with Gwen. The obvious question—"Will I see you again?"—formed itself in her mind, but miraculously she found the will not to utter it.

Instead, she only put out her right hand to touch his where it rested on the wheel.

"Don't miss your plane," she said.

"I won't." He leaned to her, kissed her. His hands touched her— her face, her blouse, her skirt. The caresses reminded her that her legs were bare, that in the bedroom of his family's house she had not troubled to put on everything, and she shivered. "Let me," he said, the words scarcely more than a whisper, his breath hot at her throat.

"Yes," she said. She believed it would always be her entire vocabulary with Jameson, and she said it to herself over and over as he moved clumsily to her side of the car and somehow crouched between her knees. She went on saying it, like a chant, as he uncovered her and bowed to her. She found the seat latch, lifted it and reclined the seatback, feeling herself released, falling, giving herself to the lovemaking. She sighed and turned her head, letting her forehead rest against the cold window of the car. She put her hands out to Jameson, stroking his hair, holding him against her. Back in the empty house where he had grown up, he had drawn her so far out of herself that she was afraid of forgetting her name—that from the time of their lovemaking she would be anonymous, dependent on Jameson to tell her who she was—but this time she was clinging to her name, to the letters on the dim street sign at the corner, to house numbers staggered above neighbors' mailboxes.

She was letting her gaze roam, languidly, and then she saw Warren's silhouette in the window of her apartment—the outline of his head and shoulders, the shadow of one hand raised between his face and the windowpane like a visor, modifying the light from the street. The silhouette stayed without moving; he was watching, watching. She wondered how much of them he could see, in so much darkness, through the car window, over the sill of the passenger door.

He sees us, Kelly wanted to say—but in a whisper, as if more than a whisper might interrupt her pleasure. Besides, what could Warren learn from them? He would invent everything anyway, take it as his own the way he had taken her dream words of the night before. He would meet Jeremy on York Street and gossip about Kelly's oblivious passion, Jameson's kisses, how lovers become victims. Or he might even go into his studio and begin a painting—perhaps a cemetery scene: a woman, laid in a grave new-opened, practicing death with a stranger.

Dorothy
and Her Friends

\\\

When Dorothy Porter was twenty and about to start her senior year of college, she had all but gotten married to a young engineer fresh out of Tufts. She had met him in the lobby at a Pops concert, introduced to him by her closest friend, Laura Rose. His name was Fred Willard; after they were engaged she regularly practiced her new names—Mrs. Fred Willard, Mrs. Frederick L. Willard, Dorothy Willard, Dottie & Fred Willard, Freddie and Dot, and so on until they had become so familiar that "Porter" sounded foreign to her ears.

They planned an August wedding, and in July rented a tiny but exquisite apartment in Needham. The invitations had gone out in June, her mother had rented a church annex—Dorothy could no longer recall which church—for the reception; the bridesmaids had ordered their gowns, gifts for the groomsmen had been picked out. Dorothy had not decided who was to give her away; it was the only plan unmade, and for a long time the only shadow across her happiness. Fathers, she felt, should be the ones to give away their daughters, but her father had left her mother when Dorothy was twelve.

Nearly every day in July she rode a bus to Needham, either alone or with Laura Rose, and Fred would come by after work. She was just starting out with the telephone company, and though the wages were small she had the idea that her future was assured. Each time she visited the apartment it was a little cleaner, shinier, had more

furniture, carpeting, drapes. At night she and Fred sat at the big dining room table bought from Railroad Salvage and wrote thank-you
notes for the presents that were already beginning to fill the front
room. After the new bed arrived, sometimes they lay on it together
and speculated about their lives, hugging each other, waving their
hands when they talked as if they were drawing pictures on the ceiling. Three or four times they stayed overnight, undressing each
other, falling asleep in each other's arms, waking in time for Fred
to go to work. At first she tried to prevent Fred from entering her;
that seemed crucial. But Fred had been insistent, and besides he was
bigger, stronger; finally she had given way to him and to her own
capacity for passion, and they made "real" love. They even did what
she later looked back on with horror: loved without precaution. Yet
that, the risk of pregnancy, seemed only to intensify the excitement
she felt in Frederick's arms.

It had, she saw now, been the happiest time of her life—filled
with promise, pleasure, ecstasy—and it all went to smithereens in an
instant, thanks to Laura Rose, who came to her a week before the
wedding and told her:

"I think you should know that Fred asked me to have sex with
him last night." She had raised her cool blue eyes to meet Dorothy's
full. "And I did."

So the wedding was canceled—the notes said "postponed"—the
hall unhired, the minister apologized to, the gifts sent back. Dorothy
missed the final fitting of the wedding gown and persuaded the shop
that surely someone else would come along to buy it and wear it.
She assumed Fred would arrange to break the apartment lease—she
wanted nothing further to do with the place, wanted the furnishings
either sold or given to Goodwill—but learned much later that he
had kept the apartment for over a month and invited Laura Rose
regularly to share what ought to have been the nuptial couch. It was
the matter-of-factness of this twin betrayal by her fiancé and her
nearest friend that stunned her, the sheer idiomatic quality of "hav-

ing sex," as spare and unembellished as sharing a cigarette, that mocked her notions of love and fidelity.

One unfortunate detail: she had forgotten the florist. On the morning of what should have been her wedding day the bridal bouquet arrived at the door, vivid and beribboned, and for the first time since Laura Rose told her the truth, Dorothy had wept.

|||| Seven years later, the first best reason Dorothy had for owning a kitten was that she felt her life ebbing away into loneliness and she was afraid of growing bitter and ill-tempered. She still lived with her mother, who worked as a cosmetics buyer for Jordan Marsh and who was herself a model for bitterness and short temper. Though Dorothy remembered her father fondly, she believed she understood why her mother had never been tempted to remarriage: it had to do with how men always betray you, but the understanding did nothing to soften her own situation.

The kitten was a Siamese, a tiny Sealpoint with a crooked tail, and Dorothy had walked past it in the pet shop window a dozen times before it occurred to her to have it. She had noticed the animal, and sometimes stopped before the glass to watch it, but there was never any suggestion of mutual attraction between the human and the animal—no love at first sight. If anything, Dorothy's interest in the cat came grudgingly, by way of a certain pity she felt for the awkward crook in its tail.

So it was partly impulse that brought her into the shop one afternoon after the start of the new year. She stood just inside the door and reached over the chicken-wire fencing to pet the kitten while she waited for the clerk to come to her. The kitten ducked away from her hand, went over on its back and wrapped its small paws around her fingers. She tickled its stomach, and the kitten responded by kicking kangaroo-like against her palm with its hind legs. Its ears were laid back; its head looked slick as a water animal's.

"How much is this one?" Dorothy asked.

The clerk shrugged. "It's kind of a runt. Say twenty-five dollars."

"What happened to its tail?"

"Maybe it runs in the family. Maybe her old lady got her tail slammed in a cedar chest." The clerk thought this was funny.

"Would you take fifteen for it?"

"Twenty-five is awful cheap for a purebred Siamese. It really is, Miss."

"But it has that tail, and the markings aren't very clear." She waited, studying the kitten half-suspended from her quiet hand.

"Twenty, and you got a deal," the clerk said.

She brought the kitten away in a shoebox, a hole punched in either end and the lid held down with tape. On her way home from the shop with the box and a bag of litter held against her, she could feel the kitten fidgeting about inside its prison, and she heard it complaining rustily to itself when she shifted the box to unlock the downstairs door of the apartment building where she lived.

Days later, on a snowy afternoon when she had just gone on relief from the switchboard, it occurred to Dorothy that there might have been another reason for her buying the kitten, and that was: rebellion. She hadn't intended to rebel; that much she knew, and yet she also knew from things people said that certain mysteries persisted in the human mind—that there was somehow a level of unconscious action in every person, and on this level decisions were made so whimsically that only the closest scrutiny could assign true causes. Assuming she was as complicated as anyone else, Dorothy thought her own hidden perversity might have had something to do with her bringing home a kitten when she knew perfectly well—perfectly consciously—that her mother despised cats. If this was so, then there was something a bit wonderful about discovering such defiance in herself.

||| Because her mother was still at work, the apartment was empty on that first afternoon. In the solemnly furnished parlor the drapes were closed against the sun; Dorothy carried Fancy directly to the

kitchen, where some slivers of daylight still lay on the oak of the cupboards. She had chosen the name, "Fancy," on inspiration—her life being so plain—and took pleasure from knowing that the name would suit whether the kitten was female or turned out later, as kittens often did, to be treacherously male. That it was not, perhaps, an appropriate name for a Siamese, she thought she might rectify in future by spelling it *Fan-si*.

Once in the kitchen, Dorothy freed the kitten and left it to explore its new surroundings while she made provision for a container in which the cat should be trained to "do its duties." Under the sink she found a battered metal pan, and into this she poured half the bag of litter. She spread out several pages from an old *Monitor* and set the pan down in a corner of the kitchen nearest to the back hall. She fetched Fancy, showed the animal the pan, and admonished it with a shake of her forefinger which the kitten swiped at with its paw—not to mess Mother's carpets ever. Then she carried Fancy into her bedroom and sat on the edge of the bed, watching while the animal moved gingerly among the furnishings of its new home. The kitten was so small, its curiosity so amusing—every fringe and shadow a toy and an adversary—Dorothy could not imagine her mother being threatened by it.

Nevertheless, after supper, when Dorothy confessed that she had bought a cat, her mother was appalled.

"Oh, my dear!" she said. "When you know how I feel about the furtive little beasts? Oh, my dear Dottie!"

Then nothing would do for Dorothy but that her mother should at least see the kitten, and so Fancy was released from the bedroom over the protests of Mrs. Porter, who seemed almost to shrink in size when the kitten sprang over the parlor doorsill.

"Isn't it darling?" Dorothy exclaimed, and she knelt on the floor and let the fingers of her right hand stalk Fancy. The kitten hesitated, crouched, gave itself to a succession of small shivers which began at its forepaws, quaked down its spine to the tip of the crooked tail, and culminated in an abrupt, all-over seizure which triggered it straight up into the air and brought it in one bound into an attack against its five-legged enemy. Dorothy giggled and pushed the kitten over on its back; Fancy drew wildly upright and danced away, stiff-legged.

"Dear God," Mrs. Porter shrieked, "it's having a fit!" She pulled her short legs up to the chair seat and brought her hands to her face.

"It's playing, Mother," Dorothy said.

Now the kitten sat in the center of the room to lick its pale ruff. Between the slow caresses of its tongue it set its blue gaze suspiciously on the twitching of its tail.

"They have such filthy habits," Mrs. Porter said.

Fancy looked up. The kitten stopped washing and began to move stealthily toward the woman's chair.

"Here, Fancy," Dorothy said, putting her hand down to the floor. The kitten glided toward her mother. "Fancy," Dorothy repeated.

Mrs. Porter held herself grimly against the chair back. "You see what they do," she said weakly. "They know when you don't like them, and they go straight for you."

Fancy stopped squarely in front of Mrs. Porter and fixed its attention on the woman's hands working nervously in her lap. Its head was lowered, and its thin neck seemed to grow longer. Dorothy was so taken with noticing how like a snake the kitten was—how it swayed and leaned and tensed—that she was almost too late in reaching out. As it was, she touched the animal at the instant of its springing, and when she caught it the momentum carried her hand weightlessly upward. She held the kitten and nestled it against her shoulder.

"My dear God," Mrs. Porter moaned. She lay against the arm of the chair. "You'll have to take that creature back to wherever you got it."

IIII But Fancy was not returned to the pet shop. After she had put the kitten safely behind her bedroom door for the rest of the evening, Dorothy set forth her fondness for the animal. She did not complain that she was lonely. She argued that after working all day or all night at the long-distance switchboard, listening hour after hour to disembodied voices, she felt genuine comfort in the presence of some living thing incapable of speech.

It was agreed that the cat would be banished to Dorothy's bedroom whenever Mrs. Porter was at home, that it would be fed there, that its duty-box was to be kept in a discreet corner of that room, rather than in the kitchen. Dorothy promised that the paths of mother and pet need never cross; within the month, Mrs. Porter seemed resigned to the kitten's presence in the apartment.

For herself, Dorothy grew increasingly accustomed to the concessions she had made on Fancy's account. Since she did not always work the day shift—and because her days off frequently came in the middle of the week—she was able to give Fancy the run of the apartment while Mother worked a regular five-and-a-half-day schedule at the department store. Dorothy took care of what little housecleaning demanded doing, or she threw crumpled paper for Fancy to do battle with; or she simply sat watching while the cat crouched on the window ledge that overlooked Brookline Avenue, switching its crooked tail and chirping small feline syllables at events beyond the glass.

When Mother was at home, Dorothy more often than not retired to her bedroom and kept company with Fancy. After the first week she bought a small wooden clothes dryer and set it up for the kitten at the side of the bed. This was Fancy's playground; Dorothy took immense pleasure—plain life indeed—from watching the cat tumble up and down the slender doweling, sometimes from too much speed and too little foresight losing its balance, hanging spraddle-legged for a breathless instant before plummeting to the floor. Even the worst of her bargain with her mother, the location of the duty-box, was hardly a problem. She placed the box in a corner, half-hidden by her dressing table. She remembered to replace the sand every other day, and she sprayed the room with an aerosol deodorizer morning and night. There was always a trace of smell in the room, but it was a slight trace; she got used to it, and probably she would have missed it.

2

Sybil Porter's chief preoccupation since the departure of her husband was religion. Currently it was Christian Science, but for years Dorothy's mother had flirted with an impressive number and variety of sects, embarked on what she called "my soul's quest." When two young men representing the Mormons appeared one Saturday morning at the front door, she let them up and listened to them for nearly two hours. Dorothy had awakened to the earnest drone of male voices—for the flicker of an instant she imagined her father had returned from limbo—had wrapped a robe around herself and peeked into the living room: here was Mother, rapt, sipping coffee and shifting her concentration from one to the other of the two men, each blond and short-haired, each in a dark brown suit, each in turn lecturing the woman about duty and obedience and the angel Moroni. The sight had not surprised her—this was only a year ago, and her mother's spiritual pilgrimage was ongoing and familiar— but she was aggravated by the young men, by their scrubbed self-assurance, their glibness. And the one-sidedness of the visit. She would have brought up questions about the Mormon attitudes toward women that she had read of in the newspapers, but she knew better than to meddle in her mother's concerns.

"How can you put up with that kind of thing?" she said later.

"They were nice young men," her mother said. "It wouldn't have hurt you to meet them."

"No, thank you. All that pretty-faced sexist hocus-pocus."

Her mother had looked away. That was in late winter, gray, with a scatter of fat snowflakes dotting the space between the kitchen window and the neighboring apartment house, and her gaze seemed set beyond the snow and the dark windows next door. "God isn't hocus-pocus," she said.

Six months later—and after a brief fling with an intense young rabbi she had first met on the subway between Boylston and Government Center, who had so illuminated her soul's quest that she followed him to the Blue Line and listened to him all the way to Wonderland—Mother settled in to Christian Science. It was as if she had come full circle, from the provincial reasonableness of the Unitarian-Universalists, through the pious Thursday-night potlucks of the Methodists, the prohibitions of the Baptists, the pomp and dead certainty of the Roman Catholics, and the grumpy literal-mindedness of uncountable Fundamentalist sects and splinters—all of this faith and threat and speculation delivered by men of every manner and shape—come at last to religion born from the mind of a woman.

"But I hope you won't get carried away," Dorothy once said to her. "I don't want you to be like one of those religious fanatics who dies from a simple thing like an appendix because she refuses to let a doctor take it out."

Her mother looked scornful. "I'm not a fool," she said.

And Dorothy had to admit—after the one Wednesday evening her mother had persuaded her to attend—that the people at the Christian Science services seemed singularly unfanatical. Ordinary people of all ages. Ordinary testimony to God and Mrs. Eddy: illnesses dealt with, fractures healed, broken relationships mended. Not from medicines, not from therapy; only faith and appropriate Bible. And if no other good ever came from her mother's religious questing, at least this time it had brought her Jinia—Mrs. Weal, a practitioner, who became Mother's only friend.

Virginia Weal was a widow lady who lived by herself in Cambridge, on Huron Avenue, in a white house set in a row of white houses with front porches and leaded-glass front doors and window boxes for geranium and marigold. Dorothy went there once with her mother, to meet a visiting religious figure over Sunday tea. Huron was a narrow street, tucked between more important routes, and she could imagine from all the maples that in summer it was a cool, heavily shaded neighborhood, and that in fall the walks and lawns were ankle-deep in leaves for children and old people to stuff into fat plastic bags for city collection.

What spiritual good Mrs. Weal did her mother, Dorothy was unable to say. The two women seemed hardly ever to discuss soul, Scripture, or church when they were around her. They talked of museum and gallery exhibits, they poked through newspapers in search of "nice" films; once in a while they sipped sherry or port—both of them getting giddy, Mrs. Porter's eyes shining unnaturally and her forehead and cheeks flushing. Yet Mother during periods of stress or depression telephoned Virginia Weal, listened solemnly to that side of the conversation Dorothy could not hear, then closeted herself in her room for as much as an hour before emerging—more calm, more "human" than before. She knew that on especially "bad" days—her mother, at fifty, was persuaded she had entered menopause—Mrs. Porter would go to Cambridge, stay an hour or two, then come home grim and philosophical.

"Your grandmother, Nana Davis," she would say with a sigh of perceived mortality, "wasted away from cancer, two years after I married your father. I watched her go, ounce by ounce—she weighed fifty-seven pounds when she died—every day smaller than the day before, paler than the day before, weaker than the day before . . ." Her mother's eyes looked through Dorothy, seeing the generations that preceded her. "That poor helpless woman. 'Let me die.' That's what she used to say to me. 'Let me die.' But the doctors were in charge; they dosed her with drugs they knew couldn't cure, painkillers that never reached the pain. Finally she passed on. 'You, too.' That's what she said with her last breath, her last strength: 'You, too.'

"But that isn't going to happen to me," Mrs. Porter said. "I know—what my mother didn't know, or her mother before her—there is Someone Else to carry such burdens, to take away from us the crosses we're too frail to bear. Virginia said to me today: 'Faith is like the sweet warmth of the sun, and whoever belittles our faith

is like a shadow cast across us.' That will save us, Dottie. Don't ever
think you're too smart to need salvation."

⦀ Her mother's other preoccupation was to include Dorothy in
various religious activities devised by herself and Mrs. Weal—possibly as an alternative to finding her a husband, men being likely to
"leave you in the lurch"—and it was not unusual that Dorothy
would let herself be coaxed back to Huron Avenue on another Sunday afternoon to meet what Sybil Porter referred to as "Jinia's Englishman."

The Englishman was a late-fortyish evangelist named Paul
Houser, and Dorothy's first impressions of him were that he spoke
well—British not so much by accent as by diction—and that he was
much better dressed than she would have expected him to be: an
expensive-looking three-piece suit, gray but not somber, with an Ivy
League shirt and narrow tie, and plain black shoes over gray socks.
Why she had expected someone less well turned out, she could not
have said, except from associating "evangelism" with Mrs. Weal and
her mother, and therefore anticipating a flighty religious figure in
string tie, brown double-breasted suit and two-tone shoes with
white socks. And Doctor Houser—it was not made clear how the
title had been conferred, or if it was legitimate—was gracious and
at ease among the dozen or so ladies who had accepted Virginia
Weal's invitation to this ritual tea.

Houser's particular insight had to do with his literal experience
of Hell, and his eventual rescue from that place by Jesus Himself.
Afterwards he had left England—and, not incidentally, a wife and
two daughters—in order to bring others to Jesus. It was a long story,
filled with oppressive detail; Dorothy listened to it from a folding
chair only slightly more comfortable than a flagpole, and she tried
to keep Houser's face in view despite the positioning of the heads
and hats of the intervening ladies. The room was warm, and swam
with a nearly suffocating mix of a dozen incompatible perfumes and
colognes.

"God cannot make stand a creature who has no backbone," Houser was saying with some fervor. "God cannot ennoble the serpent who crawls at his feet, begging to be made upright. The lost man may not be found if he cannot take of his own volition the first step back to God—and I could not. I shudder to say it. I was so lost, I did not any longer know which way was God."

The ladies seemed not to be breathing, and Dorothy was afraid that if she moved—if this folding chair should creak—she would profane the hour. What ought she to make of this Paul Houser? Was he honest? And did he make a living from this sort of performance?

⦀ When he was introduced to Dorothy, Houser said nothing—took her hand lightly, pressed her fingers, bent his head toward her. She thought he might have intended the movement of his head as a bow—and did she only imagine that for an instant his fingers insinuated a caress across her palm? If that were true, it ought to be added to his account of himself.

"I fell ill," he had told the ladies, "deathly ill, from a cause no medical doctor could trace. Was it a virus, they did not know its name. Was it some rare disease, they had no cure. Was it a fever of the brain's devising, they had no explication. But I knew. Writhing in my dank linen, my head pounding, I knew. Groaning like an animal, mouthing words which made no earthly sense, I knew."

He had used his hands to make them see—at his throat for the groaning and mouthing, around his torso for the writhing, in his hair for the brain fever—so that by the end of the recitation of his inscrutable symptoms he looked slightly disreputable, his collar partly open and necktie pulled aside, his graying hair mussed into cowlicks and snarls.

"I saw Hell itself," he said, "its towers, its tortures, its boiling lakes. I heard the screams of the tormented, the laughter of Lucifer's lieutenants. I smelled the burning flesh and hair. I felt the heat of that terrible eternal furnace, I tasted the bitterness of sulphur on my own tongue. In the inexplicable physical sickness which was comrade to my despair—I went down to Hell. I smothered there, I sweated there, I screamed my pain there; I languished in Hell's chaos."

There had seemed considerable doubt that Houser would escape; he described matters—not only the geography of Hell—so vividly and at such length that if Dorothy had not seen him, alive and lively, pacing before her eyes, she would have expected self-loathing to do him in entirely.

"And who was it braved Hell to pluck up a man who surely at that moment was very nearly the least among all Earth's creatures? Who saved this soul already damned?" Jesus, of course, Dorothy said under her breath. Jesus Christ Our Lord in All His Splendor. She sighed. And what in the world was it that made men leave marriage, abandon family—as if the truly important always lay somewhere else? Her father had stayed with Sybil Porter, had loved his daughter—his "dainty Dorrie"—through the first twelve years of her life. And then, one day, he had left both his women. "For good"—that odd phrase. Fred Willard—good heavens, he hadn't even tasted marriage, yet he had let the first temptation carry him away from it. And Paul Houser, who claimed to have had everything one expected from a good marriage: love, hearth and home, daughters, standing in the community—yet it brought him to the desperation and rejection his lecture chronicled.

For a few moments after being introduced, Dorothy entertained the illusion that it was a ghost she was confronting—not a real, flesh-and-blood, rather surprisingly boyish born-again Christian.

"How do you do," she said. "That must have been quite an experience."

In any case it was not Houser's religion she found influential; perhaps it was, more than a little, the man himself. Men—some men—had a way of giving themselves to words; they had a way of being involved, obsessed, that she found attractive in spite of herself. And Houser—surely he was scarcely aware of where he was and who was listening and what would happen next. If she could not always share his intensity—well, she was sorry; truly, she had given back her attention somewhat later—when the speech turned cooler. When Jesus arrived, just in the nick of time.

And yes, she had gone walking with Houser. It was difficult, even though she was skeptical of his autobiography, to resist his dynamism, his enthusiasm, and she wondered if he might not have surprises to pique her curiosity. The other women—did he ever address himself to men?—milled about him, plying him with tea and flutters of lash and heart, her mother not the least of these. But what could they think to say to him? He was transparent—deliberately so. He had had a mediocre life. He had run away from it. *Mea culpa.* Nobody dared ask him about his wife (abandoned), his children (spurned), his friends (rejected), his obligations (shirked).

So when he detached himself from his admirers—Dorothy was at that moment standing before the front window of Virginia Weal's house—she was in a sense ready for him.

"I'd singled you out from the start," he said to her, not extending his hand, but holding it half in front of him as if it were up to her to reach for it—and she did not. "May I fetch you tea? A sugar something?"

"Thank you, no." She sat in the windowseat. "I was looking out, watching the spring wind." If he expected small talk, she would oblige.

"Curious little house, isn't it?" he said. "Brocade, Orientals, small dark rooms and dark furnishings."

She looked at him. Fortyish, tallish—everything-ish. "Is this all you do?"

He was taken by surprise. "Please?" he said.

"This talk of yours—this—" She stumbled. "This self-revealing."

"Ah," he said. "Yes, I regret to say. This is indeed all I do." Unasked, he sat in the opposite corner of the windowseat. The Sunday afternoon light was like a thin curtain between them. "You find it insufficient?"

She shrugged. "I suppose not. Perhaps insubstantial."

He smiled. "You're certain I can't fetch you anything?"

"Nothing, thank you."

He coughed, discreetly. "Your mother talked about you. I steered her aside to pay my compliments on her daughter," he said.

Dorothy looked levelly at him.

"She remarked that you enjoy—your solitude."

"I expect you find *that* insufficient."

He reddened. "Point for you," he said. "It's none of my affair, is it?"

"But it's all right," Dorothy said. "We're both trying to be polite—and it's awkward. I've never met anyone who's actually seen Jesus Christ."

He stood abruptly. "Look here," he said, "it's a capital spring day. Why don't we go for a walk, you and I? Just close by, then back here for the amenities. I'm famished for fresh air."

To discover that he might be interested in her seemed to confirm the earlier touch of his fingers across her palm.

"It might be pleasant," she said.

"Let me make apologies for our temporary absence." And he flickered among the ladies, smiling and bowing.

|||| "It's a hallucination, you know," Dorothy said on that first day. "Not a vision."

Houser didn't answer. He walked beside her, his hands locked behind his back. The wind ruffled his hair; now and again he freed one hand to brush it away from his brow.

"You didn't literally see—or talk to—Jesus Christ. You only imagined you did. And you weren't literally in Hell, with all the sulphur and screaming, and pain even in your fingernails and the individual hairs on your head. You only saw pictures of Hell, based on things preachers have probably been telling you all your life about the suffering of the damned, and the fire and brimstone, and all the rest of it."

"You think there isn't a Hell," he said. It was not so much a question as a statement, made as they waited for a change of traffic light.

"That isn't the point," she said. "It doesn't matter if Hell exists or not—just that I don't believe you've been there." She let him take her elbow as they stepped down from curb to street. "If someone could look at Satan's guest book, your name wouldn't be in it." She glanced at him. "Not yet, that is."

He allowed himself a brief smile. "In plainer words, you're calling me a sham."

"Oh," she said, "I don't doubt your good intentions—your genuine faith—for a minute. I just can't be one of those sweet ladies who thinks you're Dante selling Bibles. But I say: Go to it."

"While Dorothy Porter's salvation comes by a different route."

"Something like that. Not from a high temperature and a fevered imagination."

"You forget that holy persons used deliberately to injure themselves—break the skin with their own fingernails or sharp objects, or wear hair shirts—and they had so-called religious experiences because the wounds infected and altered their brain chemistry."

"In other words, a vision is a vision," she said. "Get it any way you can."

"Exactly. In any case, the experience transformed my life."

"Among other lives," Dorothy said. She watched him weigh the words; like so many other things she had said to him, they appeared to baffle him.

And a week after that, she met him on the Common and walked with him to feed the ducks. This time he wore a light blue suit with a solid, dark blue necktie, so that he looked both seasonal and sober, and he greeted her affectionately—in a way calculated to remind her to be wary, to distrust Paul Houser as she already distrusted herself for being attracted to him. Sometimes she believed she saw in his eyes the look she had long ago feared Fred Willard for: a probing look that fixed her like a butterfly no matter what she was doing or saying or thinking. All men seemed capable of it; it was a one-track attentiveness, similar to a cat's concern for a sparrow.

"But don't you miss them? Your children? Your wife?"

It had become Dorothy's subject, as Jesus was his.

"Now and again." He sat on his heels at the edge of the water, tearing slices of bread into ragged morsels, building a small whole-wheat mound between himself and Dorothy. Blue pigeons lurked in the shade nearby; sparrows skittered; the families of brown ducks wheeled to and fro, a few feet from shore.

"I miss my children, mornings," Houser said. "The breakneck of getting a pair of females in and out of the bath in time for school, the natter and banter at the breakfast table."

"How old would they be?"

He pursed his mouth, tossed bread bits into the duck colony as if he might not answer. "Fourteen and sixteen," he said. "I have to do some reckoning before I realize how old they are."

"You must worry about them," Dorothy said.

"About their taste in the young men knocking at the front door—of course I do. Look here, I hope this isn't to be an ongoing exercise in conscience—my conscience, my guilt. Is it pleasure you take from that?"

"No, none," she said. "But my father left when I was twelve. I feel a—an affinity with your daughters; I know what they must feel when they think of you."

"Anger, I expect."

"Some. And guilt of their own—each girl, once in a while, thinking of your leaving and wondering what she did to frighten you away."

"Perhaps." He stood, rubbed at his legs about the knee. "Let's walk a bit—work the stiffness out."

She took his outstretched hand, pulled herself to her feet. The ground had been just slightly cold; she could feel its lingering damp-ness at the side of her skirt.

"Let's take a turn in the direction of that dilapidated graveyard," Houser said.

Dorothy walked beside him. In the waveless pond the duck fami-lies glided like tiny flotillas, the ducklings gabbling—*nattering*—endlessly.

"I'm sorry you had to come to womanhood without a father—that you lacked his admiration."

She took a deep breath. "I wonder you don't feel the same sympathy for your daughters."

A silence. A looking away. "I see," he said.

"I know this is none of my business," she said, "but I'm sure you were given much love. I'm perplexed you could have left it, forsaken it."

"Because I believe there are higher loves. Because I think a man progresses from one to another to another, always upward, always closer to an ultimate, a spiritual love. How can I go back? My family is matter, flesh; my family is mere earth."

"I see," said Dorothy. "Which I guess means I don't see. I don't think there are different kinds of love."

"All right," he said. "Different objects—some more worthy than others." The old graveyard, its thin stones streaked with time, was in shade before them. "One aspires to objects more and more worthy. Higher object: higher love."

"Ending with God?"

"Difficult to imagine anything higher, or worthier. Yes."

"But that sounds backwards to me." She pondered. "It's easy to love something worthy; not so easy to love the unworthy. And isn't that a truer measure of love?"

"Such romanticism," Houser said. He took her arm and turned her away from the gravestones. "I'd rather this not be all we talk about."

Then he kissed her. His breath was a mixture of sweet and sour—some kind of candy mint?—and for just an instant she was frightened by him. She had not stiffened exactly—though that was what chaste heroines did—but he must have felt pass through her a shiver, a glittering of tiny nerve ends he might have imagined to indicate a weakness of the flesh. The first step toward God.

3

A week later Dorothy brought Paul Houser home and went to bed with him—knowing that somewhere in this gesture was more than a little of haste, a certain insufficiency of common sense. Beforehand, in the bathroom with the door shut behind her, she washed her face in cold water, watching herself in the medicine cabinet mirror as she dried her eyes, patted dry her cheeks, forehead, chin. What would Mother say now? Dorothy wanted Paul and at the same time did not want him, as she had nearly always wanted and not-wanted a man. Probably she was scarcely different from all the others who doted on him—younger, yet neither more nor less useful to him than some sad widow closer to his own age.

If she could have changed her mind, she would have. But how did one do that under the circumstances? Act surprised to find the man in her bedroom? She slipped out of her pantyhose—crumpled them in her hands and put them into the hamper beside the sink. And what about the wife? Dorothy was the one who had brought his divorced wife up to him, arguing for the kinder connections of marriage and family. Now what was she doing? Rewarding him for being willful?

As if she were any sort of reward—inexperienced and timid to be touched, so that she thought of herself as more virginal than a real virgin; feeling, as she had felt for years, betrayed by the flatness of her figure, always wishing for ripe breasts, full hips, because men liked that, were drawn irresistibly to it, you only had to look at their magazines. If men never got enough of big breasts and wide hips and the plump golden thighs of the centerfolds, what was left over to be spent on Dorothy Porter in her cotton blouse and skirt, in a bra she didn't really require? She flushed the toilet—as if to account for her time away from Paul Houser—and went to find out.

He was lying on his back, his shoes off, his hands behind his head. Fancy was curled on a pillow near the man's head, the cat-eyes open and wary.

"Come lie against me," he said.

She sat on the bed, slipped off her shoes. "The room's such a clutter," she said. She brought her legs up onto the bed and turned into him, letting him embrace her and draw her down so that her head was against him, cradled, her face small against his chest. His white shirt was vivid in the afternoon light; she felt dazzled—as if she had lain down in a field of snow. She closed her eyes and waited for—what? To be teased, excited. To be coaxed. His hands worked rhythmically against her through her clothes; his breathing was remarkably loud in her ear, and she could feel his heart beating. Now a hand slid carefully down the back of her thighs; its fingers pulled at the skirt to draw it higher; the hand lay flat against her skin.

"Bare legs," he said in a kind of wonder.

She opened her eyes. Fancy was sitting on the far side of the bed, gazing at her, the black pupils dilating and shrinking and dilating—as if the light reflected off Houser's back altered in intensity as he caressed her.

"I'm sorry," she told him. She pushed away from him and extricated her left arm. "My poor arm is just dead."

She was kneeling beside him, rubbing her numbed arm. Both his hands were under her skirt—but motionless, like two machines whose power is cut off.

"And it might be a good idea for you to put Fancy out of the room." She smiled an empty-headed smile.

"Quite right," he said. He pronounced the words dully, from a long way back in his throat, his real attention still at her naked thighs. "Quite right," he repeated. He reached for the cat, which cuffed at him, its ears laid back, the nearest forepaw poised like a boxer's guard. "Little beggar," Houser said.

He carried the cat to the door and put it—tossed it into the hall. Then he sat beside Dorothy, sucking at a knuckle of his right hand.

"You got scratched," she said. She took Houser's hand in both of hers. It was a small scratch on the back of the thumb. She brought it to her mouth and put her lips against the red line—touching it, not exactly kissing it. It was a gesture only vaguely sexual.

"Silly nuisance, cats," Houser said. "Self-centered, haughty—think they can do anything they please, and stick you with a tooth or a claw when you interfere."

His hand tasted salty—not from blood, for the scratch was too small, too shallow, but from the patina of sweat on the skin—and it had a faint odor, metallic, perhaps of coins or keys. She remembered once having held Frederick's hands against her face and being startled by their smell and the heavy salt taste that tainted her mouth; then she had realized the smell and taste were of herself.

"Fancy can't help it," she said. "There's nothing for her to wear her claws down on. I suppose I ought to clip them."

"Or upholstery, farewell," he said.

He kissed the back of her neck. Then he moved his arm across her chest and forced her—gently; she did not resist—onto her back. Lying so, diagonally across the bed, her head on the far pillow, she could see herself—and Houser—in the dressing table mirror. Houser bent over her, his hands under her skirt gliding up the outside of her legs. She felt his fingers hook in the waistband of her underpants, raised herself, let the garment slip away from her, down her thighs, her calves. She felt no special excitement.

"Paul," she said, "this is probably not a good idea."

He put the underpants aside. "Now, now," he said. He parted her legs, laid her skirt back to expose her naked belly—a movement so matter-of-fact it fascinated her. "You're a lovely woman."

She felt otherwise. When Houser touched her, she shivered. She experienced a kind of panic, as if in the seven years since a boy—a man—had looked at her, handled her, she had forgotten what aroused her, her mind racing over the memory of Frederick Willard to determine how in spite of his clumsiness and her hurt she had been eager for anything he might do to her, and how when he at last left her alone, left her pulsing as if her sex were a second heart, she had felt cold, forsaken. She saw her face in the mirror. Stop this, the face said.

"Paul—"

She was going to say: I can't, forgive me, I'm so parched you'll hurt me, and she was wondering how she would get the words out when she realized he had stopped fondling her, had turned to stone above her, his eyes shut and his mouth open as if he, too, felt pain. My Lord, she said to herself; my Lord. He shuddered, squeezing her thighs with such strength in his fingers that she almost cried out. She watched the wet stain on the front of his trousers; it grew from a tiny dark dot into an irregular pattern as long as her hand.

She looked at the ceiling. She could hear Fancy scratching at the bedroom door, Paul's breathing growing calm. Selfish me, Dorothy thought crazily, to fret over my own pleasure.

IIII Surely it was not cause and effect, but the very next morning Dorothy woke early, conscious of an unusual silence in the apartment. She got up, opened the drapes to let in the brilliant sun that promised a renewed heat wave. When she went into her mother's room, Mrs. Porter was sitting up in bed, three pillows supporting her, a copy of *Glamour* opened face down across her lap. The white coverlet was pulled up to her neck; her bare feet stuck out at the bottom of the sheet.

"You'll be late at the store," Dorothy said.

"I'm not going in until noon. I told them I was going to have some of my vacation time—a half-day here, a half-day there." She did not look at her daughter; she seemed to be studying her exposed feet.

"Then why don't you take afternoons? When it's hot and muggy."

"Yes, I will." Her mother wiggled her toes. "Look at them," she said. "I think toes are the ugliest part of the body."

"You should re-do your toenails," Dorothy said. "You think they're ugly because most of the polish is chipped off."

Her mother said nothing; her feet fascinated her.

"Shall I make the coffee?" Dorothy said.

"When I was a young girl," Mrs. Porter said, "I had an uncle— Uncle Amos—who came to visit at Thanksgiving and always brought with him a big bag of shelled nuts. Sometimes he brought what we used to call 'niggertoes.' They had amazingly hard shells."

"Mother?"

"Nowadays you can't call them 'niggertoes.'" She turned her head to look at Dorothy; her eyes were startlingly bright. "I don't know what to call them," she said. "The names of everything keep changing."

And it was from that morning on that Dorothy found herself becoming more and more involved with her mother—curious behavior, unusual dependency, an increasing distance from former habits that made large decisions impossible for the woman. In some respects, it was as though a deeply buried maternal instinct had been awakened in Sybil Porter by the sexual rebirth—if that was what it was—of her daughter, and that she had interposed herself between Paul and Dorothy in an act of protectiveness. Now Dorothy was obliged to devote herself to her mother, who began to spend more and more time in bed.

"I have all that vacation time," Mrs. Porter said. "If I don't use it, the store will simply take it away from me."

"But what kind of vacation is it if you don't do something with it? All you do is lie around and read magazines." Lately Mother's bed was a litter of them—*Redbook, Mademoiselle, Self, Vogue, Harper's Bazaar*—all looking more or less the same: a pretty face filling the cover, an array of titles framing it.

Her mother sighed impatiently. "These are my world," she said.

Meanwhile, Dorothy's world—the world of her wishes, her reveries—was more and more Paul Houser. She wanted to tell her mother she had "prospects"—that she thought she could make a life with the man, if he should propose to her. She wanted to forgive Mother's religious flightiness because it had brought a happy outcome. But the days went by; Mother demanded increasing attention, and anything Dorothy told her might just as well be told to Fancy. As for Paul, she scarcely found the time to see him.

Late one afternoon Mother appeared in the doorway of

Dorothy's bedroom in her dressing gown, her face flushed, eyes vivid, no expression to be interpreted—as if she were looking into an infinite distance. She had put up one hand for support, and now she stood, swaying as if unsure of how to manage her weight.

"Dottie?" she said. "Dottie, would you make me a nice cup of tea?"

And then—very slowly, as if she were about to seat herself in an unfamiliar chair—she sank to the floor in a half-faint.

Now Dorothy saw for the first time what the matter was—saw the cat scratch, how swollen the knee was, how inflamed around the scratch. "Mother, you're so sick you can't stand up." She drew her mother up and sat her on the bed. "At least get into a hot tub and soak."

"That creature." Mrs. Porter plucked at the gown, as if she were trying to cover her knee, but it fell aside again.

"Mother—you have an infection of some kind. You ought to soak it in hot water, hot as you can bear." The scratch was a long one, and close beside the kneecap; it must be deep, she thought, and she could not imagine how Fancy could have done it. She touched, gingerly, the swollen area around the scratch. It was vivid pink, a color something like a television picture with too much magenta tint, and it was warm under her fingertips.

Her mother looked at her, eyes wet and bright, cheeks highlighted by fever like spots of blush. "I'd like to talk to Jinia," she said.

"I'll dial her number for you."

"No, here. I'd like to talk to her here." She turned her face toward the wall. "I miss getting out."

"That's temporary," Dorothy said. She tried to sound positive, energetic. "The first thing is to get rid of the infection. You shouldn't have kept it such a secret."

Her mother succeeded in drawing the gown over her legs. "There's nothing wrong with me," she said. "Don't interfere with things you're ignorant of."

"Mother— At least bathe."

"I want to talk to Jinia," she said.

⦀ Gradually the fashion magazines disappeared and in their place—spread over the coverlet beside her—Sybil Porter collected religious pamphlets, a Bible, *Science and Health*, and a variety of single-page "sermons and practices" supplied on a daily basis by Virginia Weal. At almost any hour of day or night Dorothy could depend on finding one of them in her mother's hands, her mother not so much reading them as holding them in her lap, her eyes staring over the top of the page blank and unblinking. Dorothy could not imagine when she slept; her light was never off, her eyes never closed. Even on the rare occasions when she was not reading—the Bible, for example, closed in her lap with the thin sermons she used for bookmarks growing between its pages like petals—her eyes were big and eerily bright.

Dorothy wondered at her concern for her mother. For fifteen years she had fantasized being free of the woman, and it was odd, now, that even though she believed she was poised with Paul at the very edge of freedom, try as she might she could not re-create that fantasy in any whole-hearted way. This surprised her. She could think it through—a personal world away from Mother—but she could not live it in her mind, and that, after all, was what fantasy meant: an unreal thing experienced as if it were real. She couldn't do it, couldn't enter into it, couldn't even rehearse it the way an actress might walk through a scene. One morning at the kitchen table she had written out on the pad used for grocery lists a kind of death sequence, a brief outline from discovery of the lifeless body to the visit of the coroner to arrangements with undertakers to *What hat for funeral?* That ended the list; she wasn't able to force herself in her thoughts back to this silent apartment, to the prospect of marrying Paul and living here without Mother.

Whatever her mother did when she was left alone, she was not lifeless, nor even in a coma one might mistake for death. She breathed—hoarsely and loudly, as if the act were one of great effort—and beads of sweat shone on her forehead and glistened like a thick polish on her neck and arms. Often she twitched like a sleeping person having a dream, but no amount of prodding and talking could rouse her. Another faint.

Dorothy wondered what to do. If she drew the sheet aside she could mark the progress of the infection. It looked horrible. The swelling was worse with every day, the skin of her mother's upper leg taut as a drumhead, the redness near the knee bright, the color rising higher and higher on the thigh as if it were eventually to consume the woman entirely, turn her from White Protestant to Red Indian. And the heat. Dorothy rested her fingers on the rigid skin; it radiated heat. Today, too, a new event was taking place: from the original cat scratch a pale, thick liquid oozed—syrup from a tree, the excretions of milkweed, the juices of grasshoppers—there was no real precedent in Dorothy's life for such a thing; it suggested matters more serious than natural phenomena. If she applied the pressure of her fingertips against the hard infection, the ooze increased. When she went for a washcloth, drenched it in cold water and gently wiped away the stuff, more appeared. It ought to be drained, she thought, but had no idea how that was to be accomplished. At least she ought to arrange some sort of loose dressing, something to absorb this repulsive discharge. She folded the cloth, laid it over the wound.

"What is it?" her mother said. "What are you doing?"

"You fainted, Mother. I was seeing if there wasn't something I could do that might—relieve you."

"Leave me alone."

"Mother—"

"Leave me alone," her mother repeated.

Dorothy withdrew the cloth. She stood, uncertainly, holding the wet cloth, looking at the deformed knee, trying frantically to think of what to do—how to help someone who rejected help. She was never sure if she dared leave her mother in the apartment alone. Sometimes the woman was lucid, almost normal in her dealings with Dorothy—demanding, impatient, preoccupied with herself and her reading matter. But other times she spoke and behaved enigmatically, recalling from the past people and events Dorothy had never heard of, or imagining she saw faces in the room, heard voices in the hallway. "Stop them," she would say. "Stop them before they break it." Then she would roll her head from side to side against the pillows, never explaining who was to be stopped or what might be broken. She had commanded a hand mirror, which lay face down on the bedspread beside her. Only once—at noontime, bringing her a cup of mild tea—did Dorothy see her use it, and she stopped still in the doorway to watch her mother hold the mirror to her mouth, breathe against the glass, wipe the thin mist away with the sleeve of her robe. She watched the action repeated five or six times, and then she entered the room as much to interrupt that as to bring the tea.

"A long time ago," her mother said, her voice slow, as if she were reading something without her glasses, "a long time ago your father's father was a rich man."

"I know, Mother."

"Do you?" She accepted the tea, set it gingerly on the nightstand. The orange-colored tea slopped into the saucer. "By the time I married your father, nothing was left except your grandmother's toilet articles. She'd been dead for a long time—" She stopped and giggled. "Nobody's dead for a short time," she said. The giggling turned into a wheezy laugh—hee, hee, hee, like a cat's sneeze—and tears bulged in her eyes. When she stopped, she had forgotten her thought, and Dorothy did not prompt her.

The infection seemed to get neither better nor worse; it oozed constantly. Perhaps the wound was purging itself and her mother would be triumphant after all, but the fits of broken reminiscence, the bouts with delirium, the moaning in her restless sleep, the high temperature and the sweating, all these continued and were frightening. Twice a day Dorothy gave her mother sponge baths—careful to be gentle around the swollen knee and thigh, though sometimes she wanted to scrub the area with all her strength, it was beginning to smell so—and now she was responsible for the bedpan because her mother could not, or would not, limp from the bedroom to the bathroom.

It was all becoming more than she could keep up with. She had begun asking for advance vacation days from work; she was often late when she did go in—she asked to work the midnight shift, since Mother was most likely to sleep during the morning hours—and sometimes she asked to leave early because she had been bothered by a premonition that her mother required help.

"They always turn out to be false alarms," she told Paul, "but they seem to be very real when I—sense them."

"Something has to be done," Paul said. His voice over the telephone had begun to sound brusque, exasperated. "My God, you and I scarcely see each other. Tell her you can't be her full-time nurse."

"I can't tell her anything, she comes and goes so. All I know is: she needs help. Yours. Mine. Somebody's."

"I'll do what I can, but I doubt she'll listen to me."

"Not that kind of help," Dorothy said. "The next time she passes out, I'll call you. We'll take her to the hospital whether she likes it or not." She paused, as if she expected Paul to object. "Please," she added.

4

Getting her mother to the hospital—out of bed; down the stairs suspended like an oversized doll between Paul and herself; half-dragging the woman into a cab, pushing and pulling her into the back seat, trying not to bang the swollen leg against any edges or corners (My Jesus, the young emergency room doctor had said, that was the least of your worries)—had been insane, almost comic.

"It's a marvel," said the doctor. "How did she do it?"

"A cat scratch," Dorothy said.

"No, I don't mean that. I mean how did she manage to let it go so far? It's the kind of infection you'd have gotten in the Middle Ages, which were a septic nightmare. I've never seen anything quite like it." He had a childish face, big-eyed and mobile.

"She simply didn't do anything for it. She has—religious beliefs."

He shook his head wonderingly. "In this day and age," he said. "If she realizes what's going on, she'll fight you."

"I expect she will." He sat beside Dorothy; Paul sat on the other side of her, solemn, listening. "Anyway, I've sedated her for the pain and dosed her with antibiotics for the infection. And I've got a call in to my resident. You've no idea how close she is to gangrene."

"No, I haven't."

"Of course the original trauma was in the joint—that's a complication—and if she did nothing for it at all, we may have to take the leg. We'll have to talk about that."

"She'll never let you do such a thing."

"She may not even be asked," the doctor said. "We may have to get the permission from you." He was trying to look sympathetic, Dorothy thought, but the eagerness was still evident in his eyes.

"Oh, no," she said. "Don't leave it up to me."

"You have religious beliefs, too?"

"I wish I did," Dorothy said, and felt guilty when she looked over at Paul.

\\\ The eventual doctor on Mother's case was not the wonderstruck young man in Emergency, but a woman in her late thirties, with ash-blond hair pulled back severely. *Marian Brandt, M.D.*, her blue nametag read. She led Dorothy into a small room containing a low table and several vinyl-covered chairs.

"Now," the doctor said, "let me finally hear your version of what happened to this leg of your mother's."

"A cat scratched her."

"That's what I see here," Dr. Brandt said. "Did you know about it?"

"Yes, but not until a couple of weeks ago."

The doctor's eyebrows pushed thin lines across her forehead. "You sat and watched it get this bad?"

"You talk as if I want her dead," Dorothy said, "and I don't. She wouldn't let me do anything. Her religion— For the last week all she's let me do is give her sponge baths. I had to wait for her to pass out, or get so delirious she wouldn't know we were bringing her to the hospital."

"Well, just let me tell you where we are, now that we've had a little time to observe your mother," Dr. Brandt said. "We seem to be of several minds, we medical professionals. Some think the leg will have to go—that the infection has gotten just too far ahead for us to win back the ground we've lost. The fainting and delirium you told Dr. Adams about—that's a reaction to the pain, I'm sure; it must have been terrible for her. And that yellowish discharge—that's an advanced symptom; it tells us the body's intrinsic defenses are pretty hopelessly outgunned. The whole business has tracked up to her hip along the lymphatic system." She stopped and gave Dorothy's hand a sympathetic squeeze. "And so it goes," she said. "Eventually it would all go black."

"She wouldn't let me do anything," Dorothy said again.

"Now—One school of thought says to amputate. With normal care she'd recover quite nicely; a few weeks of antibiotics given intravenously—"

Dorothy turned away, looked out the window. Below her was the roof of a lower level of the hospital. A man and a woman, both in green smocks, were sitting on a ledge, feet dangling, sharing lunch from a paper bag.

"The other school of thought—which is mine, by the way—says let's wait and see. Once you've cut it off, you can't stick it back on with superglue. Given what you've said, and what I infer, about your mother's notions of faith-healing, I can see the body needs a little vote of confidence. It's been preempted by a mind that didn't know what to do once it got control."

The doctor paused at the door. "That cat," she said, "is it an outdoor cat?"

"Never."

"I just wondered if it might have gotten its claws into something unusual, something really deadly."

"I can't think what."

"Well." The doctor smiled wanly. "Keep the faith. You may see your mother if you'd like."

Mother was propped against two pillows and the head of the bed was raised. Her face was flushed, but she looked more nearly normal than she had in days. The infected leg was invisible under the white sheet; the room smelled antiseptic. Out the large casement window Dorothy could see over the city's rooftops all the way to the harbor. She sat in a straight chair between the bed and the window and waited for her mother to notice her. A large television set was suspended from the ceiling by a metal frame, and a remote control for it sat on the high table beside the bed. She supposed that anyone looking into the room would see an ordinary family scene.

Periodically, Mrs. Porter licked her lips—slowly, one corner and then the other, as if only the corners were dry; she looked a little like a cat, and once when she yawned Dorothy caught herself smiling. She wondered that she could be so disconnected from her mother's agony of flesh and crisis of faith.

Her mother stirred. The head turned in her direction; the eyes collected her image; the cat lips smiled.

"How do you feel, Mother?"

"Like somebody still floating." Mother's voice was steady, but extraordinarily soft. Unusual space lay between each word. She was certainly drugged.

"I've been waiting for you to wake up," Dorothy said.

Her mother smiled wider. Her eyes glittered. "Did you think I was dead?"

"Dead?" She leaned nearer her mother.

"I'd only gone away." She did not insist by raising her voice or changing her expression; she only held Dorothy's eyes with hers. "Very far away."

Dorothy shivered and tried to smile back. "I hadn't realized."

"I left my body in the apartment," her mother said. "Just left it in bed with all the books and the cold tea, and off I went." She giggled faintly. "It was like floating, except I could float right through things—walls, doors. I floated down the steps and through the lobby door and out over the city."

"Did you?"

"It was dark. All the city lights were on. Do you remember flying over Boston with your father and me? and he said: 'The old lady is wearing her diamonds tonight.' Do you remember? You were nine."

"Of course." She didn't. She didn't recall ever flying with her father. "Where did you go then?"

"I don't know." Her mother's brow wrinkled. "Do you still have that wicked kitten?"

"Yes."

She rolled her head to the side and looked at her daughter. She blinked, as if she were having trouble locating Dorothy's face. "I want you to have it put away," she said. "Put to sleep."

IIII She supposed that it was her mother's chemically altered condition that kept Dorothy from resisting the very idea of putting Fancy to sleep. What was the point of argument, if the opponent was sedated past reason? She could not defend the cat's right to be a dumb creature. Nor—more important because it involved human creatures who were not, surely, "dumb"—could she begin to raise the question of her attachment to Paul, to gradually accustom her mother to the notion of living in the Brookline apartment without a daughter to care for her. The timing was all wrong; with Mother, it would be bad enough to mention marriage at all. Is it wise? Mother would say. How could Dorothy know? Perhaps she was only exchanging one kind of spiritual preoccupation for another.

Though in fact there seemed to be a slow but steady change in the quality of Paul's faith. He seemed, lately, to take it more casually, not—as in the beginning—insisting on it, using it to attract and involve her, but treating it instead as an aside. He talked not about salvation, but about himself and his engagements to discuss it—as if he had ceased to think of himself as the person to whom Jesus had appeared, and had become a man who had once read a story about a person to whom Jesus had appeared. Now he went about the New England states re-telling it.

She suggested that, one evening after she had left Mother, when Paul was driving to Cambridge and a narrow green space along the Charles.

"I suppose it's true," he said dubiously. "In which case I'm not so unlike the Gospel writers, putting the story together from oral histories and their own intentional imaginations."

"But you don't need to make anything up. You say you were there; it happened to you."

"In a way."

"Either it did or it didn't," Dorothy said.

"Yes, but think of the state I was in. You said it yourself, months ago. I'd been deathly ill, I'd gone past recovery—I mean to say I really and truly believed I was dead, or at least not alive—and I was terrified. I'm bound to have missed a few details, don't you think?"

"I thought the entire vision was indelibly etched on the screen of your memory," she said.

"My Lord, you can be sarcastic."

"Well, you should listen to yourself. You departed from the land of the living, you met Jesus Christ Himself. He showed you Hell in all its horrible hot splendor, and then He gave you back your life and told you to spread the Word. And now you say you missed a few details." She shrugged. "I think it's fading away from you."

They were parked, looking across the river at the moving lights of traffic reflected in the slow water. The lamps of the bridge were yellowish-pink, like torch flame.

"I think my mother knows as much about it as you do," Dorothy said, almost as an afterthought.

"About what?" Paul said.

"Death. Hell. Leaving and coming back."

He took her hand, kissed the back of it. "You still think I'm some garden-variety charlatan, don't you," he said.

"I'm sorry." She leaned toward him, let him kiss her on the forehead, rested her head on his shoulder. "I'm all wrapped up in poor Mother. I don't know what's to become of her. Just when I think I'm ready to make a clean break from home, from Mother—when I'm finally ready to grow up—something happens. This happens. I can't even talk to her about it, they've got her so sedated. It frustrates me, and I guess I take it out on you."

"I make allowances," he said. His hand touched her breasts through the linen blouse she wore. *I make allowances*, her mind echoed.

"The whole country is so full of religion right now," Dorothy said, "you hardly know what to think, do you?"

"There are many false prophets," he said.

"No—I mean: You fit right in, don't you? You're in step with this country, and it's not even your own. Just like you're in step—or you used to be, anyway—with the Beyond, and that's not your own country, either."

"That's quite clever," Paul said.

Of course he wasn't paying the least attention to what she was saying, beyond hearing the words. She knew where his mind was; it was in the fingers caressing her under her blouse, and it was weighing the right time to unfasten the buttons, to undo her, to touch the bared nipples through whose tingling she could feel her own arousal beginning. He was familiar with her, in these past few weeks every bit as familiar as Frederick.

"I don't mean to be clever," she said. Familiarity could be offensive, too. One day she and Laura Rose had found a book in Mother's stocking drawer with a story by the same man who had written *Bambi*. Laura Rose said no to it: I don't want to read it; no sentimental slop for me. But it had not been about lovable animals. It had been about a woman in a hunting party, and about the guide who had gotten her alone and began to seduce her by stroking her breasts. Hermione; that was her name. And now Dorothy was Hermione, Paul the arrogant hunter. She watched her real sensations as if they too were fictional, and in both was a—a reservation, some part of a woman's brain registering insult. In the story, Hermione had killed the man—a single rifle shot—

"I adore touching you," Paul whispered. "We've had so little time lately, I'd forgot how exciting you are."

What Dorothy remembered most clearly was the description of the man caressing Hermione's breasts, "first one and then the other." Hermione's pleasure mingling with anger and humiliation—then breaking from him—the single rifle shot—

"Wait," Dorothy said. She had never made love in the front seat of a car, didn't know how to arrange herself—her arms, her legs he had a hand between, her clothes she was afraid would be torn. "There isn't room," this last with her ankle twisted against—what?—something to do with the heater. At least Hermione had had a whole forest for her actions, hampered though she was by the long skirt of her hunting costume—formal clothes, so that the indignity of having her blouse opened, her breasts violated by that conceited man imagining she would accept his advances, would have seemed all the more offensive—so that turning the rifle on him was all the sweeter—that single, stunning shot—

"All the room in the world," Paul said. He was somehow moving under her. "Let me sit where you were—so—and you straddle me."

My God, Dorothy thought, there ought to be charts and instructions. There ought to be a chapter in the owner's manual when you took delivery of the car. She was on her knees between his thighs—bare skin; he had already shed his trousers—balanced on the edge of the seat. He had one arm around her shoulders—also bare, her blouse too far open not to have slid down—pulling her against him, his mouth over one breast, his tongue a heavy pulse mocking her heartbeat. Hermione—that mix of physical pleasure and rational disgust. Awkward. Her head close to the roof of the car—if she moved she bumped it—and Paul's other hand peeling the lower half of her, the light skirt and underpants pushed—a little frantic; she could feel his nails—below her knees.

"You're scratching me," she said.

"Sorry." He held her buttocks, let her slide down so their faces touched. His hands urged her legs apart, pushed them outside of his own, one and then the other. "Now," he said. "Just impale yourself."

Impale. Brutal word, yet she had no choice. She could feel him, erect, probing, waiting to be taken inside her; she had no place to go except—downward—his hands gripped her legs, the low roof kept her bent toward him, if she backed away even a little the dashboard nudged her spine. What would Hermione have done today? Where would she have found room to tear herself out of the hunter's grasp? Now Paul was entering her; she let herself down onto him, wondering just for a moment how, this time, would she bring herself to orgasm after he had reached his. Ah. Paul moved inside her, moved, moved, moved. The pleasure and the discomfort mingled. Even quaint Hermione would have surrendered in this confinement, would have turned the rifle on herself to save her honor, impaled herself, pulled the trigger—the single shot in the forest—

For an instant she felt genuine terror.

The interior of the car had exploded—with light, not sound, yet afterward her ears rang as if there had been a noise as well. Paul was stock-still under her; she could not have seen his face even if it were not nighttime, her vision was nearly obliterated by the flash of light.

"Good Christ," Paul said, "get off!"

"What was it?" He was pushing her, had already withdrawn from her. She clung to the back of the seat.

"My wife, my damned wife." He was getting out from under, trying to pull up his trousers, elbowing Dorothy away. Out the back window she could make out the shrinking taillights of another car.

"How can it be your wife?" she cried.

He was already behind the wheel, shirt untucked, starting the engine. "Get dressed," he said. "I'll take you home."

\\\\ For the next several days her tears began involuntarily. She would be sitting in the kitchen, drinking a cup of coffee, and unexpectedly she would taste salt on the lip of her cup. She would be clowning with Fancy, poor, guiltless Fancy, thinking how undignified a cat looks when it is on its back with its legs sprawling, and her laughter would turn to sobbing. She was dazzled still—every bit as dazzled as she had been when the flashbulb burst in her eyes in Paul's borrowed car, only it was a dazzle, a disorientation that pervaded her whole body as if she were drenched to the bone in shame and confusion. She was, she supposed, a little out of control. She could not cope with Mother's infection or Mother's God, and now she could not even deal with her own world. She waited for Paul to phone, to explain, but he did not call. Finally she faced the truth: he would never call.

She could not face the hospital. She took time away from work, but went no further from the apartment than the lobby mailbox. She ate whatever was in cans in the kitchen cupboards—cling peaches for one meal, mushroom soup for the next, hash for another—opening one can at a time and finishing all its contents before she opened the next. She was nearly a machine. At night, she brought in the pillows from her mother's bed and stood them up in back of her own; when she was comfortable against this mountain of softness she reminded herself of Mother, propped up in the bed, waiting, without knowing she was waiting, for the decision that would save her leg or take it from her. What would they do with it? Burn it up, or set it out at the curb in a garbage bag, or bury it in some corner of the parking lot and tend it until it grew into a tree bearing new limbs for grafting to other people's mothers—

"Fancy," she said, "how can you let me think such horrors?" The cat, nested between her knees, opened and closed its eyes and laid its ears back. Dorothy pulled at the coverlet, and Fancy unsheathed her front claws as if to hold it in place. I must clip those, Dorothy thought. I must not let any of this happen again.

One night she read until she could no longer keep her eyes open or comprehend the words on the page or hold a thought in her head, then fell asleep almost the moment she turned out the light. When the telephone rang—it was five-fifteen, and for several rings Dorothy listened without moving because she thought it might at last be Paul—the caller was Marian Brandt.

"It's about your mother." Silence at the other end of the line, as if the doctor were giving Dorothy time to collect herself, to place the name. Voices filtered into her wakefulness, a sound like women's heels on tile, the creak of a door opening and shutting. "You'd better come to the hospital."

|||| And so the leg was taken. Dr. Brandt paced before the lounge windows, hands in the pockets of her smock, saying words. She looked weary, rumpled, and Dorothy thought the words were not registering, not moving her, because they too were tired; they carried no conviction, they were not hard enough for hurt.

"I couldn't argue with them," the doctor said. "It wasn't that they were men, it wasn't a battle of the sexes. It was a simple matter of facts, of tests, of likely outcomes."

"You said the infection was getting better."

"It was. It was reversing nicely. But the damage in the leg, in the knee—that wasn't reversible. The extent of it in the lymphatic network—that had been too widespread. The consensus was to cut. I went along with it."

"Did you do it?"

"God, no." The doctor gazed out the window. "I assisted—I helped them. That was worse."

Dorothy sat small in the chair beside a table littered with magazines and coloring books. She thought about being needed by her mother, how nice it was that at a time when her mother had no choices, it happened that Dorothy herself had none. We'll be quite a pair, she thought. "You said you'd have to have my consent before you could do such a thing."

"We had your mother's."

That seemed unbelievable. "How could she?"

"She wasn't coerced," Dr. Brandt said. "Nobody forced her. Nobody tried to frighten her. She listened to all the facts, all the opinions, and she said: 'You know best.' I was there. 'You know best,' she said. 'I put myself in your hands.' She was perfectly lucid, perfectly alert."

"Mother is never perfectly anything," Dorothy said. "She'll regret this."

"It was a regrettable operation." Dr. Brandt knelt by the chair and put her hands over Dorothy's. "She'll be fine," she said. "I'm sorry you've wept so much for her. You'll be amazed at how fine she'll be, how quickly she'll get used to prosthesis."

"I'm sure." Dorothy said it without heart. She could not even confess that she had been weeping not for Mother, but for herself.

"I'll take you up to intensive care," the doctor said. "She'll be there another twenty-four hours or so; she'll be happy to see you."

But her mother looked blankly at her, the morning sunlight turning the foot of her bed vivid and outlining her one whole leg. "I asked to be dead," she said. "It was just like Nana Davis. They kept bringing me back."

"Of course they did. You're a young woman; you have a lot to look forward to."

"I can't be queen of the prom," her mother said. "I can't lead the grand march. I can't dance the first dance." Her mother's pupils were enormous cat eyes; her voice was strong, but monotonous. Every few moments a bubble rose to the surface of the I.V. bottle for punctuation.

"Don't be silly."

"Oh, yes," her mother said. "I can rent space in the Park Street Over and sell pencils."

Dorothy imagined she had a sudden glimpse of it all—her whole life with a woman who would make a crutch of her daughter to avoid learning to use an artificial leg.

"We'll be fine," Dorothy said. "You'll see. In a couple of weeks you'll be out on your own."

"My own what?" She turned her head away. "I'm tired. I'm tired of you."

"Virginia Weal phoned. She's coming to pay you a visit."

Mother's eyes closed. "I'm tired of her, too."

IIII Sitting in a taxi on the way to the veterinarian's office, on the day her mother was to come home to the apartment, Dorothy felt part of some inevitable movement, a carrying-back to a beginning, a zero—square one. Storybook land, she thought. *Puss in Boots* with a sad ending. Wicked stepmothers. She took the top off the same shoebox that had carried Fancy into her life and stroked the cat, her fingers tracing the hard, small bones of skull and spine, the wiry muscles flexing under the cat's skin as it washed itself. A living thing, she told herself. This is a living thing. She wondered that Fancy could be both living and *a thing*.

In the vet's waiting room Dorothy imagined that by now her mother would be settled in the apartment, the hospital attendants would have carried her lightly upstairs—joking about her delicate weight, "You're light as a feather, Mrs. P."—and arranged her against the heaped pillows of the bed. Her mother would sit as she had before Dorothy and Paul had kidnapped her, the fashion magazines fanned around her, whatever medications she needed on the nightstand, and now a walker or a pair of crutches—aluminum, probably; that was what you saw nowadays, not the old-fashioned wooden kind—stored in the corner between the window and the bed, one of the attendants wagging a finger at her, saying: "Now you be sure to practice, Mrs. P.; you'll get around fine till you're ready for a fitting." High fashion. For an instant she remembered wondering, sitting at the hospital, what they would do with Mother's amputated leg. Bury it? Was that where the saying came from—one foot in the grave? Her mother thanking the attendants; ironic, probably. Look at what my daughter has done to me. Dorothy knew she would never hear the end of that story.

She was the only person in the waiting room. The box she held on her lap, the top slid aside so Fancy could sit up, look around. How could this creature be so innocent and so guilty at the same time? She held the cat in the circle of her hands so it could not jump from her lap, could not explore the smells of animals here before. That was what it wanted to do; every so often Dorothy felt the cat's shoulder muscles tighten, a hard upward pressure against the collar her hands made.

"I can feel your purr," she said. And she could—a small vibration against her palm that intensified with each breath Fancy took. So calm, she thought, so trusting. She knew she was going to cry—she seemed able to cry for everything except her mother's misfortune. We have to be extremely kind to dumb animals, her father had once told her. We think of God the way they think of us.

When the door to the waiting room opened and a young veterinarian said, "Come in, Miss Porter," she could feel the tears well— just because she was going to have to talk about what was to happen, because it really was to happen.

"I want to stay with her. Is that all right?"

"If you want," he said.

"Do people do that? Is it foolish?"

"It isn't foolish." He preceded her into the small room with glass-front cabinets against one wall, a counter under them, a wide, stainless steel table taking up most of the available space. "People love their pets."

"It won't be horrible, will it?"

"Will the cat suffer? No. Not at all."

"I'd thought I might take her to the Humane Society. I don't have any friends to take her, care for her."

"The Humane Society probably would have put it down anyway," the doctor said. "They always have too many animals."

"Somebody told me," Dorothy said, "that this is a two-step thing. That you put the cat to sleep, and then you inject the drug—that kills it—while it's asleep. So the cat doesn't feel anything." She stroked Fancy's fine head; the cat squirmed under the doctor's hands.

"That isn't the way we do it," he said. "Get a good hold on those front paws, would you?" He opened one of the cabinets, found a syringe and filled it from a silver-topped vial no larger than a perfume sample. "It's a single injection."

"What is it?"

He put one hand across Fancy's shoulder. "It's painless, really." Dorothy was bent over the table; the cat was cradled between her forearms, her hands holding its upper forelegs.

"But what's it called?"

The vet held one of Fancy's forepaws, slid the needle into the leg above the first joint, squeezed the plunger. Fancy hardly stirred in her hands. "Sodium pentobarbital," he said. He withdrew the needle.

"How long does it take?"

"Not long."

Dorothy let go of Fancy's legs and stroked the stiff fur of the cat's head and back. The cat was on its side, head against the table, seeming to be asleep. The vet had found a stethoscope in a drawer under the counter; he stood across the table; once he looked at his watch. Dorothy stopped her hands. The silence in the small room was total and interminable, like a photograph of two people and a cat in a white and silver setting.

"It's already gone," the veterinarian said. "We'll wait a bit just to be certain."

"I felt her move," Dorothy said. "I know I did."

He nodded. "That happens—the muscles letting go." He moved the stethoscope under the cat's forelegs, up over its chest. "The heart stopped beating long ago."

She picked up the cat, tried to cradle it in her arms. The carcass was soft, remarkably heavy; it almost felt boneless. Whatever shape it had, she supplied. This was what they meant by dead weight. She held the cat awkwardly, its legs at odd angles.

"I'll take it," the doctor said. He held out his hands.

"No," she said. "I'll carry her in the shoebox."

She realized the doctor thought she was being strange; his eyes searched her face. Looking for sanity. Everything in the room was haloed by her tears. Poor Fancy. Some merciful God.

"I thought you'd probably want us to dispose of it."

"I'll—I'll take care of it." She was in the waiting room, watched herself slide Fancy into the box. She closed the lid and stood holding it in front of her with both hands. "Can you send me a bill?"

"Sure," he said.

She thought he looked genuinely sympathetic, that he didn't think she was crazy, that he saw she was distraught, that he understood she could not possibly stand here paying money to the man who had destroyed a thing—a thing—she loved. He held open the door, and smiled at her as she walked past him.

"Thank you for everything," she said, and stepped out into the street.

She had walked nearly a half-block before she began paying attention to what she was doing—carrying a dead cat through the city of Boston in a shoebox with holes punched in it. Now all she needed was to step out into traffic and get knocked down by a car—that would give passers-by and the police something to reckon with, some stories to tell their girlfriends and wives. Or even under normal circumstances—confronting her triumphant mother, saying *The lady or the tiger. Look what I've chosen.*

She stopped in her tracks—the noon traffic noisy around her, the crisp air cold against her wet cheeks, the box a presence but not much of a burden in her hands, and the fact of killing already taking on the aura of something necessary, therefore sensible. What in the world do I think I'm doing? she said to herself, and she turned to deliver the remains of the Siamese back to the vet. The world seemed filled with men willing and able to dispose of whatever might have made her happy.

5

On a Sunday morning when Dorothy Porter was nine she sat in front of the television and heard a sober-looking man say God was dead. Even now, twenty-odd years later, she remembered her shock—how she had run sobbing to her parents' bedroom (Dorrie, sweetheart, what's wrong?), had flung herself into her father's arms, desperate to hold on to him, afraid if she let go he might vanish as wholly as smoke. The man says God died—is it true? And her father had tried to reassure her—No, God is very much alive—that what the man meant was that attitudes toward Him had changed, that people now talked about God more thoughtfully and didn't she, Dorothy, think it was more respectful to talk about God as if He were a complex and interesting Power, a Force that lay in back of everything from the stars to the tiny bacteria you had to look at with a microscope, than to imagine He was just a nice, bearded Old Man on a white throne, Who sat around admiring the universe He'd made and listening for prayers that floated up from earth?

Somewhere in the middle of this explanation her mother had gotten up and gone out to the kitchen to make coffee, leaving Dorothy alone in bed with her father, weeping against his chest, saying: Why do they act as if He's not real? How can they? She thought, then, that she had never known such desolation—nor had she, until her father actually left her.

Her memories of her father were various, and she wondered how she could have held them in mind all these years, when most children would instead have recalled one great happiness, one great sorrow to tide them through the fatherless years. All of them took place in Maine—in the days when the Porters had owned a summer cottage on Mere Point—and had partly to do with what her mother even now called "your father's problem."

She remembered one day. Early in the morning—this was mid-

July; light flooded the small house and alerted the shore birds before five o'clock—she came awake out of what must have been a
nightmare. Her small heart was pounding, the pillow was damp with
her sweating, the covers were a baffling tangle of sheets and quilts
that had deserted her during the dream and left her shivering with
cold. For a long time she lay still, trying to get warm, calming herself, wondering what she might have seen in her sleep. The tide was
up; she could hear the oil drums bumping together under the long
wooden dock, and she thought there was a fog because the barking
of the Parkers' St. Bernard was muffled, a sound like someone ham-
mering nails inside a boathouse. Then she dozed, and when she
woke again it was nearly nine o'clock and her mother and father
were talking in the kitchen.

At noon they all went sailing among the tiny islands she could
see from the sunporch. The boat was new—new to them—and the
only sailboat the Porters ever owned, a nineteen-foot sloop, gaff-
rigged, her father had named *Piper.*

"Sandpiper," Dorothy said. "That's where the name comes
from."

"Maybe," said her father. "Or maybe I call her that because I paid
so much for her." He winked at Mother—how pretty she had been
in those days: long dark hair, plucked eyebrows, a tiny mole like a
deliberate beauty mark just to the left of her mouth—but Mother
had looked disapproving.

"He means," she explained to Dorothy, "that he who dances
must pay the piper."

She imagined her father was a competent sailor. He knew the
names of things—mainsail, jib, cleats and stays, tack and buoy and
gunwale—words that were strange to her and that seemed when she
saw them written down to have expanded out of themselves and
gained syllables. He was extraordinarily patient with her ignorance,
her landlubberly ineptness; he never acted as if her mistakes were
serious or stupid.

"Simmer down, Dorrie," he would say. "Think what you're

doing." If for example she was careless at the tiller, and the mainsail suddenly went all slack and flapping, he didn't berate her. "What ho, Dorrie. I said be calm yourself—not becalm the boat." Then he helped her get *Piper* into the wind and kissed her jovially on the forehead. All the while her mother knitted and looked vaguely dissatisfied with everything that happened. No one but Father ever called her Dorrie.

Late that afternoon he wanted to drive to Lisbon Falls to investigate a boat trailer that was for sale. Did Dorrie want to ride along? Yes. Did her mother want to come, too? No, Mother thought she would drive over to Harpswell with Brenda Parker and perhaps bring home some sweet corn for supper.

After they had looked at the trailer—it was badly rusted, with nearly bald tires, and she knew at once that her father wouldn't buy it—they stopped in at the local pharmacy and had ice cream.

"That trailer looked awful," Dorothy said.

"Loving hands of home," said her father. "Are you thirsty?"

"A little."

"So am I." He asked the girl behind the counter to bring two glasses of water, with plenty of cracked ice. "Ice cream makes me thirsty as hell," he said. "And you can imagine how thirsty that is."

"Why do we want a boat trailer? Is it for *Piper?*"

"No, not for *Piper.*" He sipped the ice water. "Your mother doesn't think much of *Piper;* she doesn't care for sail."

"Why not?"

"She's a powerboat person. She likes—I don't know—the speed, the spray, the noise. Something."

"But you don't."

"I don't. I like—floating, silence, sliding from wave to wave. I like knowing there's no machinery to break down except the wind—and that always fixes itself." He chuckled. "Your mother doesn't have much faith in the wind. She thinks it's irresponsible."

"I'd rather be on a sailboat," Dorothy said.

"Birds of a feather," said her father. "We're both bound to have our wings clipped."

"Is she going to make you sell *Piper?*"

"I don't know. Probably, when fall comes." He had gotten quiet then, and she had felt a surge of sympathy for this boyish man who only wanted to slide over the ocean and trust the wind. She put her arm around his waist while he paid the girl at the cash register. The register sat on a glass showcase filled with candy bars and cigars and, on the bottom shelf, a small assortment of face powders and lipsticks and perfume in purple bottles, which she contemplated sadly, her cheek pressed against her father's side.

Walking to the car, she said, "Why can't you sell *Piper* to me? I'd let you use it whenever you wanted."

"That's very thoughtful." He hugged her against him. "Just remember that a boat is always a 'she,' and never an 'it.'"

He drove back to Brunswick very fast, bought a fifth of Canadian whiskey at the green front, and spent the rest of the afternoon sitting on the sunporch, drinking whiskey and water until supper. Just having a couple, he used to say.

In those days grandfather—Father's father—owned a summer house at Christmas Cove overlooking the ocean. A quarter-mile offshore was a long, narrow island, rocky and tree-covered, called the Needle. Between the Needle and the ledges the house sat on was the Thread of Life, a channel scattered with lobster buoys.

Dorothy often came to sit by the water's edge to watch the lobstermen check their traps. If she followed the tide charts she knew exactly when to begin her watching, though in the summers when she was eight and nine and ten there was nothing special to do and she walked down to the water when she felt like it. Her father told her the lobstermen had used to mark trap locations with bottles— green or brown or clear glass—but that sometimes the summer people used the bottles for target practice and broke them, and then the lobstermen had to drag for their lost traps. Nowadays the markers were all wooden buoys, each lobsterman's painted with its unique, personal design, but if you walked along the shore you could still find sea glass—bits of broken bottles rubbed smooth and harmless by the waves.

Mornings, while her parents and her grandfather talked, Dorothy played on the front lawn and watched white-hulled boats file through the Thread of Life, out to the open water. Their sails were furled, inboard motors carrying them through the narrow channel. If she waved, the people on board waved back.

She remembered those summer mornings as both idyllic and disheartening—the beauty of them, the freedom, while here she was on land, sluggish and rooted. Even the seals that sunned on the rocks of the Needle were better off than she was: they tumbled into the bay when they felt like it, swam underwater for so long she thought they would never come up, then lumbered onto shore for more sleep, their bulk fading to a lighter color as they dried.

Almost every afternoon her father sat on the lawn in a deck chair, looking out toward Monhegan Island, drinking. *Just having a couple.*

|||| The day John Kennedy was shot, her father had gone to the cellar of the house in Portland—that would have been the house on Baxter Boulevard, because in 1963 she was eight and they lived there until she was eleven—and sat there, day after day after day, watching on television the consequences of assassination: Oswald, Ruby, the wife and children of the dead president, the funeral procession, the riderless horse, the sense of horror implicit in the raw light from the screen. He seemed entirely changed. When Dorothy or her mother spoke to him he was deaf, or he was short-tempered over everything—as if he resented both his wife and his curious daughter.

"What's the name of the man who killed him?" she remembered asking, never able to keep it in her head because it was the name of one of her animal dolls, of a Sunday comics figure, of someone in bedtime stories she had listened to before she was old enough for school.

"It doesn't matter," he told her finally. "His name isn't what counts; it's what he did that counts." Peevish, short with her. Grim. It seemed, then, that he left the dim, paneled cellar only to get himself a drink, to go to the bathroom, to go sometimes out to the garage where he did what? Nothing that she could fathom. But he would sit in the car—the dark green Chevrolet with the chrome seagull wing on the trunk lid—and stare at the back wall of the garage where the gardening tools leaned. After a while he would get out, slam the car door behind him, pour another drink in the kitchen, descend to the cellar.

"What's wrong with Daddy?" she asked her mother.

"It's nothing," her mother said. "He's just making this very important."

"Is it important?"

"Not as important as your father thinks it is."

That was not like her father—she had thought then—who was always reasonable, who never made of things either too much or too little. Yet here he sat, hour by hour in the half dark, rising to the light only to replenish his glass. When, sometimes, Mother brought him sandwiches—or sent Dorothy down with them—he accepted them absently, his eyes filled with the images on the screen.

Of these images she herself recalled next to none: the two Kennedy children holding their mother's hands—they were much younger than Dorothy, yet here they were with their pictures on television!—Mrs. Kennedy so still and expressionless; the continual sense of people and events seething, seething, like worms in a coffee can. And her father: mute, disconnected.

Less than a year later, in the summer of owning *Piper*, when she and her father sailed into the lee of Birch Island and dropped anchor to fish, when he had sat in the stern of the boat for a long time without so much as baiting his hook, when his face was unaccountably as solemn as it had been during his vigil before the television, she asked why he had been so sad. He had smiled at her, strangely, and at first gave no answer—as if he were reading back into memory, trying to know his feelings all over again.

"Hopelessness," he said finally. "As if someone had killed the way we looked forward."

"Why wasn't Mother as sad as you?"

"I don't know. Maybe she didn't understand what happened."

|||| One Saturday afternoon, Dorothy and her father had gone sailing in Casco Bay—off the Harpswell peninsula, Flying Point, Cousins Island, into Maquoit Bay where an artist had built a cedar house weathered silver-gray and hardly distinguishable from the tumbled rocks it was raised on. Down east of the artist's house they had discovered the seal—the picture of a seal, rather, done with white paint or whitewash or something lime-based on a smooth, vertical outcrop over the water. It was enormous. Sometimes even now she dreamed about it: it loomed like a cloud whose opacity she slowly entered, watching herself disappear, waking with a start to find that she still existed, that she had not after all been devoured by the creature whose intention, she imagined, was to carry her back to childhood.

They had quarreled about the painting. Her father at first wanted it to be a whale, after a book she had not read, and she went to great lengths of argument to persuade him to see the seal. By the time she had won, the image was far behind them; she thought afterward that he gave in out of fatigue, or kindness, or because he was a father. Anything for the sake of peace. Turning back, they set a course that took them to windward of Bustins Island, and so they did not see the painting a second time.

Both of them invented stories to explain the seal. It was put there by the artist who built the house on the rocks, her father said. When the artist and "that pretty lady we see him with at the green front" had done with the interior walls, they had paint left over. The stone outcropping, with its smooth face, demanded art, and on it the artist had drawn the outline of the seal, her father said, except for the highest curves of the head and back where he couldn't reach. These the lady had drawn, standing on the artist's shoulders to reach as high as she could. That explained why it looked so much like a whale, her father said, because since the lady was not an artist—only an artist's friend—she had made the head too large and forgot the whiskers. Her father expected the seal to be visible for years and years, he said, because the artist and the lady came to the rock every summer and repainted the seal as an affirmation and a renewal of their love.

Dorothy had long since understood how much wishful thinking informed her father's story; as a child, she had simply thought it was ordinary, but that her father had a perfect right to be ordinary. Her own guess, she told him, was that the Indians—Penobscots, she imagined—had done the painting, and that their paint was a concoction of ground clamshells and pine pitch and bitter juices from the guts of animals, which stuck harder and shone brighter and had already withstood the weather for at least two hundred years. Probably when the governor of Maine realized it was here he would ask the people to let him declare the seal a state monument, and then the Coast Guard would patrol it, protecting it from tourists who would want to scratch initials in it or chip off pieces of it to display on their fireplace mantels. She said she thought it must be some kind of seal god, and that the Penobscots had painted it to honor all the seals in the ocean, and also to teach the young Indians to recognize and respect the importance of seals to the tribe—how the seals provided hides to protect humans from the cold, and meat to be dried and eaten during the harsh winters, and rich fatty oils to shine bows and arrows and keep them from warping, and even necklaces and bracelets made from their teeth. She told her father she was glad Indians didn't need those things anymore, and so now there was no reason to kill seals, but she thought it was nice—very nice—that the picture of the seal was here for girls and their fathers to talk about.

At the end of the summer, *Piper* was sold to a professor at Bowdoin who moored the boat at Freeport and renamed her *Kittiwake*, and the Porters left Mere Point for the last time. Though Dorothy and her father had sailed in and out of Maquoit Bay several times before the boat changed hands, they never saw the seal again. She was disappointed; she had thought that if she could look at it once more, up close, she would find details to justify the history she had created for it, details that would prove her right. It bothered her that her father seemed not to care about evidence.

"It doesn't matter," he said. "Your story is the best one anyhow."

|||| Now, more than twenty years later, here came a letter from a law firm in Houston, announcing her father's death. Neither Dorothy nor her mother had heard from him in all that time—no picture postcards, no telephone calls, not even small gifts to mark Christmases and birthdays. He had dropped out of his women's lives as finally as if he had always been dead; Mother conducted herself as if she were widowed, and even for Dorothy the Boston apartment they shared felt complete. Of what her father's life had been, whether he had taken up residence in Texas from the beginning of his exile, what legacies survived him—the lawyers' letter gave only clues. There was promise of further communication, a suggestion of formalities to be dealt with and arrangements to be made. Apparently there was a house, a car, insurance policies. The firm would be in touch.

The following day a small package arrived—her father's "effects." His Waltham wristwatch, a brown calfskin billfold, a white-gold wedding ring, a bundle of papers held by two red elastic bands.

"I won't touch those things," her mother said. "Do what you want with them." She sat at the kitchen window in slacks and a silk blouse; an ebony cane lay on the floor beside the chair. It was Mother's morning habit to watch the change of weather and season out this narrow window, and more than once Dorothy remembered Fancy's preoccupation with the sparrows in the yard.

Tucked in with her father's papers Dorothy found a snapshot, its glossy surface cracked, its corners bent. It was the first reality of Richard Porter she had seen since her childhood; everything else was gone: anniversary presents, old love letters, other photographs in imitation-leather albums, travel souvenirs, even a dusty bottle of cognac he had bought to be opened at Dorothy's wedding—all of that had gone out with the trash while she was still in high school, accompanied by her mother's diatribe, nearly hysterical, against marriage and men.

The snapshot was from the summer of *Piper*, taken on the dock at Mere Point. Here was Father, highball glass in hand, raising the drink toward the picture-taker—Mother—in an apparent toast. Here was Dorothy, beside him, in jeans and soccer jersey and white sweater, with her long hair drawn into a single braid. In the foreground: Mother's shadow. In the background: *Piper*, with the black hull and white cockpit, the sail furled out of sight under a canvas cover.

It was appalling, from this perspective of time and death, to realize how happy both of them looked. Father looked jolly; Dorothy wore a smile that was shy but, clearly, proud as she clung to his free hand. She could only imagine her mother's expression, half-hidden behind the camera. For years Dorothy's deepest fear had been of living out her life in the company—that shadow—of her mother, unmarried and without prospects, coping as best she could with Mother's endless dissatisfactions. She had always been afraid, especially after her father left "for good," of being a failure at womanhood.

If she was not yet truly a spinster, that was merely an accident of time, Dorothy thought. Every evidence threatened the horrid truth. She was gaining in seniority at the phone company. She was past thirty, single, with a failed engagement and a foolish affair already a million years behind her, living with her mother—and where else could she go without facing unendurable loneliness? Men entered her life, and left it, as swift as rare, uncatchable birds. Paul Houser was the cruelest; one day, after she knew he had gone back to his wife, she had opened the mail to find a small white envelope containing a single negative: two lovers, a masterpiece of fearful contortion. She had not been able perfectly to read the reversed light and shadow, but she saw two forms fastened together below the waist like lascivious Siamese twins; the woman's blouse was open, her nipples gray dots on the negative, her eyes black stones. In a print, she would have looked like a cat in a corner, its eyes pure light. She had taken the negative to the kitchen and set fire to it over the sink; when the film flared she dropped it, and when nothing was left of it but shards of curled gray ash, she washed the residue away.

What was the secret of love? Had her father found it by escaping his family? On those vivid, lost afternoons aboard *Piper* he was the perfect skipper, the relaxed master of a world of sea and wind and open sky. She had especially remembered him that way, and she wondered if his death had not somehow brought her present life to a place not only of grief, but of unusual calm—if it might not mean that now, finally, she too should be free, should make a new beginning. Either that, or nothing, she thought. She studied the worn photograph, remembering what the two of them had talked about at the pharmacy in Lisbon Falls. *Either wings now, or earthbound forever.*

Barber

The girl in the barber chair is perhaps fourteen. Her blond hair is presently dark because it is wet after a shampoo; parted perfectly in the middle and combed straight, it falls to her shoulders. She is reading *Rolling Stone,* and her jaws work fitfully at chewing gum.

"I thought I'd better bring her back to you," her mother says. "She insists you're the only one who ever gets it right."

"Jill's hair is special," the barber says. He is a short, boy-faced man wearing a gold smock. On the floor not far away is a yellow Coca-Cola crate, upside down; probably he uses it as a platform when his customer is too tall.

"I don't know what it is," the mother says.

"Partly it's pH. Partly it's oiliness. Partly it's the experience of the artiste." He tips up the girl's face so she can look at him out of the wall mirror. "Isn't that right?"

"That's right," Jill says. She glances sidelong at her mother. I told you, says the glance.

"I've been taking her to my own beautician," the mother says.

"You should stay with the person who knows her hair best, Mrs. Weaver."

"She's very good."

"I'm sure she is—for you." The barber holds strands of Jill's hair out from her temples and compares the lengths.

"She was a creep," Jill says.

"She knew how to get your hair clean," Mrs. Weaver says. Her mother's voice is sharp. The word *clean* is in italics. "I don't know what she used, but it worked."

The barber smiles and snips. "Janitor-in-a-Drum will get hair clean," he says, "but what does it do to the follicles? What does it do to the ends? How does it clash with the chemistry of the hair? We're looking at protein, Mrs. Weaver. Protein—not Congoleum."

Jill takes the gum out of her mouth and holds it in the air as if she doesn't know what to do with it. The barber plucks a tissue from a box under the mirror and takes the gum.

"A disgusting habit," Mrs. Weaver says.

"Excuse me," Jill says. "It keeps me from getting tense."

"That's the truth," says the barber. "It concentrates a person's distractions. Chewing gum is like the ground wire on your television antenna: the tension trickles away, all harmless."

"It's the way she looks."

"They all do it nowadays. Even bank tellers," he says.

"That doesn't excuse it."

Jill flattens the tabloid on her lap. "Mother, why don't you go shopping or something?"

For several minutes no one talks. The only sounds in the shop are of scissors and the turning of pages. Once Mrs. Weaver sighs. Then she puts aside her magazine and stands up from the chrome chair with its thin plastic arms.

"I think I *will* do some errands," she says.

|||| Lauren Weaver is not fond of this shopping mall, whose setting is a well-to-do suburb and whose customers seem mostly to be young girls resembling her daughter. The girls are everywhere—bunched around drinking fountains, loitering in twos and threes in front of the plate-glass windows of shoe stores and frilly boutiques, moving singly among the skirt and blouse racks of Paul Harris and Marshall Field's. They are baby-faced and baby-plump, their jeans

like the skin on some exotic pale-blue fruit, their quilted jackets dyed orange and magenta and pink, like the flowers of that fruit. Their feet are in thin sneakers or shoes far too flimsy for the November weather outside. Their hair is either boy-short or impractically straight and long. It is true, what Jill's barber said, that all of them chew gum, and Mrs. Weaver marvels at so much tension collected in this confined place.

She herself feels somewhat tense in the mall environment. She does not think of herself as "old"—she belongs, after all, to a generation whose trademark was its contempt for men and women beyond the age of thirty—but the shopping mall never fails to remind her that she is too old for gum, for tight jeans, for impractical shoes that show painted toenails. Too old for things her own mother would have called "saucy." Perhaps it is this awareness of age that has prompted her to leave her daughter alone at the barber shop; anyway, it is a fact that she lied—that she has no particular errands that need doing.

At the heart of the mall is a skating rink, and she sits for a few minutes at the end of a wooden bench, looking idly down onto the ice. They are all shapes and sizes, the skaters. Fathers with small sons who fall and laugh and fall again, pretty girls of sixteen and seventeen who circle the rink with the becoming grace of birds almost ready to fly, one older couple—early sixties, she guesses—who glide across her gaze like endless lovers. In the very center of the ice is a woman in costume: white skirt covered with glitter, white sequined jacket, white skates and leotard. The woman looks to be in her late forties; her hair is tinted a vivid, unnatural yellow, teased into the shape of a dandelion bloom and striped with spokes of black. All the while Mrs. Weaver sits beside the rink, the woman keeps to the same place on the ice, spinning first on one skate then the other, sometimes fast, more often slow, head back, arms out, her vacant smile outlined with bright carmine lip gloss. Mrs. Weaver wonders if the woman is mad.

Walking back to the barber shop she pauses in front of a jeweler's window, where a selection of wristwatches is arranged against a backdrop of black velour. None of the watches displays the correct time, but she stands for a few moments to read her face in the glass, take stock of her appearance, be assured that she is probably sane. Distracted, but sane. She even goes inside the store, to contemplate showcases brilliant with gems and precious metal, and to notice how a young male clerk responds to her—how his eyes admire her, though he tries manfully to be businesslike.

||| When she gets back, the barber has put a flowered cap over Jill's head and is engaged with a crochet hook, drawing locks of the girl's hair up through holes in the cap.

"What are you doing?" Mrs. Weaver wants to know.

"Don't get crazy, Mother," Jill says. "It's all right."

"We're streaking it," the barber says. He has dragged out the Coca-Cola crate and is standing on it. "It will be just dazzling."

Mrs. Weaver sits down.

"I don't recall asking you to make her dazzle," she says.

"God, Mother," her daughter says. "Would you let a person do something nice for somebody?"

"Think of it as a present," the barber says, "to a favorite client."

"I don't know what to think," Mrs. Weaver says. Possibly she is upset that her daughter has acquired a fresh wad of gum. Or she is remembering the mad skater with the yellow hair, turning and turning on the same point of blue ice.

"It isn't like bleaching," Jill says. "Walter explained it."

Walter.

"Bleaching takes away protein," the barber says. "This is coloring, a special formulation. It puts back the protein as it works."

"What will it look like?"

"You'll love it. We've decided on just the slightest bit of rye-and-ginger. The hair will have highlights—a golden shimmer—like nothing it ever had before."

"Well—" says Mrs. Weaver. She watches the barber drawing her daughter's hair through the cap. Jill's head is like a limp wet-mop. "Perhaps I'll get used to it."

"I'm positive you will."

He finishes with the crochet hook and begins the streaking, soaking cotton balls with dye, stroking the exposed hair under his hands. Mrs. Weaver watches, silent, the magazine opened but unread in her lap. After a while her eyes wander to the window, which imposes the reflection of her daughter and her daughter's barber against the shadowy figures drifting through the mall.

"I wonder, Mrs. Weaver, if you've ever thought of frosting your hair?" the barber says. "Quite a number of ladies your age have it done." His graceful hands are suspended in the pungent air. "When those first few strands of gray begin to show up in your looking-glass."

"No," Mrs. Weaver says. For just a moment, turning from the window, she notices her daughter's sullen gaze. "I've never thought about it."

She looks down at the magazine in her lap, listening to the scrape of the Coca-Cola crate when the barber nudges it with his foot across the tiled floor.

Walter.

"It's actually quite a natural process," he says.

Jill smiles. In the wide mirror she catches the barber's eye and—does Lauren Weaver invent this?—rounds her baby lips into a soft, saucy kiss.

Parts Runner

When Chuck Mason left his wife and moved to
Cedar Rapids from Chicago, he did so with every expectation of
putting his life back together in a new place. He moved into an
apartment complex called Condos-5 with a girl half his age named
Janice. He'd met Janice in the bleachers at a Cubs game, but she was
originally from Palo, a town not far from C.R., where the state of
Iowa's only nuclear power plant was located. Chuck wouldn't have
given any thought to the plant, except that shortly after he and Janice moved into Condos-5 the postman left a color brochure entitled
Emergency Action Plan. The Plan told him that the plant did not expect to have "an emergency that would require evacuation," but included a long list of what to do if such an emergency took place. He
noticed that one paragraph instructed residents without cars to "Go
to the nearest bus stop to await the city bus for free pickup and
transport to a place of safety."

"I try to feature that," he told Terry Buscher at the shop; "waiting at a bus stop while the radiation settles all over town. You
wouldn't know if the bus was on its way, or if it had already gone past
your stop before you got there, or what."

"I thought you owned a car," Terry said. They were on break;
Terry was smoking his third cigarette of the morning. "Doesn't that
yellow Camaro belong to you?"

"Sure it does."

"Then what the hell do you care?"

"I don't." Chuck turned away from the cigarette smoke—Terry was the only one of the mechanics who still had the habit—and looked idly out the window over a styrofoam cup of coffee. The Camaro was at the far end of the lot; Terry's Blazer was parked beside it with a red-and-black sticker—*How's my driving? Dial 1-800-EAT SHIT*—on its rear bumper. "I just think it would be weird, having to depend on a city bus to save your life."

|||| Almost as soon as they were settled in C.R., Janice left him. He came home from work on a Tuesday evening and found her loading stuff into the back end of a black Ford pickup that sported a fat roll-bar and a pair of roof-mounted Marchal driving lamps. He met her as she was coming out the front door carrying a cardboard box filled with her stuffed animals.

"Oh, good," she said. "You can meet my dad."

Nothing about "I'm leaving you." No explanation. No apology. As if moving out on a man who'd left his wife for you was a perfectly reasonable thing to do.

"Dad, this is Chuck. Chuck, this is my dad."

Chuck shook the man's hand. Janice's father was about Chuck's age—*maybe exactly my age*, Chuck told himself later—and had a strong grip. He was good-looking, tall, wore denim jeans out at one knee and a denim jacket that appeared to be new. He had on tan cowboy boots with elegant scrollwork at the toes.

"Pleased to make your acquaintance," Janice's father said. "Name's Tim."

"Pleasure to meet you, Tim."

Back inside the apartment, Janice said, "I'm taking the floorlamp. It came originally from my apartment in Rogers Park."

"What the hell is it with you?" Chuck said. "What kind of a way is this for me to meet your old man?"

"But I'm leaving you the blue lamp in the bedroom."

She stood for a moment in the doorway with the brass lamp in

one hand and her framed senior-class picture in the other. The sunlight streamed in from behind her, and he felt her shadow lunge
against him.

"This is the last of what's mine," she said. "It's too bad. I think
you and Dad would've liked each other."

"Why are you doing this?"

She hesitated and half turned so that the light caught one side of
her face—a child's face, Chuck realized, and he wondered why he'd
bothered to ask the question.

"I miss Palo," she said. "I miss the farm." She lifted the lamp in
a clumsy salute. "G'bye," she said. "Maybe you should move back
to Chicago."

\\\\ Well, he said to himself, here you are: forty-five years old and
not-quite-divorced, working on foreign cars in a hick city, and living all by your lonesome. Now what?

He said as much to Terry, who shrugged and went on with a
brake job, the right front axle of an old Mercedes located just at eye
level while he tapped out the pins that held the pad retainer in place.

"You asking me to fix you up with somebody?" Terry said. "You
believe I got a sister?"

"Thinking out loud," Chuck said. He watched Terry pry out the
worn pads and blow brake dust out of the caliper with a long blast
from the air hose. "You don't want to breathe that stuff," he said.
"You ought to wear your mask when you do that."

"Fuck off," Terry said.

"Suit yourself," Chuck said.

Later on it occurred to him that it would have been convenient
if Terry did have a sister—only provided she didn't smoke like a
fiend, or walk through the world with a chip on her shoulder and a
four-letter word always ready to jump out of her mouth—for life at
Condos-5 was not terribly pleasant if you were all alone. In the
apartment next to his lived a muscular young man who seemed to
spend every weekend with a different girl, all of them blond-haired

and tawny and blooming with an aggressive good health that suggested he picked up his partners at a fitness club. Fridays and Saturdays, sometimes Sundays, Chuck lay awake and listened to the
sounds of talk and lovemaking that murmured through the wall between the two apartments; sometimes he would stand at the front
window the next morning, drinking his first cup of coffee, and watch
the girl leave the apartment house, unlock her car—the cars were
nearly always red, sporty—and drive away to her job or, possibly, her
parents. Then his neighbor would emerge, the energy of youth rippling under the blue work shirt he always wore, and climb into the
cab of his Nissan pickup with the magnetic plumbing-company
signs stuck to its doors.

IIII The parts runner was a girl named Raejeanne. She looked to be
in her middle twenties and she drove a gray Chevy pickup with a
necklace of red beads looped around the inside mirror. He didn't see
her every day, but on the days when she appeared it was usually mid-
morning, right around his break time, and after a while he managed
to contrive it so that whenever her truck slid into the yard he was
just washing up on his way to the coffee machine.

"Morning, Raejeanne," he'd say.

The first time, she had looked at him funny—wary, as if he rep-
resented a threat of sorts. The second time, she said, "How'd you
know my name?" and he'd had to confess that he'd asked Harley, the
parts manager, who she was. After that, she seemed to tolerate his
interest in her. One day she let him buy her a cup of coffee—cream,
no sugar—from the machine, and a week or so after that it happened
that her arrival coincided with the appearance of Gene's Snackvan.
"Running late," she said. "Let me buy you lunch," he offered.

"Well," Terry said to him later, "I've heard that the way to a
man's heart is through his stomach. But I'd always thought the way
to a woman's heart was by a more southern route."

"Screw off," Chuck told him, but inside he was hugging himself.

The following Friday, after he'd cleaned up at a bathroom sink that looked so much like streaked black marble you'd hardly have known it was white porcelain, the gray pickup was parked out back. Raejeanne was leaning against a fender, smoking a cigarette.

"Hey," she said. She tossed the cigarette aside and came toward him. Her walk had an attitude to it, he noticed, a swagger that was almost masculine. "You've been so good to me lately—all the coffee and stuff—I thought I'd offer to buy you a beer."

She stopped in front of him, head tilted, smiling out from under the visor of her *Discount Parts* cap.

"Sure," Chuck said. "Sounds good."

"You have a special place where you sip your beer?"

He shrugged. "You pick it," he said. "I usually drink at home."

"I'm not ready for that," she said. "How about Tony's?"

"Fine by me. I'll meet you there."

Unexpectedly, she took his arm. "You can ride with me," she said. "I'll bring you back to your car."

The truck's passenger door was locked. While he waited for Raejeanne to reach across the seat and unlock it, he wondered how much she smoked—was it a cigarette every now and then, or did she smoke two packs a day the way he had done for more than twenty years? And could he persuade her to quit?

When he pulled the door open she was making room for him in the clutter of the bench seat: invoices, a can of brake fluid, an oil-filter carton—she dragged everything to the center.

"My next-door neighbor," she said. "He's this retired guy who doesn't get out much. I help him with oil changes and simple stuff like that."

"Good for you," Chuck said.

He climbed into the cab, closed the door, pulled the seat belt across his lap. She watched him lock the belt.

"You're careful," she said.

"Older and wiser," he told her. He had to smile, because then she latched her own seat belt and smiled back at him.

"Younger and wiser," she said.

\\\\ Riding with Raejeanne was a good decision, because Tony's parking lot was jammed and she'd had to find a space on the other side of Center Point. Inside, the place was a madhouse, a half-dozen TV screens competing with the drinkers and the talkers and the players at the bar's one pool table. The air was blue with smoke; the late sun through the transom above the entrance let in a long shaft of swirling light.

The booths and tables were filled. He and Raejeanne sat with their beers at the very end of the counter, up against the snack-menu board, facing the wiener-go-round—or whatever they called that revolving oven thing.

"How long you been running parts?" he wondered.

"Nine, ten months," she said. "I'm a qualified dental hygienist, and I even did that for a while, but I quit—right in the middle of a patient. Just whipped off my mask and walked out. All those rancid mouths were getting into my dreams, my nightmares." She emptied her beer bottle into the glass. "I don't know what in the world I was thinking of, studying to be a hygienist."

"You want another brew?"

"One more," she said, "and that's my limit for drinking with a stranger."

"I'm not so strange," he said.

"How strange are you?" she asked. "I know you haven't been at the garage that long. Not even as long as I've been running parts."

"I'm from Chicago. I worked at a Buick agency there."

"'I used to work in Chicago,'" she said. "Everybody knows that song."

"I used to be married there, too. The divorce isn't quite final."

Raejeanne rummaged in her purse for a pack of Luckies, put a cigarette to her mouth. Chuck picked up a book of *Tony's Bar & Grill* matches and gave her a light.

"I wish you wouldn't smoke," he said, and he wondered if saying that out loud meant he was already seriously interested in her.

"Me too," she said. "You're not a smoker?"

"Not any more."

She took a deep drag from the cigarette, let the smoke out slowly through her nostrils. "So. Your wife threw you out?"

"No," he said, "I was the one filed. I'd had this surgery, and then a long time getting over it, and I decided I had to change my life. That was the way I thought of it, the way I said it to the lawyer: 'I have to change my life.'"

"Must have been serious," she said. "The surgery."

"I wouldn't want to do it again."

Raejeanne contemplated the tip of her cigarette, then stubbed it out. "What say we have that last beer?" she said.

It was almost a month before they made love, and when they did it was in the nature of a celebration. In the morning his lawyer had called: the divorce was final, the papers were in the mail.

"She gets everything except the Camaro," he told Raejeanne, "and my tool cabinet."

"And you're happy?"

"It's a relief. It's dragged on for more than a year."

"But she got everything you owned. Practically."

"I don't know," he said. "I've got transportation to my job, and the tools to do it with."

"You're one lucky man," Raejeanne said. "You could've let her have the car. I'll drive you to work."

They were at Tony's, holding hands, sitting in a booth near the entrance, and something about the way she said "I'll drive you to work" stirred him. Her hand seemed warmer, he felt—or thought he felt—his pulse quicken, her face blurred and he could only make out her eyes exploring his. She squeezed his hand. The two of them stood, left the bar, walked and then ran across the parking lot to her pickup.

Forever after, "driving" was the code for climbing into bed together. It would come up in the strangest places. At a movie Raejeanne would lean toward him and whisper, "Let me drive you to work," and she would lead him from the theater. Halfway through dinner at the Boar's Head he would put down his knife and fork and say, "Let's drive somewhere," and they would fidget until the waiter brought the check. Sometimes they didn't make it to either of their apartments but made love in the truck or the backseat of the Camaro—a frantic, awkward business of straddling and bruising.

But this first time was less than frantic, almost gentle. Raejeanne was quieter than Janice, more adaptable to him—as if she were remaking herself to complement him—and he tried to do the same for her. They climaxed together; it was something that had never happened to him before, and it made him dizzy.

"We fit," she said. She was resting alongside him with her cheek on his chest, her hand idling on his belly. "You think so?"

"Yes. I do."

"You know what gypper parts are?"

"Sure. Counterfeit; ersatz."

She hugged him. "Other lovers are gypper," she said. "We're the real thing. Factory originals."

She sat up and propped a pillow behind her, leaned over to kiss him on the mouth, touched his chest damp from their efforts.

"That's a terrible scar," she said.

"My surgery. I told you."

She ran her fingers along the red welt. "It's huge. My God, it runs way around to your back."

"They took a lung."

"A whole lung?"

"Well—Half. Half the right lung."

"From just smoking?" She slid down and embraced him, her warm face pressed against his chest. Her hair was a blur between his vision and the blue-shaded lamp on the nightstand.

"I guess. Mostly." He nuzzled her black hair, that smelled like flowers or herbs, and only faintly of cigarette smoke. "Asbestos too, maybe, from working on people's brakes."

"God," she said.

"Nobody ever told me I shouldn't breathe it," he said. "Now I don't. I wear the mask. I'm damned careful."

"I should hope," she said.

For months after the surgery he'd had nightmares—had waked in the middle of the night imagining he was suffocating, sat up choking, feeling all over again the deep pain of the incision that so impressed Raejeanne. *I don't want to die,* he'd reminded himself over and over. When the painkillers didn't work, he lay in his hospital bed and cried like a baby. When he was back home with his wife and the morphine fell short for him, he moved from one chair to another, one room to another, like an animal that doesn't comprehend pain and tries to walk away, leave it behind. It hurt to breathe; he would wake up at 3 A.M. convinced he was dying, drowning in darkness. Now the pain was remote and abstract, but it was no less real.

"Can you stay all night?" he asked Raejeanne.

"Oh, yes," she said. "Just you try and send me away."

||| At work he was more careful than ever, as if something new was at stake. When Terry kicked up his fogs of brakedust, he turned away, mask on, and pretended some job on the other side of the shop. When Terry laid his burning cigarette aside for a few moments, Chuck moved it farther down the bench so the smoke wouldn't touch him. *I don't want to die* became *I want to live a long time.* All because of Raejeanne.

Now when she delivered parts he stopped buying coffee for her and didn't flirt with her. He tried to stay entirely away, as if he were afraid—that he would try to make love to her right here and now, forcing her against the Coke machine while all the guys watched, laughed, clapped; pulling her into the filthy toilet and holding her on his lap facing him until they both exploded.

At night he told her his fantasies and made her laugh at his imagination. "You're so gross," she said. "I think that's why I love you." He told her how his mantra had turned more positive for her. "I want to live," he said. "It isn't enough just to not die."

"I know," she said.

"I had this doctor," he said, "this surgeon. Just before I went under, he told me, 'Remember. One of the objects of being alive is to make everything wear out at the same time.'"

"Don't lecture me," Raejeanne said. "I'll quit."

He kissed her. "Think of the money you'll save."

"Let's drive," she said. "I'm thinking of wearing something out."

Weekends, they lay in bed whole mornings, whole afternoons, loving and talking. They told their lives; they told their travels; they told the lovers who'd come into their lives and gone out again.

"Why did she leave you, do you suppose?" Raejeanne said, talking about Janice.

"Age," he said. "I remember once I said something about how she was keeping me young, and she said no, that I was making her old. I think that's why she left."

Raejeanne looked thoughtful. "I think it had something to do with her father," she said.

"And what about you?"

"My daddy's dead," she said. "You're home free."

On Mondays, when both of them had to rise early for work, they sat with their coffee at the apartment's front window and watched the newest in the next-door neighbor's parade of sleek blondes with salon tans as they trotted out to their red Miatas and Mustangs.

"They're interchangeable," Raejeanne told him. "There must be an assembly line somewhere, and this guy's put in a standing order."

Once, early one Sunday morning when neither one had got up to open the curtains, she moved close and put her mouth to his ear. "I know you hate the word," she whispered, "but I love fucking you."

"'Fucking,'" he murmured. "You make it sound like a word we could say in church."

"Maybe we will," she said.

ꟾꟾꟾꟾ He wasn't sure if it was a real dream or not; it might have been one of those sort-of dreams people had when they were neither awake nor asleep but were suspended somewhere in between, so that fantastic events seemed plausible, and ordinary events seemed like magic. Whatever it was, in the dream he was paired with Raejeanne, riding through the city in her ash-gray pickup with a Kraft-paper carton on the seat between them. *Body Parts* said a label on the carton, and just as he noticed what the label said it dawned on him that they were headed toward one of the local hospitals—probably St. Luke's, because that was the hospital nearest the shop. The rest of the words on the carton were in German, and the only one he recognized was *echt*, which meant *genuine*. He felt a strong sense of pleasure that whoever was getting this part would be getting the real thing and not some gypper substitute. It amazed him that everything in the dream was making such perfect sense, and when he looked over at Raejeanne she gave him her wide-eyed smile as if it amazed her too. The dream ended when he started coughing and felt Raejeanne touch him with one hand while she steered with the other. He sat up in the dark, wide-awake and sweating; a moment later the dream had gone out of his head completely, and Raejeanne was asleep beside him. *Finally*, he thought, and he leaned over to kiss her—her closed eyelids, earlobes, cheeks, mouth—then held her against him until the morning sunlight smothered the room.

A Day of
Splendid Omens

\\\\

I'm on my way to a September wedding in
Scoggin, a small town in Maine not far from Portland. It's Webster
Hartley—Webb, my closest friend since the days when we were at
Bowdoin together—who's marrying Prudence Mackenzie. When
Webb called me in Evanston to ask me if I'd stand up for him, he
mumbled something about making an honest man of himself—he'd
had a few drinks—and I felt a funny twinge of I don't know what.
Envy, possibly; or, on the other side of it, maybe a curious sort of
disapproval. Webb is sixty-four, the same age I am, and I suppose
some Puritan part of me rose up and clucked its tongue at the idea
of a man as old as Webb marrying a woman as young—I think she's
twenty-eight—as Pru. What if we'd known when we were in college, dating the girls from Holyoke and Smith and Jackson and
Bradford Junior, that in fact we might eventually love and get married to someone not even born yet?

\\\\ Webb is an artist—a good one, I think, but not a successful one.
He moved to Maine after his last divorce and managed to buy a run-
down farmhouse for back taxes. Then he spent the next few years
making it livable—patching the roof of the house and the barnlike
ell, shoring up the foundation, replacing broken window panes; he
dug a new well, put in a septic tank so he could have an indoor toilet. He lived alone during all that rehabilitation, living a life so or-

ganized it hardly seemed possible this was the Webster Hartley I'd
known at school. He got up with the sun, went into his makeshift
studio carrying a cup of coffee spiked with Jameson's, and painted
for two, three hours; he gave over the rest of the daylight to being
a carpenter, an electrician, a journeyman plumber. Then in the
hours after dark, before Prudence came into his life, he drank until
he fell into bed. It was edifying—I told him this—to see a man take
up the disconnected pieces of his life and use them to build a house.

I can only imagine what they live on, since Webb's income as a
painter occupies a range from slim to none—though nowadays
when he does sell a picture, he tells me he often gets something up
in the four-figure neighborhood. Perhaps he sells two pieces a year,
three in a super-good year. He doesn't have savings. He never did.

But the two of them are happy. I visited them a couple of summers ago, pulling into the yard on a Sunday afternoon in August,
the day sweltering and hazy-gold. There were white chickens in the
driveway, a fat, lazy orange cat asleep on the porch railing, a rusty
pickup truck and a vintage Chevy sedan parked between the house
and a rickety barn. Webb came out of the house in torn tennis shoes
and swim trunks, Pru in the shadows behind him, barefoot, wearing
a long-tailed man's shirt that might have been all she had on. The
baby, Melinda—she was walking, but just barely, so she must have
been what? not quite a year old?—was in cotton underpants, tot-
tering against her father's hairy legs.

You have to spend a lot of time with Webb Hartley to know him.
He's not tall, but he's big and he *seems* tall. He's broad-shouldered,
stocky, with hands so huge that if somebody asked you, you'd pre-
sume that if he were any kind of artist, he had to be a sculptor, and
ever since he entered his thirties he's worn a beard so red and so unruly he looks like a scruffy Viking warrior. Flamboyant—that's how
you'd describe him, first meeting him. But it wouldn't be long before you realized you were in the presence of a truly shy man, and
you'd forget you thought him flamboyant in favor of thinking him
reticent, or self-effacing, or politely antisocial. He has a squint to his

eyes that suggests the wariness he feels in the company of other humans; I've seen that squint disappear only when he's in front of a
new canvas, or looking at Pru across the dinner table, or sitting on
the porch steps by himself, petting the indolent orange cat in an absent fashion, his mind a million miles away.

IIII It's late afternoon when I arrive at the farmhouse. The ceremony
is scheduled for six, but the reception is before the wedding and I'm
looking forward to some hefty eating and drinking and clowning
around for the newlyweds' benefit. The day—in fact it's the first day
of autumn, the equinox—is superb. The sky is absolutely unclouded,
is perfectly, flawlessly blue; the air is warm and moves with the
slightest of breezes, only enough to keep you from feeling uncomfortable; you can smell the grasses—not the humid scent of fresh-
cut green, but a more subtle, drier odor, mingled with a distant sus-
picion of cow and horse from some unobtrusive neighbor's farm. A
knockout day to declare love unto death, a day of splendid omens.

Oddly, there's nobody around. I sit for a few minutes in the
rented car, surveying the farmyard, the house and the ell, wondering why no one strolls out to greet me. The car window is down—
the breeze touches my cheek and brow—but no sounds reach me.
No laughter, no clink of glasses, no background of a hired musician
tuning his fiddle. No cars belonging to guests—only the Hartley
pickup, rustier than ever. I'm surrounded by rare silence—or what
passes for silence in a noisy world: a soft thunder we hear that science says is the rush of blood through our bodies; a thin whine al-
leged to be the electric current that drives the nervous system. Then
other sounds disturb the quiet. The chirp of a cricket. A fly's buzz.
A barely audible rustle of leaves in the birches. A crow calling, distant, like a rusty hinge. But no human noise.

I go to the farmhouse, cross the porch to the screen door, and
knock. Knock harder. Open the screen door and tap on the glass of
the inside door with the car key. The sharp noise of the key echoes
into the birches, and the echo comes back sounding like someone

far off swinging an axe against a tree, cutting it down. I push the door open—Webb has never locked anything in his life—and call Webb's name, get no response, close the door and turn away. I wonder if I have the wrong day, or only the wrong hour.

Walking around the house, I meet a first sign of human habitation: a pet, a small brown and white terrier who is overjoyed to meet me, who jumps up to lick my hands, whose tail wags nonstop. "Hey, little guy," I say. "Hello, boy. Where's the party?" I follow the dog around the end of the ell. At the end of the long, sloping lawn the farm pond shows a few dimples where dragonflies touch and dance away; otherwise the water is quiet and unruffled.

In the backyard, finally things look festive. Three picnic tables, covered with red-checkered tablecloths, have been set end-to-end and laden with bowls of potato salad, macaroni salad, corn chips, raw vegetables, a variety of dips—all of them covered over with plastic wrap for protection from insects and air. At the end of one table are glass cups arranged in a circle that suggests they're intended to surround a missing punch bowl. On a pair of card tables nearby—also draped in red-checkered cloths—are paper plates, a few styrofoam cups, an aluminum coffee maker. On the lawn, pushed into the shade of a fair-sized oak tree, are a couple of galvanized iron washtubs filled with ice and canned beer, and I can see the corked necks of a wine bottle or two looking aloof among the cans. Tubular-aluminum chairs with bright-colored plastic seats and backs are scattered about; a few emptied beercans are in evidence, standing alongside the chairs or tipped over into the grass. On the top step under the back door of the house sits an old-fashioned wind-up Victrola, its lid open, its varnished horn aimed across the yard; a stack of shellac records is on a step below.

But no people. I stroll through the party scene with the terrier wagging at my heels, open a can of Narragansett, slip my fingers under transparent plastic to withdraw a stark cerebrum of cauliflower. I eat the blossom, toss the stem to the dog, who sniffs it and then gives me a puzzled look. I sip the beer and wonder what Webb is up to. Perhaps after a toast or two in champagne he has proposed to his guests a walk in the countryside, a procession, a one-time ritual—the wedding party tramping through the late-summer meadows to put on the last of the wildflower pollens, breathe the faint and fading perfumes of the dying season—that will lead back to the ceremony itself. That would be like him.

I sit on the steps next to the Victrola, drinking my beer, waiting for the party to return. The dog makes several circles, slumps into the grass at the foot of the steps and rests his head on his forepaws. I remember someone once told me that the point of the old RCA Victor trademark—"His Master's Voice"—is that what the terrier is sitting on, head cocked to listen, is a coffin, and the Master is dead inside it. Webb would enjoy this scene at the back of his house, the rearrangement of the trademark, its elements fragmented but the reference still clear; this is the kind of still-life subject he looks for in the world, that ignites his imagination and sends him into his studio. I pick a phonograph record off the top of the pile at my feet— *Vocalion* I can read, but the gilt lettering is too worn for me to read the fine print of the label—and put it on the green felt of the turntable. I lift the arm and turn it down to rest the needle at the edge of the record; the turntable begins moving, but too slowly to make melody. I crank the phonograph; the turntable speeds up, the music wavers and rises and becomes intelligible—a tenor voice, a sentimental song: "Believe Me, If All Those Endearing Young Charms."

|||| The day cools, the sun has made its descent into autumn, the shadows lengthen and climb the shingles of the house, the breeze drops off to nothing. By now I'm sinking into concerns of my own. Where *are* Webb and Pru? Where are the wedding guests? I walk around to the front of the house, the terrier at my heels, and sit in a Boston rocker at the end of the porch—a vantage point from

which I can look down the narrow gravel road, see what's coming toward me. For a long time I sit on Webb's porch, rubbing the ears of the dog at my feet, crooning nonsense words.

In the distance is a glitter of chrome—a car coming. I scowl down the length of the road, the low sun in my eyes, a cloud of dust behind the car colored like gold, boiling, molten. It's a blue Ford, a newish sedan that could stand washing, and it speeds past—its driver a middle-aged man, straw-hatted, with his hands holding the wheel at ten and two o'clock.

"False alarm," I say to the terrier. I lean back in the rocker, close my eyes, try not to speculate. I wonder what happened to the white chickens. I wonder if Melinda—Mindy—is old enough to be the flower girl for her parents, and how they will dress her—or *if* they will dress her.

Now another car is approaching, not as fast, and behind it is a second. They slow as they come near, the dust clouds behind them diminishing, flattening in light no longer direct. I stand; the dog startles to his feet. I walk down the two porch steps to meet the new arrivals. Because it is dusk by now, the lead car has its parking lights on.

Both cars turn into the farmyard—the first stopping in the driveway, almost running up on the lawn in front of the porch, and the second going past it to park beside the old truck. The driver's-side doors open simultaneously, and two men appear. Neither one is Webb. The man from the car nearest me trots to the passenger side and opens the door. He offers his hand; a young woman takes it and he helps her to stand. Pru. She is dressed in a pale blue dress whose color is almost neutralized by the failing of the daylight, and her high-heeled shoes are likewise pale blue. She is bareheaded, but in one hand she carries a flowered hat and a sheer white scarf. She leans heavily on the man, who turns with her toward the house. Only then does she look up; only then does she see me, recognize me.

"Alec," she says.

"What's the matter?" I say. "What's going on?"

She puts her free hand to her face as if she is going to brush aside a stray lock of her long hair, but the hair is pulled severely, formally, back. The hand seems to flutter at her eyes, her mouth.

"Webb," she says.

"What about him?" I take a step toward her. I wish I knew who this man was who suddenly seems so proprietary, who stiffens and turns his shoulder so that Pru is shielded from my question. Pru anticipates me.

"This is the minister," she says. "This is the man who was going to marry us."

"Was?"

"Webster's dead," the man says. He steers Pru past me. "Let's get you inside," he says to her.

By now the man from the other car has come up.

"Alec," he says, almost jovial. He holds out his hand; I take it, a reflex, my mind still grappling with the words *Webster's dead*, wondering if I heard correctly. "Bob Hartley," he says. "Webb's kid brother. We met once, a couple of Webb weddings ago."

"What the hell happened?"

"Heart attack."

"Jesus. On his wedding day?" I feel dizzy, and sit on the top step of the porch. Bob Hartley sits down next to me.

"Out of the blue," he says. "Right out of left field. One minute he was hugging Pru and bragging about his good luck; the next he was on his face, dead as the proverbial doornail. It was weird."

"Jesus." It is all I can think of to say. A prayer, a supplication—I don't know what. *Jesus.* Does the name give us some kind of relief from horror? "Are they sure?"

"Sure of what?"

"Are they sure he's dead?" *Jesus,* I keep saying inside my head. *Jesus Christ.*

"Yeah, they're sure. They tried CPR. They tried adrenaline." Bob produces a cigarette and lights it. "That electric-shock gizmo. He's dead all right."

"Where is he?"

"Kimball Hospital. The undertaker's supposed to pick him up tonight."

Sweet Jesus. I try to get a purchase on the day, to say anything that suggests I might have some modest control of reality. "How's Pru?"

"Destroyed; you saw."

"Where's Mindy?"

"My wife—you remember Theresa?—I dropped her and Mindy back at our motel. They were going to watch cartoons."

It seems to me it is the interior of Webb's house that is a cartoon—a caricature of what is expected to happen when someone dies. While I rehearsed my private blasphemies with Robert Hartley, two more cars pulled into the yard and emptied themselves, a parade of solemn guests passing around and between us, so that by the time he and I come inside, the front room feels crowded and there is activity in the kitchen. A screen door slams periodically; someone is ferrying food from the picnic tables to the refrigerator. Bob excuses himself, leaves me, reappears shortly thereafter staggering under the weight of one of the tubs of beer, which he slides noisily onto a kitchen counter.

"Who wants a beer?" he calls. "Who wants wine?"

This is a small room, made smaller by its furnishings. An old upright piano occupies most of the far end, bulking so large that it partially blocks a window. A claw-footed sofa covered with an afghan sits under the window that looks onto the porch, a long coffee table, littered with magazines and paperback books, slightly askew in front of it. On the facing wall: a leather chair, a brass floorlamp, a magazine rack. On the floor is a worn Oriental carpet, mostly dark red with extravagant grays and oranges.

It was the piano that was Webb's pride and joy. I was with him when he acquired it—gratis—from the Methodist Church of Holderness, New Hampshire, which wanted it moved out of the basement to make room for a projection-screen television set. Webb was beside himself; he hired half the football team of the Holderness School to do the moving, rented a pickup—he later bought the truck; it's the one that sits in the yard, rusting away even as we settle in to the evening's wake—and brought it here pretending it was a birthday present for half-nude Mindy. I've heard him play it, something he did whenever he'd had too much to drink and the light was too weak for painting. Honky-tonk, that was his specialty, and the piano—being out of tune, missing innumerable felts and having a cracked sounding board—was the perfect instrument. Had he not been so happy, so good-hearted, the experience of listening to Webb play would have been excruciating. As it was, you couldn't help but feel the pleasure of it all. He sang "The Darktown Strutters' Ball," his left hand boom-chucking away, his right hand trilling treble octaves, his voice—his awful voice—bouncing the lyrics off the room's walls and ceiling. He sang "I'll Take You Home Again, Kathleen," tremolo, while tears streamed down his cheeks. He played "House of Blue Lights" until the boogie-woogie bass gave you a headache. But how do you say to a man who's in a heaven of his own making that he should for God's sake give us a rest from all that racket?

IIII Bob Hartley presses a beer into my hand, pausing to make sure I have a grip on it, since I must seem to him not to be paying attention. He says, "Okay, old buddy?" and I snap out of it and nod. The room is suddenly warm, crowded. The wedding guests talk softly, moving between the living room and the kitchen—the rooms are separated from each other by a countertop and a bank of cupboards—pouring wine, helping themselves to food. The screen door to the backyard creaks open and slaps shut incessantly.

I lean back in the leather chair and press the beer can against my forehead. The cold feels sharp-pointed, welcome. Bob returns and sits unsteadily on the chair arm.

"Pru's lying down upstairs," he says. "She'd like to talk with you."

"Now?"

"I think so; yes."

"Shouldn't she rest?"

Bob shrugs. "She took a couple of pills. I think she's about cried out for today."

IIII Pru is leaning against two pillows in the center of a brass bed; a patchwork quilt is under her; she's clutching one of the matching pillow shams, holding it against herself like a security blanket. She's red-eyed, but not crying.

"Alec," she says, her voice small and sweet.

"Bob said I should look in."

"Please." She pats the quilt beside her.

I sit, gently, intending not to shake the bed. "Can I get you anything?"

"Thank you, no." She lowers the sham and lets go of it; she puts out her right hand toward me, but doesn't try to touch me. "Is that beer?"

"Yes."

"Let me have a taste."

"Should you? On top of—whatever?"

"They were only aspirin. Cross my heart."

I hold out the beer, but instead of taking it from me she puts her hand over mine and steers the can to her mouth. She takes a long swallow, then releases me. "I hate beer," she says. "It's such bitter stuff."

"There's sweeter stuff downstairs."

"I know. I helped buy it." She sighs, leans back, closes her eyes. "I made the punch too. With plenty of vodka."

I don't know what to say, or what she wants of me. I let my gaze roam around the bedroom: to her blue heels in the middle of the room, the scarf and hat on a wicker chair under a window, on one of the room's two dressers a beribboned plastic box with flowers inside it.

"You came a long way for nothing," she says.

Her eyes are open, and very green. On both her cheeks are faint,

thin streaks made by tears, and her lipstick is faded almost to nothing. Her hair is loose; the combs are on the nightstand nearby.

"If I can help," I say, without the slightest idea of how to complete the thought.

"You can," she says. She sits upright, swings her legs over the far
side of the bed. "But you have to turn your back while I get into
something simple."

I hear her clothing rustle. A closet door slides, hangers jangle.

"All right," she says. "I'm decent." She's in tights, a loose pink
sweater; she is tying her hair into a ponytail. "In the corner closet,"
she says, "could you get me that scruffy pair of Tretorns?"

"Where are we going?"

"I want to go to the studio." She finishes tying the tennis shoes,
takes my hand to lead me. "Come," she says. "We'll use the back
stairs so we miss everybody."

At the head of the stairs she stops so abruptly I almost collide
with her; she turns, throws her arms around my waist and hangs on
desperately. Her head is down, her face against my chest. "God," she
says. "I didn't want all these people; I wanted you, and Bobby and
Terry, just to witness."

"They'll be gone pretty soon."

"They don't know anything about any of us," she says.

⦚⦚⦚ After he'd picked up the old farmhouse from the tax assessor—
long before Pru came into his life—I visited him here, followed him
around while he boasted about what he was going to do, what he'd
already done. The studio in those first days was an impressive mess:
the ell windows had long been broken out by storms and vandals,
and half the animal kingdom of southern Maine must have been
wintering in it for years; scat and straw and nests of fur like tum-
bleweeds corrupted the space—the odor was unbelievably raw—and
off and on during my stay various of the previous tenants tried to re-
assert their squatters' rights. One morning we burst in on a red fox
couple, another time a family of raccoons like a band of gypsy

thieves surprised around a campfire. Skunks were the riskiest, Webb told me, and when one Sunday he cornered one behind the pot-bellied stove he'd just hooked up, I opted out—went back inside the house and poured another cup of coffee for myself. "How'd it go?" I wanted to know when he came back to the kitchen. "Piece of cake," Webb said. "I think I've driven that one off before; he was friendlier than most—acted like he knew me."

That was the year I stayed all summer, and by the time I left, Webb had been painting in his new studio for almost three weeks. We'd put in a skylight, caulked all the old window frames, replaced a dozen broken floorboards. We even lugged in three cords of stove-wood to take Webb through his first winter. Seeing the studio now, with poor Pru, brought all of that back, and it brought back the time I'd first met her.

The year was melting into springtime then, but the day I arrived there'd been a spectacular ice storm. The driving was ugly—I'd seen cars and trucks tipped off at the side of the roads, and I'd clutch the wheel to my chest like a life-vest, praying the rear wheels wouldn't break away every time I came to a curve—but Nature was glorious, encased in ice, glittering like cut crystal. Webb either saw or heard me coming; by the time I drove into the yard he was standing on the porch—Levi's, green-and-black plaid shirt, the same style of army boots he'd worn for close to forty years—waiting for me. He had a great black skillet—a "spider," he called it—in his right hand, and in his left a couple of brown hen's eggs he held up and waved at me.

"How many eggs in your omelet?" he said.

"Three."

I trailed him inside a house that was already full of the smell of bacon and too-strong coffee, laid my toilet kit on the magazine rack—it held magazines then—and sat at the kitchen table. The table was a recent find of Webb's; it was old and austere and heavy, made of oak and varnished to an autumnal shade of brown, and with its four high-backed chairs it crowded the kitchen. Webb poured me a mug of the coffee from a battered aluminum pot and went about his cooking duties, breaking a half-dozen eggs into an outsized measuring cup, adding a splash of water from a faucet at the sink— "Anybody tells you to add milk instead of water has never been intimate with a hen," he said—beating the mix with a fork and pouring half into the greasy spider.

"I'll remember."

"Cheese?" he said.

"Why not?"

He opened the refrigerator and brought out a fist-sized block of cheddar, grated much of it into the pan, ate most of the rest while he oversaw the omelet. "Sharp," he said. "Nice edge on it." The bacon was draining on a wad of paper towels on the counter, the coffee steamed above its low blue flame at the back of the stove. I remember how secure I felt; it came from being comfortable and attended to and needed. It had been years since I'd lost my wife, and I was still getting used to traveling alone, restless, moving in this direction and that like a hurt animal that thinks it can walk away from its pain.

"I met this woman," Webb told me. It was a statement that sounded abrupt, as if he'd been holding it in until it simply refused any longer to be contained. "In Boston a couple of weekends ago." He prodded the omelet, bent down to stove level to adjust the flame under it. "Goes by the old-fashioned name of Prudence."

"How'd you meet her?"

"Luck." He folded the omelet over, danced the spider on the burner for a moment or two, tipped it up so the omelet slid off onto a heavy white plate. He added several strips of the bacon and set the plate before me. "Karma. Life's reward for Good Behavior." He turned his back to me and went to work on the second omelet.

"Sounds serious," I said. "Is she rich?"

He seemed to study the question. "I think not," he said after a while. "Not by any worldly definition."

He set his plate on the table, brought over what was left of the bacon on its bed of greasy paper, sat down across from me.

"So you're in love with her," I said.

He took a mouthful of omelet, chewed, swallowed. "There's salt and pepper behind the mustard pot," he said. "I don't know your taste. Or your dietary requirements."

"So you're *not* in love with her?"

"I'm deliberating over the word *love*," he said. "There's a connection between us—I can't describe it." He tried his coffee, found it had cooled, went to the stove to add hot. "Like I've been only half human all this time, and Pru is the other half of me."

"Another marriage ahead?" I said.

"No," he said. "She's too good to be made by any man into a mere wife." He took a sip of coffee, scratched the beard at his chin. "You'll meet her." he said. "She's moving in with me on Saturday."

||||| On today's sad visit the studio has the agreeable clutter it lacked when Webb and I first got it into shape to be used. One end of it is a kind of carpenter's shop smelling of the pungent, fresh-sawn wood waiting to be made into canvas stretchers and frames, and of the thick brown glue kept hot in its electric pot. At the other end, under the skylight stained from years of gray weather and mottled with bird droppings, the smell is sharper: of oil paint, lacquers and thinners, turpentine-soaked rags. Prudence wends her way through the canvases leaned against the workbench, the one-by-twos and one-by-threes of pine and hickory and oak; she pauses, picks up several corner fasteners and spills them with a sound like cracked bells into an open paper box on the bench. "Webb was never neat," she says.

Now we're in the studio proper, where Webb worked. A large easel directly under the skylight, finished canvases and Masonite boards leaned and piled against the end wall, a cabinet with open drawers that reveal paint tubes and brushes of every size. The floor, where years of colors have fallen, is like a Pollock painting. Squat cans of turpentine, spray cans of plastic, line the sills of the two windows that face east.

"It wasn't my idea to get married," Pru says. "If you've wondered. I was against it. I thought we were doing fine as lovers, as people with special 'significance' for each other." She leans against the windowsill. The light from overhead makes unflattering shadows on her face, accents her eye sockets, hollows her cheeks.

"He was no stranger to marriage," I say.

"I know." She looks down and her face is all shadow. "I'd have been number four."

"I'd lost count."

"He told me all about all of them, chapter and verse. I think he really wanted me to know him, make sense of him. He told me he'd decided never to do marriage again."

"What made him change his mind?"

"Oh, I think he was trying to be practical. I think that because he was so much older—and really, he was getting awfully conscious of his age—he wanted me to have whatever benefits the wedding ceremony might bring with it. Survivor benefits, insurance, tax breaks. I don't know what."

"Age affects people," I say. Not sarcastic.

"It never bothered me. I mean he never seemed to me to act old or talk old—or *paint* old." She sighs, looks out a window that faces the woods. "I suppose, too, he wanted to make things easier for Mindy."

"He said he wanted to make everybody honest."

"Something like that." She looks suddenly forlorn, and for an uneasy moment I think she's going to just let go, just collapse, as if it's easier to be unconscious and let the world go on without her for a while. My wife used to say: *I'm tired; today I'm just going to be a passenger.* Pru raises her hands, a gesture of futility.

"And he actually loved me," she says. "God—You can't believe how much I already miss him."

I hold her. "I'll miss him for the rest of my life," she says, and then she cries and cries. I hang on while the sobs shake her, my right hand pressed against her back, pressed against the light sweater through which I can feel her warmth, my left hand cradling her head to my chest. I wonder if she can hear my heart, or if her own grief drowns it out.

After a while she stops crying, her body begins to relax, she wipes at her cheeks with the back of her hand and steps away from me. Her face is mottled and her eyes swollen. She tries to smile.

"We were a strange and wonderful pair," she says. Then she goes through the motions of pulling herself together—adjusts the tights at her waist, pushes the unruly strands of hair back from her face, takes a facial tissue from a box on Webb's cabinet to dry her cheeks, blow her nose. "God," she says, "I almost forgot why I dragged you out here."

She goes to the pictures leaned against the wall of the studio and slides one out. A blue mailbox.

"Remember?" she says.

"It was my favorite."

"Mine too. It was the first work of his he showed me Anyway, I know he wanted you to own it. He said you'd earned it."

"Maybe I have," I say.

"Oh, Alec." Now she comes back to me, not to cry but to let us join hands like the friends I believe we are. "You came here to stand up for Webb, and now you've got to stand up for me. You have to stay. You have to see me through whatever it is that's supposed to happen next."

**** "Webb wasn't a practical person," Bob Hartley is saying. "When I found out that he'd never made out a last will and testament, and here he was with this string of ex-wives, and him planning to marry Prudence—God, I could see the complications. Nightmares for everybody, and Pru could end up in the poorhouse."

Bob is a lawyer by profession—something I might have remembered if I hadn't been so staggered by Webb's death—and we are sitting in the kitchen, at the oak table, with papers and envelopes strewn between us. Bob's glasses are pushed up on his head, and he's finally taken off his necktie. At my left elbow is a half-empty bottle of Jameson's, and he and I each have a tumbler full of ice cubes tinc-tured with whiskey. Prudence is still up with us—it's past midnight, Mindy has been put to bed upstairs—and she and Theresa are doing up the serving dishes and silverware.

"Though I'll tell you," Bob says. "She may end up there anyway. My brother didn't have much to give away."

"You can't take it with you," Theresa says. She's a big-boned woman with the kind of voice you can pick out of all the other voices at a restaurant or a cocktail party. "So why own it? I think that was the touchstone of Webb's life."

"Be fair," Bob tells her. "He just needed someone to remind him that he was going alone. That he might leave a survivor or two."

"Is there any estate at all?" I ask.

"Oh, sure." He unfolds the will stapled into its blue cover. "There's this house, which believe it or not is free and clear, and the seventy acres with it. This is a valuable thing—though this is a de-pressed area and it isn't an especially good time to sell. It's a terri-ble time, as a matter of fact."

"I won't sell it," Pru says. "Mindy and I live here."

"And there's his paintings."

"Ha," Theresa says.

"Cut it out, Terry," Bob tells her. "Picasso he isn't, but he told me the last thing he sold was for thirty-five hundred. And that was a painting by a *living* artist. Dead—"

"God, stop it, Bobby." Pru throws down the dishtowel she's been using and runs upstairs.

"Shit," Theresa says. She follows Pru.

"Just as well," Bob says. "Let them cry on each other's shoulders."

"Catharsis," I say. Something about Bob—or perhaps it's some-thing about lawyers?—makes me say the obvious.

Bob looks at me. "It's peculiar. Terry didn't much like Webster, but she liked the *idea* of him. She'd like to have rolled us both into one person; Webb's Bohemian flair, my talent for making money."

"She doesn't seem to think much of his paintings."

"I've had divorce clients who act like Terry," he says. "They're still in love with the spouse but they know it won't work anymore, so they snipe at something they may very well be fond of—some habit of the spouse that used to be endearing and now seems to drive them bananas." He flips back the top page of Webb's will. "You know: denial."

I take a drink of the whiskey.

"It's a real stunner," Bob says, "to see a man drop dead before your eyes. One minute Webb was standing with his arm around Prudence, waving a champagne glass in the air, and he was saying something about how ordinary language was insufficient to express his feelings for this woman by his side. Very formal. The next minute he was on the ground at her feet." He tips back in his chair so it's leaning against the counter behind him. "You know what we did? We laughed."

I can imagine it. I can hear people saying what a joker Webb was.

"Then, of course—" He rocks forward. "Well," he says, "the rest you know." He takes a long swallow of whiskey and sets the drink aside; he brings the glasses down to his nose to read. "Anyway, everything will go to Pru, the State of Maine willing."

He fishes among the papers in front of him.

"Except that rusted-out pickup truck. It goes to some farmer over in West Egypt. Don't ask me why." He shuffles the papers, gathers them, makes them into an even pile. "And I guess the mailbox canvas is yours."

"Pru's worried about funeral arrangements," I say.

"That's easy. I talked to old man Curtis from a pay phone at the hospital. We'll have to choose a casket—something you and I should do; I don't think Pru needs to be burdened with that."

"I think her worry has more to do with the body than with the box. Webb apparently said something once about giving his body to science."

"And his brain to Harvard," Bob says scornfully. "I think that's totally unacceptable. My brother isn't going to be some medical student's cadaver. You've heard those horror stories—they cut the body completely in half, for Christ's sake."

"So I've heard." When I was in graduate school, there was gossip about a med student who cut a heart-shaped chunk of flesh out of his cadaver's buttock, and sent it to his fiancée on Valentine's Day.

"Cremation seems to me the most sensible thing," Bob says. "No fuss, no grave to tend—maybe a marker in one of those commercial mausoleums, but no perpetual care fee to pay to some cemetery rummy, maybe not even a casket—and then if she wants to scatter his ashes in some appropriate place, someplace symbolic and special—"

"Like the Ganges," I say. "And then she could throw herself on a funeral pyre."

Bob stares at me for a long moment. "Fuck you," he says. "I'm only trying to deal seriously with my brother's remains."

IIII Pru doesn't come back to the kitchen; Theresa rejoins us briefly, finds a bottle of Bailey's Irish Cream at the back of the liquor cupboard and pours herself a small glassful. Sitting at the table, she and Bob carry on a wary discussion: should the two of them go back to their motel, or should they stay—both of them measuring my presence—in case Pru wakes in the night and needs the consolation of another woman? My opinion isn't asked for. Finally, Bob gathers up his papers and they leave. I watch the car's taillights diminish in the trailing pink dust of the gravel road. Alone, I wander around downstairs, find a stray punch cup on top of the piano, a wadded-up paper napkin on the floor under the coffee table. I rinse the cup under the hot water faucet and throw the napkin into a wastebasket labeled *paper.*

Upstairs, on my way to bed I pass Mindy's room. Its door is partly open, and I pause to look inside. Among the dim shadows cast by a light that may be the moon's, I see Prudence. She is lying beside her daughter, one arm holding the child close, the small blond head nested under the mother's chin. Pru is talking softly—so softly, almost a whisper, that I can make out only a word, a phrase, nothing truly connected. I realize she is telling Mindy about Webb—about fathers and friends and, perhaps, about the ongoing complexities of love.